Morning Glory

A Novel of the
First Great Awakening

ENDORSEMENTS

Rebecca's memorable characters provide a vivid and endearing glimpse into this fascinating time in history. She has an ease in her storytelling that draws readers in and keeps them engaged until the satisfying conclusion. *Morning Glory* is a gem.
—**Robin Jones Gunn**, best-selling author, the *Father Christmas* novels that inspired three Hallmark original movies, and *Victim of Grace.*

At Home in Mitford meets the First Great Awakening. What a delightful stroll through the colonial world of George Whitefield, Ben Franklin, William and Catherine Tennent, and Jonathan and Sarah Edwards. Romantic intrigue and theological controversy with some keen insights into human longing. A good read.
—**Barry Hankins**, Professor of History, Baylor University

The first Great Awakening is an often-overlooked and yet rich and fascinating period of American history. I love how Rebecca Price Janney has brought this beautiful time of revival to life through attention to historical detail and characters you just want to root for from beginning to end! What a treat to immerse in this remarkable time period of history, walk the streets of Colonial America with Janney's characters, and meet legends such as Ben Franklin, George Whitefield, and William Tennent. Lovers of history will delight in this latest offering from Rebecca Price Janney!
—**Marlo Schalesky**, award-winning author, *Reaching for Wonder, Encountering Christ When Life Hurts*

In her newest book, *Morning Glory,* Rebecca Price Janney transports her reader back to 1739 and the early years of the Great Awakening. Henry Sharp, a young graduate of William Tennent's Log College, travels to Philadelphia to help an ailing Presbyterian minister, and a spark of love ignites between him and the pastor's daughter. However, another suitor waits in the wings. William Tennent, George Whitefield, and Benjamin Franklin figure prominently in the story. Rebecca captures the tension between the New Side

revivalists and the Old Side traditionalists. Once I started reading this book, I couldn't put it down. This is a must read for anyone longing for another Great Awakening.
—**Wendy Wirsch**, President, William Tennent House Association

Rebecca Price Janney's novel brings the First Great Awakening to life through the eyes of compelling characters. Readers can identify with these young Christians who demonstrate great faith and human vulnerability as they witness Whitefield's fervent ministry. *Morning Glory* artfully tells the true story of a revival that shaped early American Christianity and the first Great Awakening. In doing so, it brings Whitefield's passionate message into the present, challenging readers to follow Jesus wholeheartedly today.
—**Bill Curtis**, President Christian History Institute

Morning Glory, a Novel of the First Great Awakening, provides a historically accurate account that is enjoyable to read, as well as interesting and thought-provoking. Rebecca Price Janney does a remarkable job telling this story by engaging the reader with diverse characters, striking descriptions, poignant moments, and an attention to historical detail.
—**Sue A. Fairchild**, editor, author, *What You Think You Know*

It's enjoyable to see the people I've researched and written about come to life in Rebecca Price Janney's *Morning Glory: A Novel of the First Great Awakening*. I found it riveting and refreshing to walk with her characters page-by-page as they grapple with the challenges and controversies of their day. Though the book's setting is three centuries removed from us, my hope is that modern readers will discover the timeless—and in some cases life changing—lessons embedded in this engaging narrative of the extraordinary time when God "visited" America."
—**John F. Hansen**, author, *The Vision That Changed A Nation: The Legacy of William Tennent*

It's easy to forget the rich spiritual heritage of my native Southeastern Pennsylvania, but Janney's *Morning Glory* brought it to life for me through the characterizations of theological giants and their places in the supernatural drama of the First Great Awakening. Retelling the story of revival through the eyes of common believers, *Morning Glory* is sure to please lovers of Christian historical fiction and inspirational romance alike.
—**Kaylena Radcliff**, author, *Torchlighters:* Corrie Ten Boom biography

Morning Glory

A Novel of the First Great Awakening

Rebecca Price Janney

Copyright Notice

Morning Glory: A Novel of the First Great Awakening—Book 1, Morning in America Series

First edition. Copyright © 2019 by Rebecca Price Janney. The information contained in this book is the intellectual property of Rebecca Price Janney and is governed by United States and International copyright laws. All rights reserved. No part of this publication, either text or image, may be used for any purpose other than personal use. Therefore, reproduction, modification, storage in a retrieval system, or retransmission, in any form or by any means, electronic, mechanical, or otherwise, for reasons other than personal use, except for brief quotations for reviews or articles and promotions, is strictly prohibited without prior written permission by the publisher.

This book is a work of fiction. Characters are the product of the author's imagination. Any resemblance to actual events or persons, living or dead, is entirely coincidental.

Scripture quotations from the Authorized (King James) Version. Rights in the Authorized Version in the United Kingdom are vested in the Crown. Reproduced by permission of the Crown's patentee, Cambridge University Press

Cover and Interior Design: Derinda Babcock

Editor: Deb Haggerty

Author Represented by WordWise Media

PUBLISHED BY: Elk Lake Publishing, Inc., 35 Dogwood Dr., Plymouth, MA 02360, 2019

Library Cataloging Data

Names: Janney, Rebecca Price (Rebecca Price Janney)

Morning Glory: A Novel of the First Great Awakening—Book 1, Morning in America Series / Rebecca Price Janney

270 p. 23cm × 15cm (9in × 6 in.)

Description: George Whitefield preaches to America--thousands come to a saving knowledge of Jesus Christ. For Catherine and Henry, a common love of Christ draws them together.

Identifiers: ISBN-13: 978-1-948888-88-2 (trade) | 978-1-948888-89-9 (POD) | 978-1-948888-90-5 (e-book).

Key Words: George Whitefield, Colonial Era, Religion, Christianity in America, Benjamin Franklin, Revival, Philadelphia

LCCN: 2018968299 Fiction

DEDICATION

For the ministers who have especially impacted my life:
S. Clyde Robison
Peter Marshall
Richard B. Gibbons
James Montgomery Boice
Charles Zimmerman
Jim Farrell

ACKNOWLEDGMENTS

I'm deeply grateful to the people who shared my enthusiasm for this book about George Whitefield and the First Great Awakening, especially Wendy Wirsch, historian of the Neshaminy-Warwick Presbyterian Church and President of the William Tennent House Association. She is also a reenactor who portrays Catherine Kennedy Tennent, William's steadfast wife. Wendy spent the better part of a day giving me delightful tours of the Neshaminy-Warwick Presbyterian Church and grounds, including the site where George Whitefield preached to thousands, and the William Tennent homestead in Warminster, where I could almost picture Whitefield and Tennent sitting before the hearth. I appreciate her valuable insights and information about Tennent, his family, life, and ministry.

I also wish to thank Dr. Gary E. Gary, Professor of Biblical Studies at Cairn University's School of Divinity in Langhorne, Pennsylvania, for his perceptions about early American revivals. Biblical Seminary librarians Dan LaValla and Lydia Putnam dug through the archives, producing wonderful old abstracts and books pertaining to George Whitefield. Kudos!

Thanks also to my friend, Heidi Patrick, who helped me brush up on my German, making sure I used the right words and phrases. *Danke schon!*

For the unfailing prayers and encouragement of my dear friends, Sandra Allen and Marlo Schalesky, I am deeply grateful. I love you both.

To my husband, Scott, and son, David, who cheered me on and got swept up in my stories about that great revival, thanks for your support, and for the occasional reminders to, "Come back to the 21st century!"

I am especially indebted to my Lord Jesus Christ for giving me the gift and desire to write for His glory and to encourage others.

> The hand of the LORD was on me, and he brought me out by the Spirit of the LORD and set me in the middle of a valley; it was full of bones. He led me back and forth among them, and

Morning Glory

I saw a great many bones on the floor of the valley, bones that were very dry. He asked me, "Son of man, can these bones live?"

I said, "Sovereign LORD, you alone know."

Then he said to me, "Prophesy to these bones and say to them, 'Dry bones, hear the word of the LORD! This is what the Sovereign LORD says to these bones: I will make breath enter you, and you will come to life.'"

Ezekiel 37:1-5

CHAPTER ONE

There was something about the silence that disquieted her. As a city lass used to the ongoing cacophony of teaming streets, the abode of the wilds created in her a constant darting of the eyes to the edges of the primitive road. Many miles into their journey from Philadelphia, she could barely sit still when the carriage slowed in what appeared to be a dead end. The sounds of nature seemed to shoot darts into her soul. Catherine's head jerked to the side. "What is happening?"

Her brother didn't answer fast enough to suit her. "I seem to have wandered from the main road." The false lilt in his tone was not lost on his sibling.

"Y-you don't know w-where we are?" The dense, darkening thicket began pressing in on her, and she slouched as if to withdraw like a turtle into a modicum of safety.

"I wouldn't say 'lost,'" Jacob said. "Turned around maybe."

She deliberately lowered her voice to keep from screeching, her pulse the ocean's roar in her ears. "We are surrounded on three sides by trees and bushes. I think we'd better turn around."

"Yes, you're right."

When Jacob did so, however, coming toward them from the one way out stood a lithe, dark figure, which Catherine immediately recognized. She'd only seen Indians a few times in her life at Head House Square, objects of curiosity doing business at the market. In this lonely place, however, this man caused her to tremble. She noticed Jacob reach for the musket beside him on the seat.

"Hello," her brother said.

The native bowed his head slightly. "You may be lost then?"

Catherine exchanged a quick glance with Jacob. *He speaks English!*

"Yes, I am afraid so."

"To where you be going?"

She was grateful the gun lay close at hand, just in case. *Oh, Lord, please protect us.*

"To Warminster."

The Indian, who hadn't moved from the opening, shook his head. "You missed, a while back. Come. I show you."

Jacob turned to Catherine, his eyes holding a question. Could they trust him? She nodded. What other option did they have? If anything went wrong, there was always the musket. The Indian turned his bare back to them and began walking away from the enclosed thicket, the wagon rumbling after him. When he had brought them into the open, he started gesturing this way and that, his voice clear and strong.

"Do you understand?"

"Yes, thank you," Jacob said.

"Better to hurry." The Indian raised his face to the sky. "Night is coming."

"Yes, we will. Thank you again."

He nodded and crossed his arms over his chest. Catherine gave him a close-mouthed smile and bowed her thanks. When they were many yards away, her tension uncoiled.

❦

"I still don't understand why Father didn't just get Mr. Oldfield's brother to help out."

Reaching their destination, Catherine glanced over at her younger brother. "He doesn't want Mr. Oldfield. He has someone else in mind."

Jacob stared straight ahead. "I'm a disappointment to Father, aren't I?"

Catherine's mouth dropped open—her brother wasn't given to much reflection. "Why do you say so?"

He shrugged his shoulders. "I know he always wanted me to be a minister, but I just never had the desire in me."

"Well, at least you know your mind. There are many pastors who do considerably more harm than good, having no business leading churches." Adjusting her hat, she wondered whether he getting any of this. "Father believes God has other work for you."

Jacob gave what passed for a laugh. "Do you think apprenticing with Mr. Franklin is God's work?"

"If you allow God to guide you."

He turned to her and smiled. "Perhaps you should become a Quaker."

"Whatever for?" She clasped her hand to her chest.

"Because they allow women to be ministers."

Henry usually walked the twenty minutes between Mr. Tennent's house and the church, but tonight, he was on an important mission and rode his horse instead. When he arrived, he discovered a small gathering, unusual at this late hour. Peering into the near distance, he could make out the form of Mr. Harmon, the caretaker, along with the disagreeable elder who was constantly making trouble for Tennent. Henry pursed his lips, wondering if Mason were dreaming up some new scheme to kick Tennent out of the pulpit, having tried unsuccessfully on several occasions. He summoned his resolve to exhibit Christlike behavior in all circumstances while taking note of two strangers—a young man, whom Henry judged to be about sixteen, and a woman who seemed closer to his own age. Even in the fading light, he could see she was nice looking.

"Well, if it isn't *Heinrich* Sharp," Mason said snidely. "What might you be doing here now?"

"Good evening, Elder Mason. I was just wondering the same." Henry managed to keep his voice steady, but when he dismounted and tied his horse to the hitching post, he purposely stood next to the much shorter man. Sometimes, Henry let his height do the talking.

Mason took a step back and gestured toward the new arrivals. "Mr. Harmon and I are on church business. We found these weary travelers looking for Mr. Tennent, and I was just explaining how he lives not a mile from here."

The young woman introduced herself. "Good evening. I'm Catherine Harrison from Philadelphia, and this is my brother, Jacob."

"I'm pleased to meet you." He removed his hat and bowed. "I'm Henry Sharp. May I be of assistance?"

"Our father is Pastor Joseph Harrison of High Street Presbyterian Church, and he's sent us on an urgent matter."

Henry had met their father once at the Log College a while back and had taken a liking to him. Actually, he'd heard from Tennent recently about Harrison's poor health and wondered if he might be gravely ill, or even had died.

"I've just come to the church to get something for Mr. Tennent," Henry said. "I'll be glad to take you to him."

Mason sneered. "Our minister grows forgetful in his old age."

Ignoring his comment, Henry walked toward the church door, the caretaker on his heels. "Mr. Harmon, I trust you have a key?"

"Oh, yes, yes, indeed." Harmon leaned toward Henry's ear, nearly tripping into the younger man. "I'm here because of Mr. Mason. I mean no harm."

"Of course not." Henry's voice softened. He'd never known the custodian to be untrustworthy.

He walked over to the desk where Tennent kept his papers as Harmon chattered incessantly. Not knowing exactly how to find the particular notes his pastor had requested, Henry grabbed the lot and headed toward the doors, careful not to drop any of them.

"Thank you, Mr. Harmon. I have everything I need."

The little man rushed ahead to open the door for him, and once outside, Henry stuffed the papers carefully into his saddlebag. Mason seemed to be trying his hardest to wheedle information out of the young woman, but she offered only cagey responses. *Good for her! She seems to be a good judge of character.* Turning to the visitors he said, "If you're ready, I'll take you to Mr. Tennent."

Looking relieved, Catherine Harrison thanked him and climbed back into the carriage beside her brother. "Good evening, Mr. Mason, Mr. Harmon," she said with an aloof nod.

Catherine snuggled deeper into her cape while Jacob steered the vehicle alongside Henry Sharp, noting how the weather was definitely cooler here than in the city. The thump of horses' hooves as they crossed a stone bridge over Little Neshaminy Creek accompanied their conversation. She felt more awake, more talkative, now she knew for certain where they were going, a far cry from an hour ago in the deep wood. Her misgivings, however, hadn't totally ceased. Something about the elder who'd greeted them at the church made her skin crawl, his manner reminiscent of Robert Oldfield. Fortunately, this fellow Henry Sharp had come upon them on his sleek mare, putting her immediately at ease. She didn't mind he was handsome, either—a big-chested, fair-haired man who towered above the others. When the elder had called him "Heinrich," her pulse had quickened. *Could this be the man Father spoke of?*

She could smell the lighthearted scent of honeysuckle growing along the sides of the road, playing host to crickets chirping to one another as night enrobed them. Jacob was recounting the details of their adventure to Sharp, leaving Catherine to wonder whether she should jump into the conversation and confide the purpose of their journey, or wait until she was with the Tennents. She decided to delay, but in the meantime, she'd try to find out all she could about this intriguing man.

"Are you a student at the Log College?" she asked when there was an opening.

"I've recently graduated from there," he said.

"I'm curious—do all of the students come from around here?"

"Most of them do."

"Yourself included?"

"Yes. Actually, my family lives on a farm next to the Tennents. My father and older brother are also blacksmiths."

"So you grew up in Neshaminy Presbyterian Church?"

Jacob cast her a look as if to say, "Enough questions, sister."

"For most of my life. The congregation didn't start until about thirteen years ago."

"Where did your family worship before there was a church here?" She wanted to find out for sure if he was German. He might be Dutch after all. She enjoyed listening to his resonant voice, but there was no hint of any accent, so she couldn't tell about his family background. *He could be compelling in a pulpit.*

"They had to wait until a traveling minister led them in worship and brought the sacraments."

"Were they Presbyterians?" She knew she was asking way too many questions, but she couldn't seem to hold back. What might this young man think of such a bold female? Still, she just had to know if this was the man her father wanted to summon. If she knew what kind of church his family had attended before Tennent's, she might also know his nationality.

"They were German Reformed, which is similar," Sharp said. "That was the faith of my grandfather and grandmother when they came here about twenty-five years ago."

So, he is German! Satisfied her efforts had been rewarded, a new thought struck her—*What if he's not the only one at Mr. Tennent's school? Of course, if he were not, Father would have been more specific.* In her mind's eye, she could picture his piercing gaze when he looked up at her from his sick bed and commanded, "Get the German."

"Sister!"

Catherine glanced toward her brother. "Yes?"

"You plague Mr. Sharp with questions."

A blush reached all the way to her scalp. "I do apologize, Mr. Sharp. I seem to be afflicted with curiosity."

Henry gave a kind of snort, then pulled out a handkerchief and discreetly blew his nose.

"You might be interested to know, Miss Harrison, I am of a similar frame of mind."

Relief spread from her temples to her toes. After a pause, Catherine felt emboldened. "You were born here, then, Mr. Sharp?" She ignored her brother's light jabs to her side.

"Yes, in fact, we're on my family's property now and will soon reach the Tennent's." He paused then asked, "Since you're from Philadelphia, perhaps you know about Mr. George Whitefield's coming to the city?"

Catherine nodded, but before she could say anything, Jacob spoke. "Yes, we've had such news. I work for Benjamin Franklin, the printer, and we've been carrying stories about Mr. Whitefield's visit."

"When do you expect him, then?"

Catherine heard a boyish enthusiasm in Henry's voice.

"The last I heard, late October."

"You are excited about hearing him?" Catherine asked.

"Oh, yes."

"I am as well. Do you know sometimes he preaches in the fields because not all churches can hold the masses of people who come out to hear him?"

"Yes, I know. I wonder where he'll preach in Philadelphia." Then he added, "Wherever he speaks, I'll be there."

So will I.

They came in sight of the Tennent's barn where Henry directed them to hitch their horse and wagon. He put his mare in a stall, then fed and watered their animals.

"Do be careful," he said when they set out for the house. "The walkway is uneven."

For a moment, Catherine thought he might offer his arm, but instead he took her leather satchel and led the way. She tripped once on one of the rocks, and Jacob steadied her.

Henry looked over his shoulder. "Are you all right, Miss Harrison?"

"Yes, thank you."

When they reached the front door of the whitewashed house, Henry knocked, then went inside.

"I'm back," he announced, as Mr. Tennent came to greet him.

He must be very close to the Tennents to go into their home unbidden.

Henry stepped aside for her and her brother to enter.

"Well, good evening to you, Miss Harrison! And there's young Mr. Jacob. How nice of you to come!" The white-haired minister smiled as if he'd known them for years and had been expecting them.

Several men, sitting in what appeared to be the parlor, craned their necks, apparently to see who had come in. Catherine saw a look of surprise on Henry Sharp's face, which probably mirrored her own. *I can't believe he remembers me or my name.*

"Do you know these people, Mr. Tennent?"

"Why, of course I do, Henry." He took Catherine's hands and held them for a long moment. "What a pleasure to see you again, Miss Harrison."

She curtsied. "Hello, sir. The pleasure is mine."

Jacob stepped forward to shake the minister's hand. "Mr. Tennent, I am Jacob Harrison."

"You have grown to manhood since I last saw you." Tennent looked around. "Is your good father with you?"

Jacob looked to Catherine. "I'm afraid not, but he's the one who sent us to see you."

Tennent gave her a knowing look. Waving them into the dining room to the left of the door, he called out for his wife. "Mother! See who's come to visit!"

Mrs. Tennent appeared from a room off the dining area, a serene figure with a welcoming smile and kind eyes as soft as summer twilight. Like her spouse, she received her guests as if she knew exactly who they were and the reason for their visit.

"Welcome, my dears. You have certainly come a long way and must be road weary. Do come in and sit." She indicated chairs loosely arranged around a big mahogany table.

"You remember Miss Harrison." Tennent's was more a statement than a question. "She's the daughter of Mr. Joseph Harrison, of Philadelphia's High Street Presbyterian Church, and this is her brother."

Catherine felt proud when her sibling bowed as if he was remembering every lesson in etiquette their mother had ever taught him. "I am Jacob Harrison, madam."

"I am pleased to see you both," Mrs. Tennent said. "I'm guessing you've not had your supper."

Catherine remembered their small meal of soggy bread; apple cider had spilled all over the loaf as well as their cheese. "We did have some food," she said, trying to be honest. Jacob gave her a look, which Mrs. Tennent seemed to pick up on immediately.

"I'll have our servants prepare something for you right away. In the meantime, you might want to freshen up."

Afterwards, Catherine joined her brother in the dining room for a pleasant meal of rabbit stew, warm bread, and milk, while in the background, they could hear Mr. Tennent leading students from his so-called Log College in the exposition of Scripture. He appeared in the doorway just as she and Jacob finished eating.

"My good friends, would you care to join us in the parlor?"

Catherine spoke for herself and her brother. "Yes, thank you."

They rose from the table and joined their hosts and four young men, including Henry Sharp. The fire burned low, its warmth and the scent of smoldering pine offering comfort as Catherine shed still more of the chill from the journey. When they'd left Philadelphia in mid-morning, she'd just assumed they would arrive in Warminster by late afternoon, deliver their message, and turn right around to go home. Now she realized how little she knew about traveling.

"Miss Harrison, sit here by me and Jacob, there is a seat for you next to young Mr. Whiting. Now then, men, I would like to introduce some visitors from Philadelphia. This is Miss Harrison and her brother Jacob, and these are some of my ministry students—Mr. Whiting, Mr. Eden, and Mr. Thomas. You've already met Mr. Sharp."

Catherine nodded at each man, then her eyes rested upon Sharp, who smiled and bowed his head.

"The Harrisons' father, Joseph, is pastor of the High Street Presbyterian Church. Do tell us, Miss Harrison, what brings you here?"

Rebecca Price Janney

"We have come, good sir, on a matter of utmost urgency."

CHAPTER TWO

Catherine's hands quivered as she began to unfold the story of their mission. "Mr. Tennent, my father has become quite ill."

The old man wrinkled his brow. "I'm sorry to hear such news. What is the matter?"

She willed herself to speak slowly and clearly, clenching her folded hands to control her trembling. "Every winter he gets sick with coughing spells, but when the weather grows warmer, he always regains his health. This past year, however, the sickness was worse than usual, and this spring and summer were so chilly." She pictured him lying in bed hacking, her mother framed by the doorway wringing her hands and weeping. Both of them were in bad shape—her father, physically, her mother, emotionally, and she didn't really know which she considered to be in worse condition. If only her mother understood the great and precious promises of being in Christ! Catherine and her father had prayed seemingly without ceasing for Ann and young Jacob to know the new birth, but so far, they lacked spiritual understanding. As for herself, Catherine was fighting her own fears about her father's health—she certainly didn't want to be like her mother.

"He's been limited to preaching once on Sunday morning, then he spends the rest of the week recovering. Recently he hasn't been able to finish his sermons because of severe coughing spells." She paused, feeling the fire's warmth caress her legs. "I've been visiting some of our members for him, but alas, I can't preach."

"She wishes she could, though," Jacob said with a half-smile.

This caused a ripple of laughter, and she glared playfully at her brother. Then she began to relax, feeling calmer after the initial release of tension. "My father's inability to carry out his duties has become a concern to our church, and just this morning an elder came to see him about the situation. After Mr. Oldfield told us about his brother, who's a minister, and how he could fill the pulpit while my father recovered, Father had an especially bad spell. Later, Father told me under no circumstances was I to allow the Reverend Oldfield to come. This puzzled me because finding qualified ministers is so difficult these days."

Tennent nodded, his gaze inviting Catherine to continue.

"My father said he is of a different spirit."

"I know him," Tennent said, clapping his hands against his knees. "He's an Old Side."

"Old Side?" Jacob asked.

Catherine could tell by Tennent's expression he understood her brother wasn't spiritually astute.

"That's right, Jacob. Old Sides believe adherence to doctrines, creeds, and human effort are God's requirements for salvation. American pulpits are full of them, which has resulted in a generally dead faith across the colonies. Your father, on the other hand, understands how being born anew in Christ Jesus comes from repentance of sin. This is one of the main reasons all of us here are looking forward to George Whitefield's arrival this fall—maybe he'll be the spark God uses to ignite the faith of the colonies."

Catherine nodded. "Father hopes so, too. He's been trying to bring his congregation to the new birth in Christ since his own a few years ago." She paused, then spoke quietly. "That's when I came to faith in Jesus Christ as well."

Tennent smiled. "I remember, my dear."

"I believe you understand Father doesn't want the Reverend Mr. Oldfield to come and undo his work."

"Of course not, Miss Harrison. Each man in this room can attest to being at odds with other church leaders about what it means to be part of the kingdom of God. To hold to a form of religion while denying its power is a serious thing, with eternal consequences."

"Yes." She paused. "When I asked him what to do, Father told me to come here right away, that you—" she looked at Tennent, "—would be able to send someone to help us."

"Several fine men have already graduated from my school."

"Father has someone specific in mind."

"Indeed?" His eyes had the appearance of a star at first light. "Who, may I ask?"

She took a deep breath, then spoke, "He told me, 'Get the German.'"

Henry felt a sudden, bracing cold—like the time when, as boys, he and his older brother had jumped recklessly into the creek at the end of April. Another sensation followed, the kind of warmth he experienced after a hearty sip of his mother's coffee. Both carried with them something he recognized as the peace of Christ. Henry knew two things for certain—this winsome young woman was talking about him, and he was meant to go with her and her brother to Philadelphia. Maybe this was why he hadn't known tranquility about which church he was supposed to serve, although he knew which one his family wanted him to take. The Tennent's grandfather clock ticked time, and everyone in the parlor was looking at him. The room was vibrant, as if a heavenly chord had been struck. When she had spoken, Miss Harrison had averted her eyes as if she felt too shy to look directly upon anyone, let alone him. "That's just what my father told me, Mr. Tennent," she said at last. "He didn't say for how long we would need this minister, or where he would lodge—not even what his compensation would be." She looked down at her hands resting on her lap.

"Sometimes, my dear, God requires of us things that don't make sense humanly speaking, for his ways are not our ways." Tennent looked at Henry, who felt a need to say something.

"Miss Harrison, since I'm the only student here of German descent, your good father must have been referring to me."

She turned to him, her face coloring. "Yes."

"Did he say anything else?" Tennent asked.

Catherine shook her head. "No, sir. He did make the request with great authority and urgency, however. I have no doubt he knew exactly what he wanted."

Tennent gazed at Henry. "Mr. Sharp, we've been praying for your call for several weeks now, not knowing which of two churches you should serve. What are your thoughts about this new, albeit temporary, post?"

"I can almost hear a voice beside me saying 'This is the way, go in it,'" he said, paraphrasing Isaiah 30:21. "However, there is one potential problem." He looked at Catherine, knowing there were actually two, at least. "You see, Miss Harrison, I've not yet been ordained, so I would be limited in what I'm able to do. For example, I could not serve communion." He hoped she wouldn't be put off by this.

"Would this stop you, then, from coming?" she asked, her eyes widening.

Tennent broke in. "There could be trouble from this Elder Oldfield as well, depending on what kind of man he is."

"Such as?" Catherine asked.

"He could file a complaint of some sort to the Presbytery."

"Wouldn't such a thing take time to sort through?" she asked.

"Yes."

"I seem to have put you in an awkward position, Mr. Sharp." Catherine looked into his light-blue eyes. "If you would rather not come, I'll understand."

Before Henry could speak, Tennent said, "I can suggest one or two other men I have educated who've been ordained. I'm sure your father's congregation would benefit from their services."

Henry realized his teacher was giving him a way out, if he chose. He hated the way lesser spirits consistently tried to thwart God's will and decided he wouldn't give them the satisfaction this time around.

"I promised my Savior a long time ago I would follow him wherever he called me. I believe he's leading me to help your father, Miss Harrison, however uncertain the details may be. We can trust God to work all those things out to his glory."

Her amber eyes glistened. "Thank you, Mr. Sharp."

He nodded. "My pleasure."

"I've been wondering, how did my father know to ask for you?"

Henry pursed his lips. "I remember meeting him when he visited our school about a year ago. We enjoyed talking with each other very much—there was a connection between us."

"Yes, yes, and he wanted to know all about the school and my students. That he's singled you out, Mr. Sharp, is noteworthy." Tennent became animated. "I do see God's hand is in this."

"Yes, sir, I have the same conviction."

"Mind you, this won't be easy. You know the forces working against me at Neshaminy. I can only predict similar troubles for you in Philadelphia."

Henry blew out a puff of air. "I'm well acquainted with them, and I've watched you handle them with grace and dignity, Mr. Tennent. I know I can count on all of your prayers." He felt his chest swell with a feeling of invincibility.

"Mr. Tennent, there is something I don't understand," Jacob said. "My father felt strongly about not having Mr. Oldfield's brother substitute for him. Although I must confess I'm not overly fond of Mr. Oldfield, why should there be such distrust about another minister? Aren't all clergy men of God?"

"Would that they were, Mr. Harrison."

A spent log slipped to the bottom of the grate, casting sparks which flew upward. "Do you recall how your father came to know our Lord a short time ago?"

"I, uh, guess so." Jacob sounded uncertain. "Something about a new birth, he said."

"And yet, he was already a minister, was he not?"

"Yes, sir."

"You see, men have various reasons for entering the ministry. Perhaps they want to do some good in this world. Others enter the church because their families wish them to do so. Some serve because the Lord God has called them. Your father wasn't a Christian when he became a pastor, but there was rejoicing in heaven when he repented and gave his life completely to the Savior. Now he's as solid in his faith as any man, or woman, I have known."

"And what of those who are not, uh, Christians?" Jacob asked.

Henry could tell the young man was having difficulty wrapping his mind around these concepts and began praying he would come to understand the truth being expressed.

"They're creating much division within the church," his mentor said. "They hold to the traditions and teachings of men, rather than to the work of regeneration. Far too many church people profess with their lips, while their hearts are far from God."

"And the Reverend Mr. Oldfield is such a man?" Jacob asked.

He nodded. "From what I know of him, yes. You must understand, Satan does some of his greatest damage in the Church, which he despises. When you think about it, though, this makes sense. He already has the people outside of the faith in his grasp. To harm Christ's Church is to inflict the most bitter damage."

Seeing Catherine frown, Henry sought to reassure her. "He's a defeated enemy, Miss Harrison. The very gates of hell shall not prevail against the Church." He was pleased when she smiled at him.

Tennent motioned for everyone to come closer. "We need to have a time of prayer for Mr. Sharp. If you would, my son, kneel right here."

Henry's fellow students, Mrs. Tennent, Catherine, and Jacob gathered around him in a bulging kind of circle, but there was nothing sloppy about the crisp, bold prayers filling the room. He couldn't wait to get to Philadelphia.

Catherine Tennent took charge when they finished. "My dear, Miss Harrison, you and your brother must be fatigued by your long journey and the deep concern for your father."

"Actually, yes, we are." Henry noted the way Jacob's eyes seemed to be disappearing into his forehead.

"Come with me. You'll sleep in our second bedroom upstairs, and Mr. Harrison, I'll put you on the third floor with the students."

"Thank you, Mrs. Tennent," Jacob said.

"Mr. Sharp, I assume you'll be going home tonight?"

"Yes, madam."

"One of the students will bring the Harrisons over in the morning. Tell your good mother I'll prepare food for your journey, since there's such short notice."

Henry bowed. "Thank you." He looked upon her lovingly, knowing he wouldn't be seeing this dear woman for possibly a long time to come.

She touched his cheek. "You are as dear to me as a son."

Henry disliked waking his parents, but he lifted his right hand and knocked, calling softly, "Mama. Papa." On his third attempt he heard, "Heinrich? Is that you?"

"*Ja.*"

"*Komm heren.*"

He opened the door as his parents sat up in the bed his grandfather had carved years ago.

"*Wie spät ist es?*"

"After eleven."

"Are you well?" She sounded anxious.

"*Ja, Mama. Mir geht es gut.*"

She patted the side of the mattress, and he sat down as he'd done many years ago after being frightened by bad dreams or bumps in the night.

"I have something to tell you." He inhaled. "God has shown me the direction I must take."

"You have decided on the Bedminster church, then?" she asked, all alight.

He knew how badly she wanted him not only to stay close, but to minister to their own family members as they came from Germany and settled in the neighboring community. Although not an easy task, in the next few minutes, he told them all about Catherine and Jacob Harrison's visit to the Tennents, and their father's urgent plea.

"I knew I must go when she said he wanted her to 'get the German.' Mr. Harrison meant me."

Silence. He could almost hear them breathing. Were they going to disapprove? He hoped not because he knew he couldn't disobey the Lord's call.

His father said, "I'm not one to argue with the Almighty, but this seems *verruckt*. You have two good calls from German congregations, including one involving your own flesh and blood, but *Gott* requires you to go to the English in Philadelphia, and for how long, who knows?"

Henry could see the outline of his mother's head nodding in the darkness.

"Where would you live?" she asked.

"What will they pay you?" his father asked in turn.

"I'll find out soon, probably tomorrow." He wished he knew so they could be more settled about the situation.

"What kind of a man is this minister?"

"A *gut* man, Mama. I met him when he came to see Mr. Tennent, and I felt a strong connection with him. I want to help him."

"I am concerned, Heinrich, that this other man, the elder, may make trouble for you, since he wants his brother to take the position."

He could feel his temperature rising. "This other pastor is not right with God. We have too much of church people not being right with God."

"*Ja*," his parents said at the same time.

Their family had looked with heartache upon developments at Neshaminy Presbyterian Church as Mr. Tennent's opponents had tried repeatedly to remove him as pastor because they considered him a zealot.

"We must not let such men win these battles," Wilhelm Sharp said. Then he asked, "Will you be ordained, then?"

"*Nein*. Rather than being a call of the presbytery, my service is a favor to a brother in Christ."

"Then you cannot act fully as a minister there." His father's voice rose.

"This is true." Henry couldn't argue with this. "From a human standpoint, this makes little sense, but I'm convinced God is calling me to go, and he already knows the end from the beginning."

His mother sighed. "Will this harm your chances of taking one of the other churches?"

"I don't think so, Mama."

"I wish I knew how long you must be away."

Henry tried to soothe her. "Perhaps Mr. Harrison will regain his health soon, with the burden of his duties lifted. Then I could ..."

Then he could what? Go to the Bedminster church, or the other one? In his spirit, he felt like he'd come to a high, stone wall barring him from seeing any further ahead.

"First things first," he said.

CHAPTER THREE

Dorothea Sharp was looking pleased with herself. She'd risen before the cock's crow to bake her son's favorite German bread, adding cheese, bratwurst, pickled cabbage, and a few bushels of fresh vegetables and fruit to the food she was sending with him to Philadelphia.

"Mama, we're not going to sea," he said, kissing her cheek.

"You'll be hungry in Philadelphia."

"I've been to that city, and I assure you, they have food there."

Undaunted, she shooed him away to carry out her maternal mission. While Henry went off to pack, his father came into the room with a firm set to his jaw and a wrinkled brow.

"Heinrich, I'm satisfied to leave you at the mercy of our loving God, but not at the mercy of men. *Hier*." He handed over a leather wallet.

"*Was ist das?*" Henry asked.

"You don't know how you will be paid, so this will help you not to want for anything."

Henry's voice was husky. "*Vielen Dank, Papa.*"

"*Bitte seh*r."

Following an abundant breakfast, William Tennent sent Catherine and Jacob off with a blessing and prayers for their father's health. "Above all," he concluded, "may Jesus Christ be praised and glorified."

"Thank you, Mr. Tennent. I will try to keep his glory ever before me."

Jacob looked at his feet, as if he didn't know what to say.

"That is where you will find peace—and rest for your soul."

"You've been so kind," Catherine said.

Tennent smiled at her, then shook Jacob's hand. "See well to your sister, my son."

"I will, sir. Thank you for your hospitality."

Catherine wondered what kinds of conversations might have transpired the night before between her brother and the Log College students while she slept soundly in the guest room. Now, in the promise of a new day, she dared hope all might be well at last for her father, their family, and his church. Even the earth smelled fresh on this early autumn morning. She thanked Catherine Tennent for the ample supply of food she was sending with them and embraced her before leaving. Not ten minutes later they arrived at the Sharp farm, Jacob giving a low whistle.

"Wow, sister. Mr. Sharp's family appears to have some means."

"Indeed."

She wasn't sure what she had expected, but certainly less than what met her eyes. As the wagon lumbered up a dirt lane, she noticed a blacksmith shop to the left and just beyond, a barn and several other buildings. Commanding the most attention was an elegant stone house with two-toned shutters at each of the windows. Chunky sheep bleated in a field as Henry Sharp looked up from cinching his saddlebags.

"Whoa. Whoa." Jacob pulled the reins, bringing the horse and vehicle to a stop. "Good morning, Mr. Sharp."

"And a good morning to you, Mr. Harrison." Henry doffed his black beaver hat and walked over to them. "Miss Harrison."

"Good day, Mr. Sharp."

"I believe this will, indeed, be a good one." He looked toward the blue sky. "We have favorable weather for our journey. So, did you both rest well?"

"Yes, thank you. Mrs. Tennent is a fine hostess."

"She surely is." He suddenly looked like one of the sheep in his pasture. "Do you have room for a few things?"

Catherine noticed a leather trunk by the front door, along with assorted casks, baskets, and a barrel.

Jacob handed the reins to his sister as he jumped down. "Is that everything?"

"Actually, there are a few more baskets besides those."

"Oh, okay, then," Jacob said.

She watched them haul everything to the wagon, noticing as well how nice Henry Sharp looked this morning with his dark blonde hair pulled into a neat pigtail. Wearing a navy coat, linen waistcoat, and tan breeches, he loomed over her brother, who wasn't exactly short. Catherine guessed the young minister must be several inches over six feet tall.

Jacob grunted as he lifted the rest of the copious supplies into the wagon. "One thing is certain. None of us will go hungry—not even if this journey takes eight days instead of eight hours."

Henry laughed. "I do apologize. My mother enjoys feeding people." Their task complete, he looked toward the house. "Ah, here is my dear family now."

A small group gathered near the wagon, and Catherine looked at each one while resisting urges to stare. She wanted to see what kind of people Mr. Sharp came from, wanted somehow to like them. Although Mrs. Sharp was rather short and plump, very much unlike Henry, her son had her blue eyes. The father was tall, but slightly stooped, probably from a life of honest toil, with flaxen-colored hair, a long nose, and comfortable smile, all like his son.

"Miss Harrison, Mr. Harrison, may I present my family?" Henry walked over to his parents. "This is my mother, Dorothea Sharp, and my father, Wilhelm or William. These are my brothers, Christian, William, and Peter, and my dear sister, Sarah."

The little girl curtsied to Catherine, who smiled first at her, then at the rest of the Sharps.

An old man hobbled out the front door and joined the group, supporting himself with a walking stick.

"*Opa*, I would like you to meet Miss Catherine Harrison, and her brother, Jacob."

A cow lowed in the near distance as the elderly man's eyes took in first Jacob, then Catherine. Grinning, he said "*Sie ist sehr hübsch!*"

Sarah clapped her hand over her mouth, and Henry's mother gave her father-in-law a thorough scolding in German. The brothers snickered, and Henry gazed into the sky, red-faced. "You must excuse my grandfather, Miss Harrison," he said. "At his age, he speaks his mind. I assure you, his opinion of you is favorable."

"I see." She and Jacob looked at each other and shrugged. She would have to learn some German.

Dorothea Sharp stepped forward bearing a large basket protected by a cloth of many colors. In accented English, she said, "I am sorry to hear of your father's sickness. Please accept these gifts for him." She held the container up to the wagon, and Henry sprang forward to help Catherine lift the heavy object. "There are bread, broth, preserves, and biscuits."

"You are very kind, Mrs. Sharp. Thank you, on behalf of my family."

The older woman nodded. "Above all, I offer my prayers."

"We must be going," Henry said. He embraced his mother first, then his tearful sister. "Do not worry, *liebling*," he said, chucking her chin. "I will return before you know." He shook hands with his grandfather and brothers, and just as he grasped his father's, the elder Sharp glanced at Catherine, who heard him whisper, "I think you will have your hands full, Heinrich."

The journey to Philadelphia passed far more quickly and pleasantly than the previous day's wanderings. Henry Sharp's presence reassured Catherine as she provided a rundown on the church and its members. She was yearning to know more about him, such as when he had come to know the Savior and what interests he had outside of the church, but she held back because of her interrogation of the night before. When they experienced periods of silence, his horse keeping pace with the wagon, she rested in them, rather than feeling any sense of awkwardness. For as much as she liked to talk, Catherine also needed time to think her own thoughts.

One thing she was wondering about, which she was reluctant to discuss without first knowing her parents' wishes, was the immediate matter of where Mr. Sharp would be lodging. Although their three-story manse had plenty of room, she knew having a young man of marriageable age under the same roof as herself wouldn't be proper. The very thought caused her cheeks to flush, and she became vexed when he asked, "Are you quite well, Miss Harrison?"

"I'm fine, thank you."

Yes, having this handsome fellow stay elsewhere would probably be the better way to go.

Henry had always liked Philadelphia—from the time he first went there as a boy traveling with his father on business. Something important always seemed to be underway, which was the case for him today and would be again soon when George Whitefield came.

"There's the church," Catherine said, pointing to the building, "and the manse is next door."

Across the street from the Courthouse, High Street Presbyterian was a clean-looking brick and wood structure with a tall spire. Nestled in its shadows stood the three-story brick manse with white shutters, and just down the street flowed the Delaware, whose docks rang with the sounds of buying, selling, and bartering. Masts of tall ships lent a nautical feel to the city, situated between the wide Delaware to the east and the sleek Schuykill River along the city's western boundary.

Jacob brought the wagon to a halt on the cobblestones, and Henry located a hitching post along the sidewalk. Dismounting, he secured his mare. "I'll feed and water her," Jacob said. "Then I'll put her in our stable around the back for now."

The gesture touched Henry. "You are very kind, Mr. Harrison. Thank you."

"I'll make sure no one disturbs your belongings until you know where you'll be staying."

"Again, I thank you."

Jacob gave him a quick nod.

"Allow me to assist you." Henry relieved Catherine of her satchel.

"Thank you, sir."

He reached into the wagon for a few of the parcels Mrs. Tennent and his mother had sent for her family, then he followed Catherine to the front door at the same level as the street. When they went inside, he felt the coolness of the entryway, slightly dark at this hour as the sun dipped lower in the sky. He heard voices coming from a nearby room and coughing from upstairs.

Catherine called out. "We're home, Mother." He watched her remove her hat, and the cap underneath came off as well, revealing tousled, light brown hair. She quickly replaced the covering and hung the hat on a peg, looking down at the floor as if she were feeling self-conscious.

An older version of Catherine, except for her dark hair, walked down the hall toward them, a little girl trailing behind her, who smiled in their direction. A man accompanied the woman and girl, his rich-looking clothes lending an air of importance. Yet another person, an attractive young woman about Catherine's age, followed behind them.

"Oh, you're back! I was so worried!" The tearful woman embraced her daughter as if they hadn't seen each other in months.

"Hello, Mother. Hello, Margaret." As Catherine hugged them, she also greeted the young lady. "Why, Elizabeth, how good to see you!"

Henry eased the packages to the floor, preparing for introductions. He couldn't help but notice the man's gaze fall upon Catherine first, then himself.

"Good day, Mr. Heath," Catherine said.

He bowed. "I see you've brought the minister, Miss Harrison."

"Yes. Allow me to make introductions. Mr. Sharp, this is my mother, Ann Harrison."

He bowed over her proffered hand. "I am pleased to meet you, Mrs. Harrison."

"The pleasure is mine, Mr. Sharp."

He watched her sniffle into a rumpled handkerchief. *She's barely holding herself together.*

"And this is my sister, Margaret."

Henry was charmed when the little girl, who looked very much like her brother, curtsied then giggled.

"I am honored to make your acquaintance." *She seems to be about the same age as my dear sister.*

The girl ducked behind her mother.

Catherine continued. "This is our very good friend, Francis Heath. Mr. Heath, this is Mr. Sharp."

Henry gripped the man's hand as the fellow said, "I'm glad to know you, Mr. Sharp. We've been anticipating your arrival."

"And this is my dearest friend, Elizabeth Worthington."

"I am pleased to make your acquaintance." The coquettish flutter of her eyelashes wasn't lost on him.

"As am I."

A woman, slightly bent with age entered.

"Good day, Lena. This is Mr. Sharp, who will be assisting Father. Mr. Sharp, our servant, Lena."

Henry nodded at the woman who curtsied.

"How is Father?" Catherine's eyes darted toward the stairs.

"Come and sit." Her mother gestured toward a parlor with golden drapes the color of once-ripe corn and a faded Turkish-style rug. "Mr.

Sharp." She indicated a chair he judged to be their best, and she sat across from him with Heath by her side. Catherine and her sister sat on a small sofa flanked by Elizabeth. "Lena, will you please bring some refreshments?"

"Yes, madam." She hurried out of the room.

Henry thought Catherine appeared anxious and guessed she must be torn between wanting to hear an update and rushing to see her father for herself. He certainly would be in her place.

"How was your journey?" Mrs. Harrison asked through swollen eyes. She didn't seem especially keen to know, judging by the way she wasn't making eye contact.

"Quite well." Impatience laced Catherine's voice. "Mother, please, how is he?"

She shook her head. "He had a difficult night."

"I must see him." She shot up from the couch. "Will you please excuse me, Mr. Sharp?"

He stood, joined by Heath. "Yes, of course."

"She's very devoted to her father," Mrs. Harrison said.

Judging by the look he saw Heath give Catherine, Henry realized he might have to keep any attraction he might feel for the bright young woman very much in check.

CHAPTER FOUR

The first thing Henry noticed upon meeting Catherine's father was the smell, the same odor he'd first encountered in his grandmother's room shortly before her death. Although this startled him, he displayed an unruffled demeanor. Joseph Harrison was, after all, a much younger man than his grandmother had been, nearer the prime of his life. His bony face and eyes rimmed in dark circles, however, betrayed the pastor's age, which Henry guessed to be around forty.

He watched as Catherine helped Harrison sit up. "Father, I've brought Mr. Henry Sharp to you—the minister you requested."

Her voice held a triumphant note, and Henry observed a look of relief that washed at least ten years off the man's appearance.

"Mr. Sharp," he said, his voice hoarse. He offered a weak handshake then cast a glance at his daughter and smiled. "Thank you, daughter."

"You are most welcome, Father. Now then, I will leave you two to get further acquainted. I'll be in the next room if you need me."

After she left, Harrison asked, "Will you please open a window, Mr. Sharp? My wife thinks fresh air will harm me, but I beg to differ. I will cover for you if she should catch you in the act." He grinned through a cough following the exertion of this speech.

"Of course, sir." Henry hastened to carry out the duty, and soon, the sounds of people on the street below filtered into the room. He sat in the chair next to the bed and waited for the pastor to reveal what was on his mind.

"I cannot thank you enough for coming, Mr. Sharp." The voice was low, the words halting. Henry leaned closer to catch each one falling with such effort from his lips. "Your presence relieves my mind and spirit considerably." He coughed, but quickly recovered. "Have you left family behind?"

"My parents and siblings are in Warminster on a farm adjoining the Tennent property."

Harrison nodded, and between coughing spells told Henry about his years at High Street Presbyterian Church, including his initial lack of spiritual insight. He confessed to having been a good churchman—but without spiritual understanding—clearly grieved over what he considered "wasted" years. When he explained about the elder who wanted his brother to take over the High Street pulpit, his eyes opened wider. "I would rather die spending every last portion of my strength than inflict upon my people a man who knows little more of the Savior than a drunken sailor." He coughed violently, and Henry wasn't sure if he should do anything to help. As soon as he recovered enough to continue, Harrison spoke.

"God continually put your name in my heart, although we had met but once. I can imagine how strange Catherine's appearance and summons must have been for you."

Both men grinned. "I know the Lord sometimes works in mysterious ways. I've been contemplating two calls to ministry, having just finished my course work with Mr. Tennent. One seems very obvious to my family, but I've had no 'This is the way, go in it,' from the Lord. After hearing about your situation, I had sudden clarity." He felt good discussing his own dilemma with someone removed from the situation.

"Oh, Mr. Sharp, this greatly heartens me. Will you be good enough to hand me that?" Harrison gestured toward a glass of water on his nightstand, and Henry obliged, remaining silent while the pastor sipped.

They discussed Henry's wages, which Joseph assured him would be fair, then the matter of where he would be staying.

"There is a widow in my church who at times boards guests, but then young Mr. Heath offered his home."

"Mr. Heath?" Henry repeated.

"He and his father are great friends, as well as members of my church—Magistrate Edward Heath is my clerk of session. Your stay at his home will be a contribution to the church." Spittle ran down Joseph's chin, which Henry tried to ignore. "He has not yet experienced the new birth, but he is honest and honorable. I pray you will not have trouble, but he would defend you if trouble there be."

Harrison slumped against the headboard, and Henry sensed their interview was coming to an end. He wanted to know one more thing.

"Your good daughter has told me Old Sides outnumber New Sides in your congregation. I must preach what the Lord lays on my heart, though some may take offense."

"Exactly what I have done." Harrison's voice was reduced to a whisper. "I think my people consider me a harmless eccentric." After another wrenching cough, he added, "Preach whatever the Lord lays upon you, Mr. Sharp. Allow Him to take care of the consequences." He drank again from his glass. "In this city, there is great indifference toward the things of the Lord." He paused, inhaling as if to catch his breath. "My flock contains many kinds of people, from the influential to the servant class. The Lord loves them all, and so do I."

Henry got the message—do not show favoritism. Fortunately, he was not one to do so.

Joseph coughed for several seconds, the bed shaking underneath him.

Henry rose. "I must go, Mr. Harrison. You need to rest." He had something else on his mind but wasn't sure if the minister could go on.

"Not just yet." His voice was even huskier. "There is something else you should be aware of."

"Yes, sir?"

"Catherine has often assisted me on pastoral visits. Please make use of her talents. She should first take you to meet the widow Doran."

"I will do so gladly," he said. "Might I bring up a certain other matter, sir, before I go?"

"Yes, of course." Harrison coughed more.

"Are you aware I have not yet been ordained?" He looked to see if the man was surprised, but Harrison's face remained impassive. "There will, then, be limitations to my own work among your people."

"I suspected, but the Lord was clear about calling for you. After I rest a while, perhaps I'll regain my strength and will administer communion."

Henry breathed a little easier, hoping the minister's sanguine outlook matched reality.

"One thing more." He leaned toward Henry.

"Yes, sir?"

"Magistrate Heath should call a session meeting after church. Introduce you to the elders. Soon." He began coughing again and wilted back onto the pillows. "If—he—has a question—have him come to me."

"I will, sir. Allow me to pray for you before I depart."

Harrison gave a weak smile. "Thank—you. I—will—pray—for you as well."

◈

Henry descended the stairs and entered the parlor where candles now burned, casting a soft light and waxy fragrance over the room.

Francis Heath stood. "Is everything settled, then?"

Henry watched as Catherine's glance darted from Heath to himself. "Is what settled?"

"I believe Mr. Heath is referring to his family's generous offer of lodging."

He turned to the man, who appeared to be about his age, perhaps a tad older. "I thank you for your kindness."

The men bowed to each other. "Our pleasure."

Henry couldn't discern Catherine's thoughts on the subject. Her mother, on the other hand, smiled for the first time since he'd met her.

"Mr. Sharp, please consider the manse your second home," she said. "You are welcome here at any time—there is no need of an invitation."

"Thank you, madam." He noticed Catherine's friend, Elizabeth, grinning at him. She was a handsome woman, if a bit showy in an outfit he judged to be better suited to a performance than a house call.

"Perhaps we should be going then?" Heath said. "Jacob has offered to bring your belongings to my home, and he must be getting himself and the wagon back to Mr. Franklin."

"Yes, of course. Uh, Miss Harrison, your father wishes me to visit a Mrs. Doran tomorrow, and I wonder if you might wish to introduce us."

Her amber eyes reflected firelight. "Yes. You may call for me after breakfast."

◈

"He seems like a nice young man," Ann Harrison said after he left.

"He is, indeed!" Elizabeth clapped as if she were young Margaret's age. "Oh, Catherine, I had no idea he would be so fine-looking!"

Although she was used to her friend's flirtatiousness, at this moment she found the comment annoying. "He is a wonderful young man, Mother. His family was very kind to me as well."

Her mother frowned. "When did you meet them? I thought you were staying with the Tennents."

She took a few minutes to explain the details of her trip to Warminster, describing how Henry Sharp's family home and businesses adjoined the Tennent's property. Just as she was finishing, someone knocked on the door.

Ann Harrison looked about her. "Where is Lena?" The servant failed to appear. "Oh, bother."

Catherine rose and placed a hand on her mother's shoulder. "I'll get the door." When she saw who was standing on the other side, her heart squeezed, yet she also thanked God she'd returned from Warminster when she did. "Mr. Oldfield. Do come in."

"Miss Harrison." He bowed and removed his hat, holding on to his ebony walking stick.

Her mother entered the foyer, her eyes like a startled fawn. "Good evening, Mr. Oldfield."

"Good evening, Mrs. Harrison."

"Won't you come in?"

"I have but a minute to share some good news—my brother can be ready to preach next Sunday. I am certain we can make do this weekend—one of the elders can always fill in."

Catherine had to handle this diplomatically, yet firmly. "Mr. Oldfield, you are too kind."

He offered a self-satisfied smile. "I am only too happy to help." He started for the door, but she stopped him with a light touch on his right forearm. "If you please, Mr. Oldfield, my father was unable to fully speak to you yesterday. Nor did my good mother yet know his plans when she gave you to understand your brother's services might be needed."

His eyes narrowed. "What are you trying to say, Miss Harrison?"

"My father has already secured another minister's help. I do apologize for the misunderstanding and for your trouble. Please convey this to your brother on our behalf."

He cocked his head. "Well, I do wish I had known in advance. Just who is this other minister? I know most of them in these parts, since their numbers are scarce."

Ann Harrison found her voice. "He comes to us from Warminster, sir."

"Warminster?" His eyes completely disappeared.

"Yes, a Mr. Henry Sharp."

"Henry Sharp? I do not know of him. Perhaps my brother does."

Catherine was eager for him to leave before her mother could say the wrong thing. She didn't want Robert Oldfield to know Henry Sharp was a product of Mr. Tennent's school, at least not right away. She wanted him to have a sporting chance.

⁂

The Heaths lived a quarter mile from the Harrisons in a three-story, red-brick house with an arched doorway. A servant greeted them and reached for Henry's satchel, forging up the stairs to an elegantly furnished, second-floor bedroom overlooking the street. Once he got settled, Francis stopped and offered to take Henry on a tour of the house, introducing him to staff, which included two servants, the Heaths' valets, a housekeeper, and a cook. *I will never remember all these names.*

"I can recommend a man with impeccable references to you," Francis said in the parlor afterwards.

"For what purpose?"

"Why, to be your valet, of course."

"Thank you, but I am a man of simple needs."

Francis pinched his lips together. "Ah. Well, then, let me know if you should change your mind."

At dinner, Francis explained, "My father and I both have offices here. I'm studying law under him and have taken on a few clients, but I also dabble in the import and export business."

"He is becoming quite successful too." Edward Heath's chest expanded.

Henry told them about his family and his call to the ministry.

"Well, we are happy to have you, Mr. Sharp," the elder Heath said, "although I must confess, we expected Robert Oldfield's brother to help us out." He dabbed at his mouth with a starched linen napkin. "Our good Mr. Harrison had other ideas, however."

"Yes, sir." Henry examined the place setting to see which fork he was expected to use next, not feeling compelled to explain Joseph Harrison's reasons.

"He is a good man, a man of integrity," Francis said. "We have become very close in these last few years since my mother died."

Seeing Francis pick up a certain fork, Henry followed his lead, feeling the weight of the gleaming silver in his hand.

"Are your parents still alive?" Francis asked.

"Yes, they are, thankfully. It must be hard not to have a parent, or a wife." Henry looked at Edward.

"Indeed. If not for Mr. Harrison, I don't know how we would have managed our grief. My wife died peacefully because of him, and he comforted us throughout the dark days following."

"We have become like family," Francis added with a smile. "I'm hopeful we actually will become family before long."

As Henry savored a bite of seasoned beef tenderloin, he also chewed over something else—did Catherine return Heath's ardor? Furthermore, the Reverend Mr. Harrison would rather die than allow an unconverted minister to fill his pulpit. Henry couldn't imagine he'd want his daughter to marry someone who didn't share her depth of faith.

CHAPTER FIVE

Henry had expected city people to sleep until well after sunrise, so he was surprised on his first morning in Philadelphia to discover the household already up and about at five o'clock. Outside his window, horses clopped against the cobblestones, carriages rumbled, and people called to one another. He stumbled out of bed and washed his hands and face with the water a servant had put in the room, though Henry didn't know when. He ventured to the dining room to find Edward Heath at breakfast, reading a newspaper. He stood silently, waiting to be recognized.

Edward looked up. "Good morning, Mr. Sharp. Did you pass the night well?"

"Yes, thank you, sir. And yourself?"

"Never better. Please sit down." He placed his newspaper on the table and motioned toward a chair. One of the servants hurried to pour a cup of tea for Henry, and when he thanked her, for some reason, she blushed.

"I confess, Magistrate Heath, I'm taken aback to find Philadelphians up at this hour. I thought only country people were on the job before break of day." He smoothed a fresh napkin onto his lap.

"The exception is my son, who is never up before the cock crows." He sipped his tea. "How do you like the city?" With his right leg carelessly draped over his left knee, Heath gave the appearance of a man who knew what he was about.

"The city affords much excitement."

"Let's hope you don't have more than you can handle." Heath spoke with a glint in his brown eyes. "What's on your agenda today?"

"Miss Harrison is going to show me the church, then we'll visit a Mrs. Doran."

Heath smiled. "Eleanor Doran is a veritable pillar of our church, the wisest woman I've had the pleasure to know." He leaned closer. "A word to the wise—be sure to speak loudly, for the years have diminished her hearing."

Henry nodded and took a drink of tea, a hearty English blend. When the magistrate rose, Henry followed suit.

"Please sit down, Mr. Sharp. I must be going, but you take your time. Our home is yours."

He went to the manse at nine o'clock after working on his sermon for a couple of hours. Catherine greeted him.

"How is your father this morning?" Her mother came up behind her. "Ah, good day, Mrs. Harrison." He bowed to the lady of the house.

"To you as well, Mr. Sharp."

His thoughts quickly turned back to Catherine, who looked especially lovely in a bright yellow dress. He willed his mind in a more neutral direction as she smiled and pulled on a pair of lace gloves.

"I'm happy to report he passed an almost peaceful night. Your presence has greatly relieved his mind. You may see him after we return if you like. He's still asleep, which is quite rare."

"This is good news."

"Indeed," Mrs. Harrison said. Even she looked more serene. "How is the weather this morning?"

"Most agreeable," Henry said. "Just the slightest bit chilly, but the sun promises to warm the rest of the day."

"I might just need my cape, then." Catherine reached for a green one hanging on the wall to her left and draped the woolen garment across her shoulders. "I'll see you in a few hours, Mother." She kissed her cheek and left with Henry.

In the brief walk to the church, he noticed Catherine kept lagging behind and figured his strides amounted to at least two of her own. "Please forgive me, Miss Harrison. I fear my pace is too much for you."

She smiled up at him. "I've never known anyone your height before."

He laughed. "Few people have. One of my Log College friends claims I'm descended from the Nephalim."

She frowned. "The Old Testament giants?"

"The very ones." He was pleased when she broke into a grin.

When they reached the church, Henry opened the unlocked door for her, feeling the cool stillness of the unoccupied house of worship.

"The sexton is probably here, but I don't expect anyone else." They paused in the narthex and looked around. "I grew up here and am exceedingly fond of this church."

She certainly was an elegant young woman who'd been raised in the sophisticated ways of the city. He suddenly felt out of place in his homespun clothes, something he'd never given thought to before. *Perhaps Francis Heath can suggest a tailor for me. I'm going to need some clothes better suited to the city.*

"The church reminds me a great deal of my own back home." He paused. "May I look around?"

She waved her right hand. "That's why we're here."

Catherine waited in the last pew while Henry walked down the center aisle, his shoes clicking against the wooden boards. The white pews on either side faced front toward a goblet-shaped pulpit, and a large Bible rested on the altar. Clear octagonal windows filled the space behind the sanctuary. The place smelled of burnt candles and something like peace itself. He climbed the stairs to the pulpit, looking out over the empty church, imagining himself giving the sermon on Sunday morning to a packed house. Catherine smiled in his direction. One thing he knew, if he was to keep his mind on his message, he wouldn't be able to look at her very much while he spoke.

"Is the church to your liking? Is there anything you need for Sunday?" she asked when he rejoined her.

"Very much. I believe I have all I need, thank you."

"Shall we visit Mrs. Doran, then?"

He pushed back an impulse to offer his arm as they left.

Eleanor Doran lived nearby in Elfreth's Alley, a charming street made up of red brick townhouses with window boxes spilling late summer blooms over the edges. On the way, they met an older man who greeted Catherine and gave Henry a quizzical look.

"Good day, Mr. Trent." She paused. "I would like to present Mr. Henry Sharp, who will be filling in for Father while he recuperates. Mr. Sharp, this is Mr. Trent, a member of our session."

The men shook hands. "I am pleased to meet you, Mr. Sharp." His grimace said otherwise. "This is a new development."

"I believe Father will have the opportunity to regain his health with Mr. Sharp here. Oh, and Father wants there to be a formal session meeting after church this Sunday for the elders to greet Mr. Sharp."

"Were I not in a hurry, I would enjoy talking with you further, Mr. Sharp."

"I regret you are, sir."

"Until Sunday, then." Trent took off at a clip, looking over his shoulder once.

Catherine sighed. "Mr. Trent would be a lot more agreeable if he could make up his mind which side he was on, new or old." A few minutes later, she paused before a three-story house with bright blue shutters. "We've now arrived at the home of a good and faithful servant." She went up two steps and knocked on the door, Henry pausing below until a young Negro woman appeared. "Good day, Sally. I've brought someone to visit Mrs. Doran, if she's available."

"Yes, miss." Sally nodded to Henry. "Please come in."

As she stepped aside, they entered the graceful home where he removed and handed his hat to the servant. *I wonder if she's slave or free.*

"I will bring her to you in the parlor." She slipped off quickly while they sat across from each other on embroidered chairs, the black background having faded to a dark gray.

Henry's spirit took in not just the understated elegance of mahogany furniture and silver candlesticks, but an intangible tranquility. The widow appeared five minutes later, and he rose as the women embraced.

"How is your father this day?" she asked.

"He slept well, thank you, Mrs. Doran. He's not coughing quite as much this morning." Catherine smiled. "Perhaps the arrival of our new pastor will help turn things around." She motioned for him to come closer. "I would like to present Mr. Henry Sharp of Bucks County."

He took the widow's tiny right hand with its wrinkled skin and bowed. "It is a pleasure to meet you, madam."

"The pleasure is mine, sir." She waved the same hand toward the chairs, and Catherine and Henry sat. He was surprised when he and Catherine started pulling their seats closer to the elderly woman at the exact same time. Looking at each other, they laughed at the spontaneous gesture.

"Welcome to Philadelphia, Mr. Sharp, although you have likely been here before."

Henry noted her gravelly voice and the way she sat up as straight as could be managed for a woman of advanced age. He raised his voice. "Yes, madam, I have had the pleasure on several occasions."

She nodded. "So, you come to us from Mr. Tennent's school."

"Yes, madam. Do you know my good pastor?"

"We've met a time or two. I have high regard for him. When Mr. Harrison's condition warranted an assistant, I assured him we would be best served by having someone from Mr. Tennent's school."

Catherine spoke up. "My father and Mrs. Doran are close. She's often advised him."

The lady smiled. "I used to be an active woman in my younger years. Since I've grown old, God has given me a smaller sphere, and I spend most of my time praying for the needs of his people and our city." She closed her eyes for a long moment. "I believe he is about to answer many of them." When she opened them again, she said, "I am sure you are aware, Mr. Sharp, that George Whitefield will be preaching here this fall?"

"Yes, madam. I'm quite eager to hear him."

"God will use him mightily to wake up our sleeping people. He's already begun to rouse them from slumber through Mr. Harrison." Her eyes bored into his. "I'm sure he will work in you as well."

Her words felt like a call to arms. "Thank you for your confidence."

Sally reappeared with a tea tray, and after passing out porcelain cups and plates with delicate-looking biscuits, she quietly left the room.

"I don't mean to contradict you, Mr. Sharp, but I am more confident in the One who bestowed your pastoral gifts upon you than I am in you, yourself."

He felt heat rise to his face. "Your point is well taken." This woman was a force to be reckoned with.

Catherine fixed Mrs. Doran's tea, using a generous amount of sugar and cream, while Henry took his black.

"Have you had much experience preaching?"

"For two years, I've supplied pulpits while training with Mr. Tennent."

She nodded. "What characterizes your preaching?"

Catherine offered her a biscuit, but she held up her hand. "Not for me, thank you."

Henry had never been asked this question before and didn't want to be in any way glib, not with her. "I explain the Scripture passage using stories to illustrate the main points, following our Lord's example." He hesitated. *May as well tell her the truth.* "Some would say I'm too casual because I like to speak of everyday people and everyday things."

She closed her eyes, pursing her lips. "You may expect opposition."

He nearly choked on a biscuit, startled by her directness. He took a long swallow of tea to wash the crumbs down.

"Still, Mr. Sharp, you must obey God rather than man. Our city is in some ways like Israel during the time of Samuel, when the word of the Lord was rare. Mr. Harrison has made progress, and our church has tolerated him because he is so loved. A few have responded, but others still sleep." She placed her cup and saucer on a table containing a worn Bible. "God will use you to awaken some, but the Devil will not take this lightly. I am praying for you, as I am praying for Mr. Whitefield. The fields are white unto harvest."

CHAPTER SIX

He stood before the congregation, Bible in hand, accompanied by Magistrate Heath and a contingent of butterflies occupying his midsection. The sun streamed through the transparent eastern windows of the church, and a baby in the fifth row from the back hiccupped. Catherine and Ann Harrison sat in the front left pew with Jacob beside his mother. Henry nodded to acknowledge them, pleased when Catherine smiled. Just behind them was Francis Heath, waving a fly from his face. Henry was surprised to see Mrs. Doran and Sally down in front on the other side of the aisle since the widow had said she was unable to get out much. Clearly, she'd made an effort to show her support for him, something he greatly appreciated. Henry could tell by the surprised expressions on many faces that his presence was jarring.

Edward Heath addressed the congregation in what Henry thought must be his courtroom voice. "Good morning. As you know, our good pastor, Mr. Harrison, has been ministering to us while enduring a prolonged illness. This past week was especially difficult for him, and he has requested this young man to fill in for him until he regains his strength. I am satisfied with his qualifications and honored to welcome him this morning."

Henry was grateful for the judge's unmistakable seal of approval.

"Please join me today in welcoming Mr. Henry Sharp, who comes to us from Bucks County. Although he has received offers from other churches to be their pastor, Mr. Sharp has kindly consented to minister to us in our time of need."

He extended the right hand of fellowship. "Welcome to High Street. I look forward to your ministry among us."

Henry bowed to the magistrate, then to the congregants.

Heath continued. "Before Mr. Sharp brings us the message, I would ask members of the session to stay behind after the service to meet him." Then he nodded to Henry, who ascended the steps to the pulpit, placed his Bible and notes on the lectern, and spread his hands across the smooth wood. "Thank you, Magistrate Heath. I look forward to meeting many of you after the service and in the days to come. Let us pray." He closed his eyes and lifted his face. "Gracious Lord, we give Thee thanks on this beautiful morning for beauty of the earth Thou hast created and for Thy many blessings upon our lives. We are grateful for Thy presence with us today, and we beseech Thee to reveal Thyself to us through Thy Word in such a way that we may leave this place knowing Thee more clearly and loving Thee more dearly. Amen."

He raised his eyes to them. "Our text this morning is from Ecclesiastes three, verses one to eleven. Hear the Word of the Lord. 'To everything there is a season, and a time to every purpose under the heaven …'" At the end of the passage, he concluded, "'He hath made everything beautiful in his time: also he hath set the world in their heart, so that no man can find out the work that God maketh from the beginning to the end.'"

He kept the Bible open when he ended the Scripture reading. "There are, according to this Scripture, seasons in all of our lives, those of prosperity and poverty, war and peace, joy and sorrow, life and death, sickness and health. Each of them is determined by our sovereign God, to whom all life owes its origins, its sustenance, its beginnings and ends. We come to know various aspects of his divine personality as we go through each of life's seasons, as he attends our way, rejoicing with us, sorrowing with us, ever guiding us into the newness of life that is ours in Christ Jesus, our redeemer and friend."

Henry paused, gripping the pulpit as he surveyed the well-dressed, attentive congregation. No one seemed to be looking down or fidgeting, although more than a few sat with their arms crossed and their lips set in straight lines. He had expected as much.

"The seasons of life affect churches as well as individuals, including their pastors. Those engaged in the Lord's work are not exempt from trials. Indeed, the sun beats upon the heads of the righteous, as well as the unrighteous. This congregation is going through a somber time due to Mr. Harrison's illness. As he has ministered faithfully among you these many years, now we must take a turn in caring care for him."

Henry deliberately used the word "we" to identify himself with the people. He continued speaking of God's presence throughout life's seasons, then sat down after he finished with a prayer. At the end of the service, he lifted his hands waist high to deliver the benediction, rather than above his head, a privilege he could only exercise with ordination. "And now, the Lord bless thee, and keep thee: The Lord make his face shine upon thee, and be gracious unto thee: The Lord lift up his countenance upon thee, and give thee peace.' Amen."

The organ began playing the postlude as Henry strode down the center aisle, glancing quickly toward Catherine, whose smile cheered him. At the back of the narthex, he stood near the stairs and greeted dozens of people, most who wished him well.

"That was a fine sermon, young man," said one grey-haired man with a fuzzy cast in his right eye. His wife, minus a few teeth, laughed nervously and curtsied.

"This will give our pastor an opportunity to recover," said one stout man whose buttons strained against his waistcoat. "Thank you for coming to help us."

"I am glad to be here, sir," Henry said.

"I was not expecting someone as young as you," another woman said, looking him up and down.

A young man pumped Henry's hand. "That was a fine sermon."

Finally Edward Heath touched Henry's right arm and addressed those who lingered in the narthex. "If you will excuse us, Mr. Sharp and I have some business."

Henry bowed as he left and followed the elder to the sacristy where six men waited, exhibiting a range of facial expressions and postures. He was clearly on display.

"Gentlemen, it is my pleasure to present Mr. Sharp to you. Mr. Sharp, these are the members of High Street's session. On your left is Mr. Robert Oldfield."

Henry reached out, and although Oldfield took his hand, the elder's grip was like that of a lifeless trout.

"This is Mr. Nicholas More."

"Mr. Sharp," he said, pressing his lips together.

"I'm pleased to meet you, Mr. More."

"Mr. Samuel Worthington is next, then Mr. George Shipman, Mr. Charles Dash, and Mr. Daniel Miller." Heath paused while each man shook hands with Henry, some with smiles and nods, others through gritted teeth. A church divided against itself.

"Just last week, we decided a temporary replacement should be found for our minister," Heath said.

Nicholas More piped up. "If you will excuse me, Magistrate, I was led to believe we were getting Mr. Oldfield's brother." He didn't look at Henry as he said this.

A few of the men nodded, murmuring things like, "Yes, that was our impression as well."

Henry prayed silently. *Lord, help me conduct myself in a manner worthy of the gospel.*

"I made the proposal to Mr. Harrison myself earlier last week," Oldfield said. "I thought we had an understanding."

"Mr. Oldfield, I believe you may have misunderstood," Heath said. "This was something you wanted to happen, and while Mr. Harrison considered your offer, he chose not to accept it. He is still our spiritual head, and he desired to call Mr. Sharp."

Oldfield straightened his shoulders and frowned, clearly put out.

"Where did you say you were from, Mr. Sharp?" asked rotund Daniel Miller, appearing eager to smooth the rough edges.

"From Warminster, sir."

"And you have just completed your studies?" Henry nodded. "Did you go to Yale? Harvard perhaps?" Miller looked hopeful.

"No, sir. I was educated by Mr. William Tennent at his fine school."

Oldfield sniffed, as if there were a bad odor in the room. "Few consider his Log College a 'fine school.'"

At first, everyone was quiet, then everyone started talking at once until Heath raised his hands. "Gentlemen! Gentlemen. One at a time if you will."

Henry half expected the judge to pull a gavel out of his waistcoat and start pounding on the wall.

"I have heard much of this school," Mr. Shipman said. "I'm eager to know how one of its graduates preaches."

"I cannot understand why Mr. Harrison did not choose someone of your brother's abilities." More looked at Oldfield before giving Henry a once over. "And someone more suited to city life."

"But I thought Reverend Oldfield was from the country," one of the men said, apparently without guile.

"He only preaches there, but he is far more suited to a city church," Oldfield said. Then, completely unexpectedly, he smiled and shook Henry's hand. "Mr. Harrison has spoken, and we must honor his decision. Welcome, Mr. Sharp." His words said one thing, but his eyes told a different story.

The men returned to their families waiting in the narthex, and Henry saw Mrs. Harrison and her daughter talking with some women. The minister's wife greeted him. "Mr. Sharp, what a fine job you did today. I look forward to sharing your message with my husband, who was much in prayer for you."

Henry bowed. "Thank you, madam. Please tell him I am grateful."

"You may tell him yourself. Won't you join us for the midday meal?"

Henry felt nonplused. "I would enjoy nothing more, Mrs. Harrison, but I have already accepted an invitation. Perhaps another time?"

"Why, yes, of course." Her eyes darted from him to her daughter. Elizabeth Worthington and her family joined them, Catherine's closest friend grinning.

"Well, Mr. Sharp, might you be ready?" her father asked.

"Uh, yes, sir."

Henry bowed again to the Harrisons, wishing they had asked sooner.

Catherine tried not to gape when Henry Sharp said he was dining with the Worthingtons. Instead, she purposely held her lips close together and willed her face into a placid expression or what she hoped would at least pass for one. *Why should I be surprised? After all, Elizabeth's father is a church elder and is just trying to provide a proper welcome. They probably don't want us to be burdened with entertaining when Father is so ill.* She had just about convinced herself this was the case when Elizabeth flashed a jubilant smile at her. The young woman had never been quiet about her desire to marry before the age of twenty-one, which she considered practically dotage. Apparently Henry Sharp was in her sights. Catherine found the situation amusing, too fond of her friend and secure in her own femininity to feel threatened. She walked the short distance home with her mother and Francis Heath. Almost everyone expected her to marry him, including her mother, and he wouldn't be a poor choice—handsome, witty, bright, a good churchman, promising lawyer, and a successful businessman. She studied his dark brown hair under the finest of hats, a man of average height and weight with light green eyes and an easy smile. Until the last couple of days, she wondered if somehow God would claim Francis for himself, and then the last barrier to their relationship would dissipate. She wondered if he would then stir her senses in other ways as well. She watched Henry Sharp's retreating form and realized she couldn't deny she was taken by him, not just by his striking appearance, but by his strong love for Jesus Christ. *I have no idea how long he'll be with us. Once Father becomes well, I may never see this man again.* She stumbled on a cobblestone, and Francis steadied her. She was at odds with herself. Of course, she wanted her father to recover and quickly. Of course, she wanted Elizabeth, and Francis for that matter, to be happy. Perhaps she was frivolous for even thinking Henry Sharp might be attracted to her, but then, could he be drawn to someone as flighty as Elizabeth? She sighed.

"Is something troubling you, Miss Harrison?" Francis asked at the front door.

She forced a smile. "I will be fine, thank you."

He searched her face, an eager schoolboy. "Is there anything I can do?"

"Not at this time, Mr. Heath."

"Would you like to have dinner with us?" her mother asked.

"I should like nothing more."

Catherine held in a deep sigh.

CHAPTER SEVEN

His visiting over for the day and the next sermon all but completed, Henry sat at the table in his room to write to his family. In the three weeks since he'd been gone, he'd managed to jot just a few lines and wanted to give them a more detailed account of his life and ministry. Placing the paper on the table, he dipped his pen into the pungent ink from Mr. Franklin's store.

> My dearest family,
>
> I trust this finds you well. You must be busy with the fall harvest. Mama, I can almost smell cinnamon and apples as you prepare your butters and preserves. To taste one of your pies would delight me. I wish I could be of help to you, Papa, as you and my brothers bring in the crops and prepare for winter. I know not how long I shall be in Philadelphia. Although Mr. Harrison shows signs of returning health, he is far from well. Thank you for your many prayers on his behalf. He and his family treasure them, as do I, for I have grown daily more fond of him and his family.
>
> I am kept quite busy, as High Street is a thriving church whose ministry in the city inspires me. Not a day goes by here but the people perform charitable acts for those afflicted by grief, disease, poverty, and imprisonment. Although the elders and deacons do most of these labors, I have also become involved in ministering to those less fortunate. Just last week, I was called to the death bed of a sailor, who having become severely ill at sea, was putting his affairs in order and asked for a minister. I helped the man compose a letter for his family back in England, then I inquired about his spiritual state. He confessed he felt terrified because he had done regrettable things in his young life, and I was able to tell him Jesus Christ had died for his sins. He eagerly accepted the Savior's atonement, and he died peacefully the following day.

> I performed his small funeral service, the first in my ministry. Very few came, as he had no friends in the colonies, but Miss Harrison accompanied me.

He smiled at the thought of her in a situation many females would've avoided at all costs. Although she was a refined young woman, she had the ability to make herself at home in every setting in which he had seen her. She would make a fine minister's wife. He shook his head to clear such musings from his mind. While he didn't know how she felt about Francis Heath, how Heath felt about her was an open book, and Henry was, after all, a guest in the man's home.

A breeze from the river riffled the page. He'd been closing the window at night in spite of his preference for fresh air because the street noises kept him from falling asleep, but in the light of day, he kept it open. Yawning, he wondered when he would get used to the city's constant clamor. Perhaps he would take a nap after finishing and posting the letter. The outside din somehow didn't disturb him as much during the day because he expected the noises then. First, he wanted to finish the letter.

> As I mentioned earlier, I am staying at the fine home of Magistrate Edward Heath. My room is very comfortable, and the magistrate and his son have made every effort to help me feel welcome here. The son's name is Francis, and he is four years older than I. His mother died a few years ago, and although they are making the best of things, they miss her a great deal. Mr. Heath, the younger, is studying law with his father, and he also involves himself in shipping interests. He isn't one for boasting, but I can tell he has had generous returns for his labors. He very kindly introduced me to his tailor, who is making some new clothes for me.

Henry paused and looked through the lace curtains to a team of horses pulling a full wagon.

> Along with the Heaths, a handful of servants live here, including two women who give me many occasions for mirth—although I try hard not to laugh because they take themselves so seriously. Both are advanced in years and have served the Heaths for most of their adult lives. Mrs. Daley is the head of the household staff, and Mrs. Clydesdale keeps her searching for headache powder on a regular basis. I fear the latter is growing forgetful as evidenced by her recent misdoings.

Henry laughed at the memory.

> Last week, Mrs. Clydesdale was serving an oyster salad when she tripped and dumped the contents into Magistrate Heath's lap. Knowing how vexed Mrs. Daley becomes and how emotionally sensitive Mrs. Clydesdale is, he manfully kept his thoughts to himself. After the shock of the incident wore off, and Mrs. C went running in tears for a towel, the three of us men could barely restrain ourselves. Seeing the magistrate in his condition was a revelation to me—I like a man who doesn't take himself so seriously he can't laugh at himself.

Unlike Robert Oldfield.

> Although Mrs. Clydesdale had been banished from serving, she displeased Mrs. Daley once again in the kitchen by stuffing a chicken with newspaper instead of bread pudding. I do pray for the dear woman to be able to continue in service, which means a great deal to her. Lest you fear I am not eating well, Mama, I assure you I am. City people may not have the groaning boards of the country, but with fresh seafood at hand and a lively farmer's market, they eat just as heartily. I have had several occasions to dine at the homes of church members who have gone out of their way to make delectable meals for me.
>
> Mr. Harrison is still quite sickly, but his family assures me they see improvement. I try to visit him daily, and we pray for each other. I do hope he is well enough to hear Mr. Whitefield preach when he arrives sometime at the end of October or early November. I am so looking forward to hearing him myself.
>
> I trust everyone is well at home. Know I miss you very much and pray for you upon my every remembrance. Please give my best to Mr. and Mrs. Tennent. I will try to write more frequently.
>
> Your affectionate son and brother, Henry

He folded the pages of the letter and stuffed them into an envelope, which he addressed and sealed. He decided to lay down for a quarter of an hour before going to the post office. Although the bed ended at his calves, he managed to fit most of his body onto it, letting his head sink into the down pillow. Feeling a breeze float across his face, he recited the Lord's Prayer to himself and fell asleep before he'd finished. He awakened with a start an hour later at the sound of a crash downstairs, followed by Mrs. Daley's loud scolding and Mrs. Clydesdale's mournful cries as she scurried up the back staircase. He got up, splashed his face with water from a bowl on the wash stand, and picked up the letter to mail.

"Watch your step, Pastor." Mrs. Daley was on her knees with a whisk broom cleaning up what appeared to have been a large vase, as well as the flowers and water therein. Her hair had come loose around her face, as if she'd been in the act of tearing it out.

"Allow me to help you." He bent down to pick up the flowers and some large pieces of porcelain.

"You are too kind, Pastor. I can get the rest. No need for you to spoil your clothes." She looked into his eyes. "You might say a prayer for Mrs. Clydesdale, though. I hardly know how to use her anymore." She sighed. "In her day, she could out-cook and out-clean me, but in the past few months, she has become a nuisance." Lowering her voice, she added, "I just hope she doesn't become a danger as well."

"I am praying, and I know you'll do right by her and the household."

"Thank you, Pastor Sharp. I'm at my wit's end." She smiled. "Actually, she can still out-bake me."

"My mouth waters at the very thought of her gingerbread."

The light wind that had soothed him to slumber had since gained strength as he walked from the Heath residence on Chestnut Street to Mr. Franklin's post office and print shop on High. Rolling clouds portended rain, and upturned leaves were as parched tongues thirsty for a drink. He felt the seasons turning, and he welcomed the change, having enjoyed Bucks County's magnificent color and bounty in the fall as far back as he could remember. Gone was the stifling humidity alternating with arid conditions when crops shriveled for want of rain, conditions in which his father's forge felt like the very fires of hell.

"Good day, Mr. Sharp." A middle-aged man in fine clothes tipped his hat as they passed on the street. He couldn't recall the fellow's name, but he'd seen him in church the past three Sundays.

"A good day to you as well."

The man slowed his step. "I feel a storm coming."

"As do I. Well, then, I look forward to seeing you in church on Sunday."

Henry wondered why the man was shaking his head as he walked away. Arriving at Mr. Franklin's, Henry smiled when he spotted Catherine

Harrison standing at the counter talking to the proprietor. When she smiled in his direction, his knees felt strange.

"Ah, if it isn't the good parson," the postmaster said. "Good day to you, Mr. Sharp."

Henry removed his hat and bowed. "Good day, Mr. Franklin. Hello, Miss Harrison." He wondered where Jacob was.

"I'm pleased to see you, Mr. Sharp. How are you this day?"

"I am well, thank you, and you?"

"The same, thank you."

"I was just inquiring after Mr. Harrison." Franklin pushed a pair of glasses up on his nose.

"And I was telling him Father has been sleeping more soundly—in fact, quite a lot. I believe he's on the mend."

Henry had a bad feeling about what was actually happening, but he kept silence. "I'm glad to hear the optimistic report."

"We're so grateful for your service, Mr. Sharp."

"I'm glad to be of help. I plan to visit him when I finish here. Actually, if you're going home, Miss Harrison, I'll be glad to accompany you."

"Yes, I am. Thank you."

"I understand you're quite popular, Parson, at least in some circles." Franklin's eyes twinkled.

"Pardon me?" Henry wasn't sure what he meant, but Franklin was laughing.

He waved a pudgy hand. "Never mind, never mind. I would keep my powder dry if I were you, however. Now, then, how may I serve you?"

Still puzzled, Henry handed him the letter. "I would like to mail this."

Franklin inspected the letter. "I can get this out by the close of day."

Henry picked up a copy of Franklin's newspaper. "And I'll have one of these. I do enjoy reading your publication, Mr. Franklin. So, what do I owe you?"

Franklin calculated the cost, and as Henry counted out his money, the printer said, "I have a bit of news that didn't make this edition." He leaned over the counter, the edges of his rolled-up sleeves stained with ink. "Your Mr. Whitefield is due to arrive in another three weeks."

He felt as he had as a boy when his mother had pulled sticky buns from the oven. "That is good news!"

"He has certainly made a sensation in England and in the southern colonies. Although I'm a bit dubious about a wandering cleric, I promise to keep an open mind."

"From what I've heard, Mr. Franklin, you won't be disappointed. One thing I wonder about—where will Mr. Whitefield preach, given that he draws such large crowds?"

"He isn't loath to speak in the open fields, Mr. Sharp."

Henry quietly considered whether he might not offer the pulpit of High Street to him, but then the door opened, and Elizabeth Worthington appeared, looking as if the wind had stolen her breath. Her large round eyes opened even further at the sight of Henry, but her usual delight was missing. "Catherine, I need to speak to you."

"Why, yes, of course. Mr. Sharp and I were just about to walk to the manse. Would you like to join us?"

The young woman sidled up to Catherine and whispered, a little too loudly, "I need to speak to you—alone."

"Mr. Sharp, would you mind going ahead of me?"

"Of course not." He shook the postmaster's hand. "Good day, Mr. Franklin. Miss Worthington."

"Now, then, Elizabeth, why all the secrecy?" Catherine held onto her hood to keep the wind from blowing the cloak off.

"I've just heard the most dreadful news." Elizabeth clasped her friend's forearm.

Catherine was growing alarmed. "What news?"

"Mr. Sharp is an imposter!"

CHAPTER EIGHT

Catherine's breath caught in her throat. "Whatever do you mean?"

"Susanna More just told me."

The glow in Elizabeth's cheeks betrayed a kind of pleasure for being the bearer of important news.

Catherine placed a hand on her right hip. "Just what did Susanna have to say about this?" She'd never been terribly fond of the known gossip.

"She said his real name is something like Johann Eberstark, and he is not a true minister but a German pretender who goes around preaching for the money." Elizabeth sniffed. "And to think how fond I was of him!"

She'd suspected all along her friend fancied Henry Sharp. Elizabeth had no idea how drawn Catherine also was to him, but every time Elizabeth mentioned her admiration, Catherine chafed. Nor was she buying any of this nonsense about him. "You're basing your opinion on hearsay and jumping to conclusions all too blithely. Just where did Susanna get such information?" She had her own suspicions.

Elizabeth clasped her hands. "I don't know. Perhaps, then, it's not true?"

"Of course it isn't!" Susanna's father, Elder More, may have had something to do with the vicious report. He was someone who regularly, though subtly, opposed her father in session meetings, being staunchly Old Side. She would have to be careful not to jump to conclusions. "Elizabeth, I must ask you not to spread this malicious rumor."

"I fear Susanna is not being so circumspect. News like this is bound to spread quickly."

"Nevertheless, please say nothing more, except in Mr. Sharp's defense."

Elizabeth nodded. "You have my word. Oh, this is just terrible! Mother will never allow me to see him now. At this rate, I'll die an old maid."

Catherine had run out of patience with the conversation, as well as with her friend, and excused herself, walking briskly to the manse where Henry awaited her. She found him in the parlor with her mother and sister chatting calmly, her family members with needlework spread on their laps. Henry rose when she entered, his presence filling the room.

"Is Miss Worthington well?"

"She'll be fine, but I need to have a word with you, Mr. Sharp." She gave her mother a pointed look.

"Shall I tell Father you will be up to see him?" Ann Harrison asked Henry.

Catherine answered for him, avoiding his eyes. "Please tell him we'll be by to see him a little later."

Her mother looked at her sideways. "Come along, Margaret. Perhaps you can read to Father from the Bible, if he is awake."

The little girl carefully placed her sampler on the chair and followed her mother. When they were out of earshot, Catherine invited the minister to sit down.

"I'm afraid there's some bad news, Mr. Sharp. My friend has just told me about a rumor circulating about you."

He frowned. "A rumor?"

"The daughter of one of our elders told Elizabeth you're an imposter." His brows arched as she continued, finding the words she spoke so distasteful she wished she could have spit them out. "She said some nonsense about your real name being something like Johann Eberstark, and that you're not actually a minister."

Henry exhaled, as if to expel the lie.

Catherine continued. "Susanna More's father is an Old Side who was fond of my father before his new birth. Since then, the two have been politely estranged."

They were both silent.

"Things have been quiet in your first weeks here, Mr. Sharp, lulling us into believing there would be little opposition to your ministry."

Henry rose and walked to a window, looking outside.

"What should we do?" She gladly relinquished her take-charge attitude.

"I don't think we should tell your father unless we have to. News will come to your mother soon enough, but if we can spare Mr. Harrison ..."

Catherine was touched to hear his first concern was for her father, yet even this proved worrisome. "Do you think he's too weak for such tidings, then?"

Henry turned to her and spoke in a soothing voice. "I think he's vulnerable, and we shouldn't burden him with church affairs unless truly necessary."

For the first time since he came, Catherine began to accept her father wasn't improving as much as she'd convinced herself he was. Grief squeezed her heart, but she refused to dwell on the matter just yet.

"Naturally, I'll discuss this with Magistrate Heath," Henry said, "but before then, I suggest we pay a visit to Mrs. Doran."

She jumped to her feet. "That's a very good idea. I'll tell Lena so Mother knows where I've gone."

They left the manse and walked to Mrs. Doran's. The old woman was seated in the parlor sipping a cup of tea, a dog-eared Bible open on her lap. Sally was nowhere in sight, but from the smell of roasting lamb, Catherine surmised she must be in the kitchen. The pastor's daughter attempted the requisite politeness, but the widow waved her hand in a gesture of impatience. "My dear, you have not come to pay a social call. Something has happened."

Catherine and Henry looked at each other as if to say, "Who should go first?" Then she charged ahead, pushing aside thoughts she should've let Henry begin. "Mrs. Doran, a rumor has started about Mr. Sharp, told to me by Elizabeth Worthington, who named Susanna More as its source."

The old woman closed her eyes. Whether she was praying, or thinking about what to say, Catherine couldn't tell. Some moments had passed in which the only sounds were the grandfather clock chiming in the entryway and Sally moving about in a neighboring room. Then she spoke. "I thought something like this might happen, Mr. Sharp. The Enemy does not often stand still when God's people are about his business. What, then, is the rumor?"

Catherine opened then closed her mouth when Henry answered. "The essence is I'm an imposter who goes by an assumed name, and I am not actually a minister."

"I see." Mrs. Doran tented her hands and looked past them toward a window. Birds fluttered about a holly tree outside. "Tell me, Mr. Sharp, is there any truth to this?"

"Of course not!" Catherine cried.

Henry glanced at her, then addressed the widow. "They seem to have found and twisted certain information about me, Mrs. Doran."

Catherine controlled the impulse to spring out of her chair. "Whatever do you mean, Mr. Sharp?"

"Miss Harrison, my name at birth was not Henry, but the German version, Heinrich, and my first name actually is Johannes. Likewise, my family used to be Scharfenstein, but when my parents got married, they started using Sharp because it was more American."

"I remember now!" Catherine blushed at her outburst. "I beg your pardon, but I'm excited about my sudden memory of my visit to Warminster and how one of those men at the church referred to you as Heinrich."

Henry frowned. "Mr. Mason is an elder who has a special disdain for students of the Log College in general and my family in particular because we support the school. He's been trying to get the presbytery to dismiss Mr. Tennent because he disapproves of his so-called revivalist tendencies. Whenever I see Mr. Mason, he calls me Heinrich because he thinks it vexes me."

"And does it, Mr. Sharp?" Mrs. Doran asked.

"No, my lady. I'm proud of my German heritage, just as I'm also honored to be an American."

"What about the Johannes part?" Catherine asked.

"It's customary for German families to give their sons the first name of a holy man of God, usually a biblical person, and the name is then often attached to each son. The middle name becomes the one he's known by. In my family, we use Johannes, although none of my brothers is known by that name or even by 'John.'"

"How would someone get such information about you?" Catherine wondered aloud. "I would think only your family, or those close to you, would know."

Henry pulled at his chin. "I have my suspicions. Perhaps someone at your church has been in contact with someone from Neshaminy."

"That makes sense, especially if you have enemies in both places," Catherine said.

"And what about the charge of your not being a minister, Mr. Sharp?" asked Mrs. Doran.

"Madam, although I have completed my ministerial training, I've not yet been ordained, which is common knowledge. Had I accepted a formal call from another church, I would've been properly ordained and installed by now."

The widow nodded. "I see. Some may say because they do not recognize Mr. Tennent's school, you are not truly a minister."

"That's just twisting words, though!" Catherine exclaimed as she gave a small hop in her chair.

"Nevertheless, Miss Harrison, not everyone accepts this school as a proper training ground for Presbyterian pastors," Henry said.

She sighed, sinking back into her seat. "While I understand, I don't accept it, and I am troubled that a church elder would do such a thing."

Mrs. Doran remained calm. "Miss Harrison, we do not know who started the rumor, and we must be careful not to begin our own hearsay. Remember, even our Lord had among his closest disciples a betrayer. This is nothing new." She added after a moment's pause, "Perhaps we should think more about how to deal with this threat than how it started."

Although Catherine still considered knowing who was behind the rumor important, she'd learned never to take what the widow said lightly.

"What would you suggest, Mrs. Doran?" Henry leaned forward, dwarfing the tiny woman's body, but not her spirit.

"We will pray for wisdom." She bowed her head, and lifted her papery voice. "Our gracious Father, Thou hast said when we lack wisdom we should inquire of Thee, and Thou wouldst not scold us but instead provide what we lack. We need to know Thy will in this unfortunate circumstance. Protect Thy servant, Henry Sharp, as he responds to this rumor. Help him, we beseech Thee, to honor Thy name and seek Thy solution. In all ways, may we honor Thy great name, in which we pray. Amen."

Prayer cleansed Catherine of a desire for vengeance, and she wondered what Henry might be thinking. When he looked back at her, she reddened, wishing she'd been more discreet.

"I'm still of the opinion we shouldn't involve your father, Miss Harrison, although I believe your mother should know."

"I agree, Mr. Sharp."

"Mrs. Doran, my next step will be to contact Magistrate Heath."

She nodded. "You can trust him."

Edward Heath calmly sucked a clay pipe, its spicy fragrance filling the room. After he had returned from his responsibilities for the day, Henry told him and Francis about the rumor while they sat in the young man's office.

"This is detestable!" Francis pounded his ledger book with his right fist. "Who would do such a thing?"

"Unfortunately, I can think of several people," his father said. "Trouble has taken longer than I expected to come, but now that it's here, we must take action before undue damage occurs. I especially agree we should keep this from Pastor Harrison if at all possible." He leaned over his son's cherry desk and drew a quill from its holder along with several sheets of paper. "I'll compose a brief message for each of the elders, requesting they come here tonight."

"I'll gladly distribute the letters, Father."

"As will I," Henry said.

"Thank you, but I will send one of the staff." He rang the servant's bell from Francis's desk, resulting in the immediate appearance of his valet.

"Yes, Magistrate?" The middle-aged man, every inch as elegant as his master, bowed.

"Henson, I want you to take these letters to the church elders straightaway. I believe you know where they live."

"Yes, sir."

"And have Mrs. Daley prepare the parlor for an emergency session meeting."

"Right away, sir."

"I'll go to the Harrison's," Francis said.

Henry noticed the judge smile. "Yes, of course, just go as you normally do but be sure to say nothing of this until I send Mr. Sharp after the meeting."

The words rang in his mind as Henry went to his room to pray. He'd noticed how often Francis visited the manse and how eagerly Ann Harrison received him. If he was reading the situation correctly, the pastor's wife was keen to make a match between Catherine and the young esquire. What he didn't know was the state of Catherine's mind toward Heath. Reaching the top of the stairs, he opened the door to his room and sat on the side of his bed, resting his elbows on his knees. The two seemed to get along well, even to enjoy each other's company, but would she settle for someone outside of her intense faith? He ran a hand through his hair as if to clear his thoughts, smiling as he recalled the many pastoral visits they'd gone on together and the times they'd stopped by Mrs. Doran's home for conversation and prayer. Catherine would make him a good wife. If he were totally honest, not only her spirit engaged him. He loved her mass of hair and those intriguing eyes, and found as he sat there, he wasn't able to think straight.

Sinking to his knees, he prayed. "Lord, you know how I feel toward your daughter, Catherine, feelings I've strenuously tried to keep to myself. I've striven to behave honorably toward her, as well as to respect those who have given me a home and my daily bread, but I must be honest with you, Lord. I believe she would be a wonderful wife who is better off with me than Francis Heath."

Henry broke off his prayer, startled by the realization that he'd probably be taking her to a small church in the country. She was born and bred in the city, with all its advantages, and Francis could maintain the kind of life she'd always known, and then some.

"Lord, I ask for wisdom and guidance, and for strength to keep at the proper distance from her. I beg you to show us all—myself, Catherine, and Francis—Thy will so it may be done here, as it is in heaven."

He knew which way he hoped God would answer, but he vowed to follow the will of the Almighty, no matter what.

CHAPTER NINE

Samuel Worthington was in a huff. With fists dug into his sides and nostrils flaring, he bellowed, "Are you suggesting, Magistrate, that I started this so-called rumor?"

"Calm yourself, Mr. Worthington. What I am saying is Miss Harrison heard this account from your daughter, and we are here to clear the matter up, as well as get to its source."

"Well, then, according to my Elizabeth, Susanna More contacted her this morning." He cast a sharp look in her father's direction.

"I would like to know how and where Miss More received her information," the magistrate said.

Henry sat quietly off to the side of the candlelit room while several elders shared volleys. Nicholas More cleared his throat. "Eh-hem! Gentlemen, my daughter is not one for idle gossip."

The other elders guffawed, the magistrate covered his mouth for a long moment. The young woman's father continued, undaunted.

"You may rest assured, if Susanna says something, you can depend upon its veracity."

Henry had the feeling Nicholas More was hiding something, but he had determined not to speak unless spoken to. He had witnessed the dignity with which William Tennent faced his own detractors and was determined to emulate his example.

"How many of you were aware of this situation before being called here?" Heath asked.

To a man, all of them were. "And how, may I ask, did you find out?"

"Mr. More came to see me at my shipping office," Charles Dash said.

The excitable and stooped Daniel Miller attempted to straighten up. "Yes, and he visited me at my home."

The magistrate turned to Oldfield. "How, may I ask, did you learn about this, Mr. Oldfield?"

The elder lifted his chin, assuming his signature superior look. "Shortly before my arrival here tonight, my wife informed me this story was spreading in the marketplace, and may I add, this is a most regrettable situation, Mr. Sharp."

Henry didn't trust Oldfield as far as he could throw him. He nodded out of civility. "This is a deliberate attempt to besmirch Mr. Sharp," Dash said. "There is absolutely no truth to any of it, is there, Pastor?"

Henry glanced at Edward Heath, who closed his eyes and nodded. "My esteemed elders, if you would permit me, I would like to address this matter."

All but two of the men bobbed their heads up and down. Oldfield and More remained impassive.

Henry repeated the story he had told Catherine about his family name and German customs.

Afterwards Mr. Worthington spoke. "Now I understand that part, but what about this charge about you not being a minister?"

Henry spread his hands. "I suppose that's a matter of interpretation, sir. As you know, I recently completed my theological studies at Mr. Tennent's school, a rigorous course I might add. While I have preached many times, I've not yet been ordained."

Four elders opened their mouths at the same time, and Heath raised a hand. "One at a time, gentlemen. Mr. Sharp is clearly innocent. What I would like to know is who would be privy to information that became twisted into a rumor?"

Henry spoke. "I'm guessing someone has made an effort to contact a member of my home church to investigate my background." Robert Oldfield caught his eye and quickly turned away.

"This is something I would expect from a heathen, not from a church member, let alone an elder of this church." Heath's words splashed over them, temporarily dousing the conversation.

Oldfield was the first to speak. "Magistrate, I sincerely doubt you will find any of us guilty of such a thing."

Heath stared him down—the air seemed to flicker and spark. "And may God help him if I do."

A moment passed before Samuel Worthington broke the tension. "All nonsense aside, Magistrate, I am concerned our church's needs might go unmet because Mr. Sharp isn't ordained."

Nicholas More nodded. "Nor has he has been properly trained in the first place."

Henry's hands tightened in his lap, a nerve in his temple twitched. Nothing of the rumor had bothered him until now, but this comment was an attack against Tennent. Old Side Presbyterians considered his school to be little more than a rustic "log college," unworthy to produce ministers of the gospel, whom they believed should be "properly" educated at Harvard, Yale, or abroad. They didn't seem to care Mr. Tennent held them to the highest standards of academic and spiritual excellence.

Edward Heath rose. "Gentlemen, I can vouch personally for Mr. Sharp's integrity and his fitness to shepherd our people in Mr. Harrison's absence."

The show of support touched Henry. *Thank you, Lord, for letting another man's tongue praise me, and not my own.*

"This was always meant to be a temporary solution to a temporary situation."

"Begging your pardon, sir, and not meaning to cast aspersions, what shall we do about the Lord's Supper? We need an ordained pastor to administer it," Worthington said.

Heath shook his head. "Our church polity allows for an elder to administer the sacrament in extenuating circumstances."

For a moment, Henry thought the matter had been addressed and dismissed, but not all of the elders were finished airing their concerns.

"Magistrate, there is another matter, if you will please."

"Yes, Mr. Dash?"

Henry had the impression the judge had to make an effort to keep from sounding impatient.

"As you know, during Mr. Harrison's illness, we are not only paying his salary, but Mr. Sharp's. While I hesitate to say anything, might this not present a burden on the church?"

Was this Dash's concern alone, Henry wondered, or did the others share his opinion? Was this matter legitimate or one more ploy to unseat him?

More piped up. "Mr. Dash raises an important point for us to consider."

"I hardly think after all Mr. Harrison's years of faithful service, in which he has never been overpaid I might add, if we cannot provide for him and his family in their hour of need, and support a substitute, we are a sorry bunch indeed." Heath's searing expression dared anyone to contradict him.

"Gentlemen, I believe we should adjourn with prayer." Then the meeting was over.

As Henry said goodnight to the elders, a few whose handshakes were decidedly firmer than the others, he wondered what might happen should Harrison not recover. He saw the minister on a daily basis, and the man was in bad shape. Henry also was beginning to believe Harrison may have underestimated the placidness of the Old Side in his church regarding his theological perspective, especially some of the elders. At best, not too far beneath the surface of this governing body, perhaps of High Street Presbyterian's entire congregation, lay indifference about the necessity of the new birth. At worst, there was contempt. Should Joseph Harrison not get better, Henry knew he'd have a major fight on his hands. His hands formed fists—he felt up to the challenge.

CHAPTER TEN

"Good evening, Mr. Sharp, do come in." Catherine opened the door wider to admit him, shivering from the October chill.

"Thank you, Miss Harrison." He handed his hat to her, which she hung on a peg.

From upstairs, she could hear her father coughing, unable as yet to accept the truth of his condition. The harsh spells stoked her mother's fears about what would happen to them if her husband died. Catherine had no answers beyond her trust in God to see them through. If only she was able to convince her mother.

"How did the meeting go?" she asked.

"I would say pretty well, although we didn't determine exactly how the rumor began."

She tilted her head. "I would say you have an idea, however."

"I think someone has been in touch with those at Neshaminy who oppose Mr. Tennent's ministry, and therefore, my own."

In his face, she detected a shut-door expression.

"Who is it, Catherine?" Her mother's voice wafted from the parlor.

She led him to the room where her mother sat with Margaret and Francis Heath, who stood and shook Henry's hand. As usual, the youngest daughter of the house giggled when faced with the tall pastor.

"My goodness, Miss Margaret, you are getting to be quite the young lady," Henry said, bowing.

"Thank you, sir." She blushed coquettishly.

"Yes, and this young lady needs to be going to bed." Ann Harrison called out, "Lena!"

The servant appeared in the doorway. "Yes, madam?"

"The hour is late. Would you take Miss Margaret upstairs for me?"

"Yes, madam." She caught Henry's eye. "Good evening, Pastor."

"Good evening to you, Lena."

When they ascended the stairs, Catherine gestured toward a chair.

"I suppose you've heard, madam, there was a session meeting just now," he said, sitting down.

"Yes, I have, Mr. Sharp, and I knew all about the report as well." Ann Harrison twisted her lace handkerchief. "I've barely eaten all day."

Henry cocked his head. "Then you heard the rumor early today?"

"Mrs. More told me in the market place."

"I've reassured her, Mr. Sharp, she'd heard a lie," Catherine hastened to say.

Ann clucked her tongue. "That Susanna More is a trouble-maker! She's just vexed Mr. Sharp has demonstrated no interest in courting her."

Catherine's jaw dropped. "Mother!"

A glance at Henry told her he had no idea what her mother was talking about, and she was pleased how unaware he was of his attractiveness. Perhaps he really didn't understand how his striking figure affected the opposite sex. She wished she didn't see him in such a light either, but there was no denying her feelings, though he'd never given her any indication he felt the same way about her. All they discussed were church matters and George Whitefield's impending visit. *If only I felt for Francis as I do for Henry.* She glanced in the direction of the young barrister, aware of his eagerness to have her, to offer not only his unwavering devotion, but any amount of worldly security.

Francis interrupted her thoughts. "What was said at the meeting?"

Henry provided a detailed summary, at the end of which Ann Harrison began to cry, especially after the part about the church being burdened by two salaries.

His face flushed. "I fear I've upset you, madam. Magistrate Heath quickly put the matter to rest, and you have nothing to fear."

"Don't fret, Mr. Sharp. Mother upsets easily these days," Catherine said. She knew her mother's strong memories of poverty following her own father's death long ago still haunted her. Only God could drive away such demons. Catherine's own efforts to soothe her mother had fallen away like so much chaff. At times, she felt as if their roles were reversing, and she was mothering her mother.

Francis patted the woman's hand as if she were a child. "All will be well, Mrs. Harrison."

"Thank you, Mr. Heath. You must forgive me." She sniffed into the handkerchief.

Catherine was aware the focus of attention had turned from Henry's situation to her mother's volatile emotions. "So, Mr. Sharp, is everything settled then?" She nudged the discussion back toward him.

"I believe so. The Lord Jesus has a way of working all things together for the good of those who love him, including troubling things."

"Of course all will be well," Francis said. "Now the rumor has been resolved, we can rest assured Mr. Sharp's ministry may continue for as long as need be."

Catherine interpreted the look he gave Henry to mean, "You can tell me more when we get back to my house."

"Mrs. Harrison, I wonder if I might see your husband."

She almost sprang from her seat. "Oh, Mr. Sharp, you aren't going to tell him about any of this!"

"Why, no, madam. In fact, I highly recommend we don't let him know of this at all," Henry said. "I simply wish to pay my respects and to pray with him."

She let out a sigh and sat down again. "Yes, certainly. Of course."

Henry rose. "Please excuse me, then."

"Do you want me to wait for you?" Francis asked. "I could walk back with you."

"Yes, thank you."

Catherine watched as he took the steps two at a time, then looked over at Francis, who was, some would say, equally pleasing to look at. His smile certainly contained the sum of his feelings for her.

At first, Henry couldn't tell if Joseph Harrison were asleep because he lay so still. His face appeared considerably paler than usual in the candlelit room. He was breathing, wasn't he? Henry's heart sped at the thought the pastor might be *mort*.

"Mr. Sharp." The weak voice both startled and relieved him.

"Yes, sir."

"I was hoping to see you today." He moved his head on the pillow, and Henry noticed he hadn't been shaved for a few days.

"How are you, sir?" He sat on the chair and moved closer, taking the man's cold hand, ignoring the potent breath.

Harrison smiled. "I could be better, but I have no complaints. My concern is for Ann."

"Yes, I understand."

"If only she knew our Savior, Mr. Sharp, she wouldn't let worry for the future consume her." He coughed, then wiped his lips with the back of his right hand.

"If you like, I'll speak with her."

"Please try to convince her our good Shepherd knows how to care for his flock." A few moments later, he asked, "How are things with you, and the church? How often I turn to him in prayer for you."

"You're very kind, sir, and I am quite well, endeavoring to be half the pastor you and Mr. Tennent are."

"You'll be much more than half, Mr. Sharp." The amber eyes, so like Catherine's, glowed.

Wanting to inject cheer into the exchange, he changed the subject. "I'm happy to report Mr. Whitefield will be here shortly, according to Mr. Franklin's best estimates."

"Ah, this is good news indeed. When is he expected?"

"Within a week or so." He paused. "Mr. Harrison, might we offer Mr. Whitefield the use of High Street church in which to preach?"

"A wonderful idea, son!" He coughed, then spoke again. "I would be honored to have him in my pulpit. I shall just have to get well, so I can see this prince of preachers."

The pastor's words warmed Henry. "That would be very good, indeed, sir."

Harrison lapsed back into himself, as if climbing into the present world had wearied him. "Well, then, thank you for coming to see me. I need so little now, except the presence of my loved ones, and prayer. Will you pray with me, son?"

Henry wondered if Joseph might be seeing far beyond his present situation into eternity itself. After praying for the minister and receiving his blessing, Henry went downstairs.

"Well, then, are you ready to go, Mr. Sharp?" Heath asked when Henry entered the room.

"Yes, thank you." The invitation released him from any obligation to say more than he wanted just now, which was nothing. Catherine, however, looked at him with her frank expression, but he managed to avoid her gaze, knowing he couldn't fully keep what he suspected away from her. He bade her mother good night, and Catherine followed him and Francis to the hallway.

"Thank you for coming. I'm glad the meeting went well, and you got to see Father."

Henry bowed. "I am at your disposal."

"Do you think he-he ... Do you think he's improving?"

He wasn't one to lie. "I think he's peaceful."

Henry was relieved when Francis spoke up. "Be well, Miss Harrison. Get some rest, and I'll see you tomorrow."

As they left, Henry saw her standing in the doorway looking after him.

Catherine lay awake into the morning's small hours praying, then fretting. She wanted to bring her errant thoughts into conformity with the character of her Lord, who trusted everything to his Father in heaven. She'd start nodding off in a semi-peaceful state, then be awakened by her father's coughs and lie there staring out the window until he lapsed once again into exhausted slumber. His irregular sleep had made it nearly impossible for her mother to get enough rest, so she was now using the extra bedroom down the hall. She, Catherine, and Lena took turns with Joseph on different nights of the week. Tonight, Lena was on duty.

Catherine climbed out of bed and knelt, her knees resting on a braided rug over the oak planks. Leaning her elbows on the mattress, she folded her hands. "Oh, Lord, you've promised to be with us in the night watches, so I know I'm not alone. I confess my fears to you for the present, as well as the future. I'm fearful about my father's condition. Please comfort him and provide the strength he lacks." She rested her forehead against her hands. "Precious Savior, my mother also is in need of comfort and strength. Please reveal yourself to her, giving her eyes to see you clearly. May the scales of unbelief fall from them as they did Paul's.

"Dearest Lord, please assist me so my spirit doesn't give way to my mother's fears. You know all things, especially how she keeps in her heart the hardship she knew when my grandfather died. Please help her to know you're with her and will be with us at all times. I sometimes fear, as well, what might happen to my family should Father, should Father ..." A sob caught in her throat. "... should he not survive this illness. Lord, what would happen in your providence? Would my brother be able to support us?" Another thought came, unbidden, yet one waving for her attention, a banner on a breeze. "Father, I know Francis Heath would love to take me as his wife, and he's a good man, who wouldn't allow Mother or Margaret to go destitute. He would treat me well, and my life would be pleasant, but Lord, he doesn't know you, and your Word speaks of not being unequally yoked with unbelievers."

She shifted her weight to ease the pressure on her knees.

"I confess to you, Father in heaven, I'm exceedingly fond of Mr. Sharp, but I can't be certain he returns my affections. He's about your business, and so many young women are also fond of him. Although he appears to enjoy my company, and we work very well together, he hasn't led me at any time to believe he sees me as Francis does. In fact, Lord, Francis may have told Mr. Sharp he's set his cap for me, thus discouraging our pastor."

She heard Lena moving through the hallway and waited to see if the servant needed her help. When her father's door opened and closed, Catherine decided not to investigate.

"Father, I'm so tired. Thank you for listening to me prattle. Into your hands, I commit my spirit and all of my concerns knowing your yoke is easy and your burden, light. Amen."

When she awakened the next morning, Catherine opened her two windows and breathed deeply of the cool autumn air. She washed and dressed in a state of peace, knowing her Lord would supply all her and her family's needs according to his glorious riches. Walking softly to her father's room, she opened the door so as not to awaken him if he were asleep, and finding him so, went downstairs. She was surprised to see her mother standing at the front door with Mrs. Oldfield.

"Do not fret, Mrs. Harrison," the woman was telling her. "I assure you, no matter what may happen, you have nothing to fear."

Catherine caught the elder's wife's eye. The woman frowned, said a curt "good day," and left. "Good morning, Mother." She kissed her wet cheek.

"Good morning, Daughter."

She looked past her toward the door. "What was Mrs. Oldfield doing here so early?"

Her mother blew her nose into a delicate handkerchief. "She often comes to visit and is such a comfort to me. I just don't know what I would do without her."

Catherine's spine prickled. Something was up.

CHAPTER ELEVEN

"So, tell me, Mr. Sharp, just what is your opinion of this George Whitefield fellow? You often speak of him, and now the entire city is abuzz over his coming." The magistrate pushed aside a newspaper bearing headlines about the English preacher.

He, Henry, and young Heath sat at the table following breakfast, a genial fire reducing the chill in the room. Mrs. Clydesdale hovered over him, slowly pouring coffee the second he'd drained his cup. Henry held his breath until she'd successfully fulfilled her task, then watched as she minced her way toward the kitchen. Francis leaned back in his chair. "I'm aware of his renown throughout England for preaching in the fields, and how he's both loved and reviled."

Henry nodded. "From what I know of him, Mr. Whitefield is about twenty-five years of age and has an extraordinary gift for preaching God's Word. Wherever he goes, crowds throng, and often churches aren't large enough to contain him." He chose his next words carefully. "Nor is he always welcome in them."

Francis frowned. "Does he really incite mobs?"

"I wouldn't say so. However, some dislike his frank way of presenting our need to have a saving encounter with God. Also, his listeners are prone to expressing deep emotions when they're convicted of their sinful state."

His friends lapsed into partial silence, apparently mulling over what he'd said. Finally, Edward pushed back his plate and leaned into his chair, his trim figure attesting to his disciplined approach to eating. "I suppose, then, he would agree with Mr. Harrison's view that going to church is not the mark of a true Christian."

"I like how Mr. Tennent puts the matter, sir. Imagine a mother gives birth to a son in a barn, and he grows up among the animals. He becomes so well acquainted with them he carries about their aroma." Henry paused while the men chortled. "Even so, he hasn't become an animal himself.

Similarly, if a person is born and raised within the church, knowing and observing its traditions and practices, he's not actually a Christian until he's met the risen Lord Jesus."

The magistrate reached for his coffee cup while Francis stared at his hands, folded on the damask tablecloth. Henry wondered what was going on in their minds, and in their spirits. *Lord, please help me minister to them. Help me know how to give an answer for the hope you have placed within me.*

"This puzzles me somewhat," Francis finally said. "How can one actually know Christ when he no longer walks among us? Such a thing doesn't seem reasonable."

"Before he died, Jesus told his disciples he wouldn't leave them fatherless, but after he ascended into heaven, he would send the Holy Ghost, the third member of the Godhead. He is the Spirit of Jesus, able to live within the very depths of our being." Henry took a deep breath. "Apart from him, we can know about God, but not actually know him."

Francis nodded, thoughtful. "I think I see what you mean, Mr. Sharp."

Henry's heartbeat quickened. If Francis Heath accepted the new birth, Catherine Harrison might be more inclined to accept him as a husband. Henry sucked in a deep breath and prayed he might consider this a secondary matter when weighed in the balance of Francis's salvation.

"When will this Mr. Whitefield arrive?" Edward asked.

"Mr. Franklin tells me at any time." Henry cleared his throat. "Magistrate, might we make Mr. Whitefield an offer of our church should he not have a place to preach? I've discussed this with Mr. Harrison, who is favorable."

Edward nodded. "Yes, yes, quite. I've been meaning to ask you how our pastor fares. I regret with courts in session I haven't been able to visit this week."

Henry looked down at the gleaming wood floor. "I fear he's weakening, sir."

He pursed his lips. "That's difficult to hear." If possible, Edward Heath sat up straighter. "Mr. Sharp, I've hesitated to inform you of a certain matter, but I fear more trouble is brewing concerning your ministry."

He braced for the worst.

"As you know, two years ago, the Synod of Philadelphia passed an act requiring all candidates for ministry to have a college diploma before their ordination trials could commence."

Henry recalled how upset the decree had made William Tennent, who saw the act for what it was—a tactic designed to cut off from ministry the men he'd trained.

"A small number of our members have appealed to the Synod to see if this might apply to our present situation."

Francis shot up from his seat and, bumping the table, caused crystal and silverware to clatter. "That is reprehensible!"

"Unfortunately, Son, the measure may just stand from a legal viewpoint."

This truly was a serious matter. What might happen to his dream of being ordained if the Synod should find him unqualified? Of course, Henry thought, there was always the New Brunswick Presbytery, controlled by New Sides.

"My son and I both support you, Mr. Sharp, and we'll do everything we can to assist you. About half of the elders agree this is wrong, especially during our pastor's grave illness."

Francis shook his head. "I'm appalled."

"I'm grateful to you beyond words, Magistrate." These good men were putting their own reputations on the line. Although they couldn't yet be counted among the Lord's truly redeemed, Henry thought of Jesus's words—"whoever is not against us is for us."

A shriek from the back of the house brought the men to their feet as one.

"Holy smokes!" Edward cried.

His hapless housekeeper dashed into the room pulling at her cap until it nearly covered her eyes. "Oh, Magistrate!"

"What is wrong, Mrs. Clydesdale?" His voice blended notes of annoyance and alarm.

"A spider, Magistrate, a spider as big as your fist, sir." The woman shivered as if feverish. "I cannot return to that kitchen knowing the beast is waiting for me." Her frantic gaze darted from one man to another.

Henry smiled into his palm, not wanting to hurt her feelings for the world.

"I'm certain Mr. Henson can dispose of the spider for you," Edward Heath said. "Please find him." He turned to the others as she fled upstairs in search of the valet. "Well, gentlemen, if you will excuse me, I must be getting to the courthouse."

Before retreating to their chambers, Francis began telling Henry about his flourishing business, how he provided financing for Philadelphia's import and export trades. "My success puts me in a good position to marry," Francis concluded with a smile. "Then perhaps some problems at the manse can be settled."

"Yes, I suppose they would be," Henry said, forcing himself to seem happy for him. Shortly afterward the young lawyer left the house, and Henry decided to write his mentor a letter before going visiting. He wanted to tell William Tennent not just what was happening at the church, but about Mr. Whitefield's impending appearance.

> My dear Mr. Tennent,
>
> I beg your indulgence for not writing sooner but dealing with the needs and challenges of High Street Presbyterian Church has demanded most of my attention. I trust you and Mrs. Tennent are in good health and are continuing to experience God's peace and strength in your season of grief following Eleanor's death. I always admired your faithful daughter and think of her with gladness. Please remember me to Mrs. Tennent, and to the students under your care.
>
> I am sorry to report Mr. Harrison grows weaker as the days grow shorter. Initially, he showed signs of strengthening after my arrival, but he has slipped considerably since then. His mind is alert, and although he inquires as to the condition of his flock, his concerns mostly are those of another world where there is no sorrow or sighing. I have not given him a full report of church matters as I fear they would undermine his fragile state. To you, however, I will render such an accounting in order to secure your prayers and advice.
>
> While some early false reports about my being an imposter have successfully been put to rights, I fear they opened a Pandora's box of discontentment. The most often heard complaint is my German heritage, which many consider a shocking offense, and that I should be taking care of my own people.

He refreshed the ink, careful not to smudge what he'd written.

> Others maintain I am lazy, or I preach too long or am entirely too familiar when speaking of the Almighty. There are members who are angry I call respectable citizens "sinners."

He smiled to himself thinking of his strongest allies, the matrons of the church who often scolded their men for brow beating the young pastor. Then they'd present him with pies and puddings.

> Over many years Mr. Harrison won their respect and trust, and he was able to win a small number to the true faith. He held them together, but now that he's ill and I am here, they're following the pull of their sinful desires. Not only do they swipe at me, but at each other.

> I also hear Mr. Oldfield's brother is in town, on what business I don't know. No one doubts he desires High Street's pulpit.

He looked out the window, watching a couple walking together down the street as he considered how Mr. Oldfield was likely trying to push his brother forward.

Catherine ...

Henry groaned at his mistake. Although he thought of the pastor's daughter in familiar terms, he was careful to address her properly before her and everyone else. He quickly added "Harrison" after her name and continued.

> ... tells me her mother has many dealings with Mrs. Robert Oldfield, who continually assures Mrs. Harrison all will be well. Miss Harrison has shared with me her concern that the elder's wife may have something specific in mind, though she doesn't know what. By all accounts, this is a most disagreeable time for High Street, and at times I become mildly oppressed, but I know our Lord is at work here, and I remain unmoved. As you often say, our battle is not against flesh and blood, but against the powers at work in the spiritual realm. I have always admired your grace and dignity when dealing with hard people at Neshaminy, and I'm striving to follow your good example. Perhaps with the coming of Mr. Whitefield, the Holy Spirit will do a work here.

Henry stretched his long arms and legs before completing the letter, telling his pastor about the English minister's arrival and inviting him to stay at the magistrate's home, as Edward had instructed Henry. Just then, Henson's form filled the doorway. "I beg your pardon, Mr. Sharp, but there are people here to see the magistrate. Since he is not here, and the men came on church business, I thought you might like to receive them."

Henry's skin prickled. He was a cat preparing for a fight. "Who are they, Mr. Henson?"

"I do not know them, sir."

"Please send them in." He stood and prayed for wisdom and a right spirit. The valet reappeared some moments later with two young men whom Henry guessed to be about his own age. Each was well-dressed and wore a pleasant expression, causing Henry's gut to unclench, although one of them completely filled the hallway with his presence.

"Mr. Henry Sharp, may I present Mr. William Seward and Mr. George Whitefield?"

CHAPTER TWELVE

He searched vainly for words—finding himself face-to-face with George Whitefield momentarily muted him. He opened his mouth but could not seem to command his tongue. When he recovered his senses, he moved forward to shake the men's hands. "Welcome, sirs. Welcome to Philadelphia. I'm Henry Sharp. Won't you please come in?" He gestured toward the parlor and stepped aside to let them enter ahead of him.

"Thank you, kindly, Mr. Sharp," Whitefield said. "I'm happy to be here at long last."

"Please sit down." Henry indicated two wingback chairs.

"Thank you," Seward said, looking as if he could be comfortable anywhere. Whitefield appeared to be easy-going as well, but without saying more than a few words, he dominated the place.

Henson appeared in the doorway, his face bright, eager. "May I offer refreshments, Mr. Sharp?"

"Would you care for something, gentlemen?"

Whitefield answered for them both. "No, thank you very much. We've just taken our meal at the boarding house where we stayed last night."

Henson bowed, then backed away slowly.

"This is quite a surprise, Mr. Whitefield, Mr. Seward," Henry said. Looking from one to the other he asked, "When did you arrive in Philadelphia?"

"At about eleven o'clock last night." Whitefield possessed a polished, bell-like British accent.

Henry spoke around his smile. "The entire city has been preparing for your visit." He studied the men, who bore a small resemblance to each other except for Seward's lighter hair and the minister's smaller physique. He tried not to stare, but one of Whitefield's eyes was off kilter and lent an intriguing aspect to his overall appearance. Henry wondered whether this was an accident of birth or the result of a mishap. *Don't stare, man! Speak to them.*

"How long did your journey take?"

"My little family and I spent eleven weeks on board the *Elizabeth*," Whitefield said.

"I trust the voyage was as pleasant as such an arduous journey can be."

Henry wondered what he meant by "little family." Was Whitefield married? He'd always assumed he was not.

"I found the journey so, but my companion here would tell you otherwise." His eyes twinkled as he glanced toward Seward.

"Let's just say, Mr. Sharp, I rejoiced greatly when we landed. Have you ever made the crossing?"

"I was born in America, Mr. Seward, but my parents have told me about their arduous passage when they came here many years ago."

"Where are they from?" Whitefield leaned forward in his chair, resting his arms on his legs.

"Heidelberg, Germany, sir."

"Ah. An excellent city!"

Seward jumped into the conversation, steering them in a different direction. "We arrived so late last evening, we went to the first respectable-looking lodgings we could find, but today my good friend and I are searching for a house to rent. Our ship's captain suggested we check with Magistrate Heath, but we didn't wish to disturb him so late last night."

Henry smiled. "I'm a boarder here myself."

"Is that right?" Seward asked. "How did you come to be here?"

"I'll try to make a lengthy story brief." Henry filled them in on the details of his coming to Philadelphia. When he finished, Whitefield nodded, his lips pressed together. "And how does your Mr. Harrison fare?"

Henry half closed his eyes and cocked his head. "Not well, I am sorry to say."

For a long moment, the only sounds were those of the staff going about their cleaning chores in nearby rooms. Henry caught a glimpse of Mrs. Clydesdale across the hall dusting a vase on which no dust was ever allowed to accumulate.

"That is sad news," Whitefield said. "How have you been doing in his absence?"

Henry had difficulty believing George Whitefield should be taking an interest in himself. "I've had my good and bad moments. You see, Mr. Whitefield, Mr. Harrison and I believe in the necessity of the new birth, while others don't understand or are openly hostile."

Whitefield crossed his arms over his chest. "How would you say most of the city is situated spiritually?"

"I believe our congregation is a version in miniature of Philadelphia, sir. Many are wedded to tradition, with a small number being truly Christian. The greater part of the populace cares little for religious matters."

Whitefield's unusual eyes narrowed. "Just as I suspected. The fields are white unto harvest, Mr. Sharp, and I commend you for the plowing you're doing."

Seward spoke. "You say the church elders may have you dismissed?"

"I believe this is a possibility, Mr. Seward. I know some are looking into the matter because I wasn't trained at one of the American colleges."

Whitefield leaned forward, resting his hands on his knees. "And where did you receive your education?"

"My pastor and teacher, Mr. William Tennent, has been training men at his school some twenty miles north of the city."

"Then I must meet this gentleman!" he exclaimed. "I like him already."

Henry grinned. "He's been looking forward to meeting you too, sir." The magistrate came through the front door just then, followed by Hanson, who had no doubt gone to fetch him. The men rose, Henry made introductions. When they'd settled back into their seats, Henry explained the purpose of their visit to Edward Heath, who listened with his customary intensity.

"I would be pleased to open my home and my staff to you both for as long as you have such a need," Heath said.

Whitefield gave a small bow. "Magistrate, you are a most generous and kind man, however, I must tell you when people discover I'm staying somewhere, they often come to visit, unbidden, at odd hours. There are at times unsavory characters who seek me out as well. You might be disturbed by the comings and goings of my little family."

"I assure you, Mr. Whitefield, I'll be honored to have you stay under whatever circumstances."

"I'm most grateful, sir, but there's another matter. I've come here with not only Mr. Seward but my secretary, John Syms, several orphans, and three of their caregivers. Mr. Syms is with them as we speak."

Henry couldn't imagine this quiet, esteemed house full of urchins.

"The children will be leaving in a few days, sailing to the colony of Georgia where I'm in the process of establishing an orphanage."

Henry had a sudden idea. "If I may, perhaps we could send the children elsewhere. What about Mrs. Doran?"

"An excellent idea, Mr. Sharp!" Heath addressed Whitefield and Seward. "She is a delightful widow from our church who enjoys all kinds of people. She can no longer get out as she would like, and she enjoys having the world come to her. Since you have staff to care for the children, I think she might be agreeable."

"I am obliged to you, Magistrate."

"I can take you there straightway," Henry said. "Where are the children now?"

"They remain on board the ship." Whitefield turned to Heath. "I assure you, we will pay for our accommodations as there is much expense involved."

Heath nodded in a disinterested sort of way.

Seward's shoulders straightened, as if he'd just put down a heavy load. "We meet many friends in our travels, but we also have had our disparagers."

Henry grinned. "I, too, am acquainted with those."

An hour later, Henry, Whitefield, Seward, and Syms sat in Mrs. Doran's parlor waiting for her decision, which didn't come as quickly as Henry expected. He was beginning to consider other options when a sudden smile broke through her wrinkled features.

"I should be delighted to hear the laughter of small children in my home."

Catherine took a breakfast tray to her father, relieving Lena who'd kept the night watch, and whose puffy eyes revealed her need of rest. Her mother had taken Margaret to the Oldfield's on yet another social visit there. The Oldfields had become her mother's source of strength, which sat on Catherine's spirit like so much greasy sausage. As she climbed the steps, she recalled when she was Margaret's age and had enjoyed a close relationship with her mother—a time when they laughed easily and worked side-by-side in the home and in ministry, before Ann insisted on holding fast to religious traditions rather than the One to whom they bore witness. If she were honest, at times Catherine resented her mother, especially when she struggled with fear. She knew her mother's solution was marriage to Francis Heath. Other than matrimony, she had no other options. Her thoughts careened onto a different path. What would happen to Henry Sharp if her father did pass away? While the church ladies favored him, the younger ones in particular, most of the men had become increasingly fractious about Henry's ministry—some for, others against.

Entering her father's room, she found him slumped part way up, as if he'd tried to sit up the entire way, but weakness had thwarted him. His face was drawn, the color of day-old bread. Unbidden tears coursed down her cheeks, and through the blur, she saw her father reach out his arms for her. She placed the tray on the chair and lowered herself gently into his embrace so as not to cause him further pain. She hadn't intended to, but she let herself weep as he held her.

"There, there, my dearest girl, shhh, shhh," he said, his voice filled with his native Scotland. "All will be well."

When she spent her tears, she sat up on the bed and beheld this man who was dearer to her than life. "Forgive me, Father." She dabbed at her eyes with a handkerchief.

He coughed. "For what, my dearest daughter?"

"For ... for not being strong."

"Tears and emotions are gifts from God when words fail us."

"What will I do without you, Father?" As soon as the words were out of her mouth, she regretted having said them. "I, I did not mean ..."

Joseph held up a hand, its blue veins like tributaries on a map. "Let's speak frankly to one another." A coughing jag compelled him to stop for several moments then, "I'm at peace about this sickness being unto death yet am uneasy for you, your mother, and Margaret. Jacob is on his own now, and my only concern for him is to know Christ." He paused, catching his wispy breath. "How is our Margaret's soul?"

Catherine willed away tears so she could speak clearly. "She displays a general curiosity about our Lord."

He nodded, smiling. "This is a good beginning. Will you continue to train her in the ways of the Lord?"

"Yes, Father."

"And don't give up on your dear mother. Some take longer than others to enter the kingdom of God, but I'm confident one day, she'll stop drinking from puddles. Her thirst will be quenched in rivers of living water."

Catherine liked the poetic turn her father's words had taken, a reminder of his engaging preaching style. "I won't give up on Mother."

"Now, for you, Catherine. How is your heart?"

She folded her hands on her lap. "I'm mostly peaceful, Father, but at times my spirit gives way to fretting about what will happen if, when …"

"I die. When I die. Don't be ashamed to say the word, Daughter. It is appointed unto every man once to die, and my time is near. My soul rejoices at the thought of seeing my Savior." His eyes saw what she could not, somewhere in the distance. Then he returned to her. "My concern is for my family, and my church, but I am confident that he who began a good work will be faithful to complete it. I'm not afraid, but I see you are."

"Not always, Father, but sometimes late at night. Then the Lord ministers to my spirit."

He nodded. "While I move toward the glories of heaven, you must deal with the things of earth."

"Yes."

"What are your prospects?"

She shook her head. "I'm not sure what you mean, Father."

He coughed, wiped his lips with a trembling hand. "You're of marriageable age. You will make a fine wife, Catherine."

"Thank you, Father." Should she follow him into the territory she kept avoiding?

"How do you feel about our friend?"

"Our friend, Father?"

A laugh sputtered into a cough. "Francis Heath. He is courting you, is he not?"

She couldn't hide from him. "Yes, I believe so."

Joseph smiled. "That young man is here often enough. He would make a good husband, and I like his dedication to my daughter, but …"

She completed his sentence. "He doesn't know Christ, merely knows of him."

Her father nodded. "While I would have no worries for your material welfare, I would not be confident about your oneness in Christ."

She wrestled with herself. Should she tell him what a daughter would ordinarily entrust to her mother? Her hesitation quickly vanished. "Father, there is something I don't quite know how to say." She fingered a loose thread on his quilt.

"Tell me whatever you wish."

"I like Mr. Heath well enough, but I don't … I'm not …" She reached for the right words. "He doesn't make my heart flutter." She didn't see her father nod. "How important is that?" She searched his expression for the answer.

"To some, this matters little." He reached for her hand, and she willed herself not to withdraw involuntarily due to the shock of his protruding bones and the chill of the thin flesh. "For you, Catherine, I believe this is of consequence and nothing to feel ashamed about."

Surprising herself, she lifted his hands to her face and caressed them. When she gently laid them on the bed, Catherine thought the conversation was ending, but her father hadn't finished.

"While I understand his lack of spiritual understanding, I believe there is less wrong with Francis Heath than there is something right about someone else."

Her mouth was open, but nothing came out—an unusual combination for her. She saw the twinkle in his watery eyes. *He knows.*

"How do you know?" she whispered.

"My eyes still see, Daughter." They lapsed into temporary silence. "Do you know how he feels?"

"I don't, Father. He speaks of little but the church, but when we make visits, I feel well matched. Comfortable, something like putting my hand into a glove that fits exactly right." Her voice became husky. "Has he, has he spoken to you?"

"Not yet."

Although her father sounded as if he were certain of Henry Sharp's inclinations, Catherine didn't know how this could be. Only in a few unguarded moments had she found him staring at her with a look beyond courtesy. How could a woman go on such an assumption?

"My dear daughter, he is living under the Heaths' very roof, and since Francis doesn't hide his intentions, Henry Sharp feels it dishonorable to try to claim you."

The room suddenly went brighter, but only for a moment. Even if her father was right, where did this realization leave her? A young woman couldn't speak her feelings ahead of a man.

"Daughter."

She gazed at him, her heart swelling. "We'll commit this to the Lord, who loves us more than we know."

CHAPTER THIRTEEN

In the darkened room down the hall, Ann Harrison lay on her bed covered by a quilt, her knees drawn practically to her chin. The curtains and blinds were closed.

Catherine found her father's chamber far more pleasant. "Are you well, Mother?"

"I am with my friends." She was speaking to the wall. "When I return, my head aches."

Catherine gave a small huff, knowing which friends she meant. "I'm going to take some jam I made to Mrs. Doran."

Ann waved her away. "Yes, yes. Take Margaret with you and close the door, so I may have some peace."

She means she doesn't have to hear Father coughing. Anger fired her insides. She couldn't get out of there fast enough.

A brisk wind swirled her skirts. From the docks in the near distance, Catherine saw British flags snapping on their masts, the fresh air enlivening her. On this third day of November, the weather held a hint of winter—a persistent sun did battle with puffy gray clouds. She and her sister, who seemed almost giddy to be away from the house, greeted a few parishioners, stopping just long enough to inquire after their health and answer questions about her father as vaguely as she could manage. She found concealing her feelings difficult, but she didn't particularly care to bare them either, unlike Elizabeth. Avoiding unwanted attention from a leering sailor—"Now, there's a lass!"—she hastened toward Elfreth's Alley, relieved the man hadn't trailed her and Margaret. When she reached Mrs. Doran's house, something wasn't right.

"What's all that noise?" Margaret peered into a window on tiptoe.

"Come away from there!" Catherine yanked her sister and knocked on the door.

"Miss Harrison! Miss Margaret!" Sally was breathless, her swarthy complexion matching the flame in her eyes. She opened the door for them to enter.

Catherine could not have been more surprised if she'd discovered a whale in the middle of the widow's parlor. A variety of strangers—two women in their twenties or thirties, along with several laughing children—were making merry with Mrs. Doran. Another lady hustled a little boy to the back of the house. From the way he clutched at his pants, Catherine could figure out their destination. There were also a few men in the room.

"Why, good afternoon, Miss Harrison. Margaret." Mrs. Doran seemed ten years younger.

Catherine stood at the edge of the room with all eyes on her and her sister as she glanced from face to face. When she spotted Henry Sharp, she blushed in shame, as if he could've known she was just talking about him with her father in the most intimate of terms. A look passed between them, and she felt further disconcerted when she realized one of the three well-dressed men in the room looked at Henry, then Catherine as if he *knew*. She felt as though her heart had been undressed, and quickly rearranging her innermost being, turned to the lady of the house. "Good day, Mrs. Doran." She elbowed Margaret, who was gaping at everyone.

"Hello, Mrs. Doran." Her sister curtsied.

"I am delighted you stopped by. There are people I'd like you to meet."

Catherine wondered who they were and where they'd come from. She'd never seen the likes of them before, and she knew most of Philadelphia's regular citizens at least by sight. The children appeared to be under the age of ten and although their clothes were not of the finest quality, they were clean and the children, well groomed. The two jars of jam she carried in her basket suddenly seemed like a drop in the ocean. She handed them to Sally.

"For your pantry," she muttered.

"I didn't expect you to have company," she said as Sally disappeared with the basket.

"Nor did I. Do sit down, and I will introduce you and your sister."

One of the urchins, a boy of about seven, jumped up and offered his seat before any of the men could do so. "'Ere, miss. 'Ave my chair." His English accent was heavy, lower class.

"Thank you." Catherine sat, and Margaret sank to the floor on her knees, demurely tucking her dress under herself while the other children looked her over.

"Ladies, gentlemen—and children—I would like you to meet my dear friend, Miss Catherine Harrison, and her sister, Margaret. They're the daughters of our pastor, Mr. Joseph Harrison, of High Street Presbyterian Church."

Catherine nodded as the two young women bowed their heads. "Pleased to make your acquaintance," they said almost in tandem.

"I'm likewise pleased. I admit I'm astonished to find a crowd. Mrs. Doran's home is usually, well, quieter."

The widow chuckled. "Yes, and more's the pity, too. Now, then, Mr. Sharp, would you please introduce these fine gentlemen?"

"Miss Harrison and Miss Margaret, I would like you to meet Misters Seward, Syms, and Whitefield."

"Whitefield!" Catherine sprang from her seat, immediately regretting the outburst. "Are you *the* Mr. George Whitefield?" She sounded more like Margaret than the grown woman she was.

The minister laughed and slapped his thigh. "Indeed, I am he, Miss Harrison, and I am very pleased to meet you." His voice was high, captivating. He kissed her proffered hand, and she once again sat down feeling as though she'd just disembarked from a rough carriage ride. "I've heard much about your good father from Mr. Sharp and the Magistrate."

Again, her impulsiveness took over. "You've met Mr. Heath!" *Lord, please put a guard about my tongue.*

"Indeed, I have. He and his fine son have invited my friends and me to board with him during our sojourn in Philadelphia."

She looked at Henry, who smiled back. She knew how much he'd been anticipating Whitefield's arrival, and now to have him staying under the same roof—she guessed Henry must be beside himself with joy.

"I'm happy to hear this good news, Mr. Whitefield. Magistrate Heath and his son are outstanding citizens." She avoided looking at Henry as she made mention of Francis.

Margaret blurted, "Who are all of these children?"

Catherine elbowed her. Apparently, her sister suffered the same affliction when it came to speaking her mind.

"These are my family, Miss Harrison," Whitefield told her. He gave all of the women and children's names and concluded, "They'll be going ahead of me in a few days to Georgia, to an orphanage I'm starting there."

"What a simply wonderful ministry, Mr. Whitefield," Catherine said, trying not to study his features too hard and finding the task almost impossible. *He has the most intriguing eyes!*

Eleanor Doran smiled. "They needed a place to stay for a few nights before their ship departs, and I offered mine. I do love the sound of children's voices."

Catherine missed the look Henry gave her.

"Sure, I'll get him." Jacob Harrison raised his eyebrows in the direction of his sister, who'd brought Henry Sharp and three strangers into the shop. They had the look of the sea about them, as if they'd just blown into port. Margaret had stayed at the widow Doran's to play with the orphans. Jacob disappeared up the stairs to Ben Franklin's personal quarters.

"Mr. Harrison is apprenticing with Mr. Franklin," Henry explained.

"So, he didn't fancy the ministry?" Whitefield asked, smiling.

"No, sir. He favors newspapers and printing." Catherine's nose tickled from the pungent odor of fresh ink and newsprint.

"God needs people in all sorts of professions," Whitefield said.

Moments later, Franklin tromped down the steps, smoothing his hair and fastening the last button on his waistcoat, Jacob following close behind. "Why, my dear Miss Harrison!" He looked first at her, then at Henry. "And Mr. Sharp. Good day to you both."

"Good day, Mr. Franklin," they said together, then burst out laughing.

"Ah, I see you are of one mind."

Although he was teasing, Catherine looked down at her feet, wondering if there was to be no end of her exposure. *What must be going through Henry's mind?*

The young minister made introductions. "Mr. Franklin and Mr. Harrison, I would like you to meet the Reverend George Whitefield and his companions, Mr. William Seward and Mr. John Syms. They arrived just yesterday from England."

Franklin's eyes opened wider, and he thrust his large hand toward the men. "I am very pleased to meet you, indeed, Mr. Whitefield." Then he shook the other men's hands. "Mr. Seward. Mr. Syms. Welcome to Philadelphia."

Jacob greeted the visitors along the same lines. Catherine noticed her brother peering at the pastor's one unusual eye and wished she could elbow him. Whitefield smiled. "I am delighted to be here. What a fair city and so full of life! Mr. Sharp and Miss Harrison have been escorting me about town, and they insisted I meet you."

"I've been anticipating your arrival, sir, having read many accounts of your preaching in England." A puckish look passed between them.

"Hopefully, they were accurate."

Catherine liked how he didn't say "favorable." She already liked Whitefield, who seemed to be not only genuine, but indifferent to his own importance. *Henry has a similar way about him.*

Franklin scratched his chin. "I have read, sir, you've caused nothing short of a sensation, preaching to large crowds, even in the out-of-doors, and I might add, up to twenty-five thousand at a time."

"God has blessed me with many opportunities to preach, and I look forward to many here."

"And I look forward to hearing you." Franklin held up a copy of the *Pennsylvania Gazette* so the minister could see the headline, "Renowned English Preacher Whitefield to Speak in Philadelphia."

"You are most generous, Mr. Franklin." He bowed. "I have been treated quite civilly here thus far, having met Mr. Penn, the proprietor, the Anglican church's commissary, and of course, the misters Heath. I feel quite at home in Philadelphia after traveling about like Abraham, who left his kindred and his native country to follow God's call."

"I am curious, Mr. Whitefield, about your ability to be heard by so many people at one time and over the din of such numbers."

"I suppose you will just have to come and hear me for yourself." His eyes gleamed.

"*Touché!* In the meantime, I would be honored, sir, if you would consider having me publish your sermons while you're here."

"Ah, Mr. Franklin, thank you, yes. I understand you run the most reputable newspaper in these parts." He turned to his companions. "Blessed be God's holy name! He's surely sent his angel before us to prepare the way, and in such a way—far above our expectations. I fear we should be tempted to say, 'It is good for us to be here, let's build booths for each of us,' but we must move soon, and learn hardness like good soldiers of Jesus Christ."

Whitefield was such a compelling figure in everyday conversation, Catherine could barely wait until she actually heard him preach. Her skin prickled with the expectation of God doing a mighty work in Philadelphia.

"When do you plan to begin preaching?" the printer asked.

"As I'm Anglican, I must first arrange matters with the vicar. I'll be meeting with him shortly and hope to start just as soon as I can."

Catherine wished the evangelist were Presbyterian so High Street Church could play him host; she hadn't considered this before. As if he were reading her thoughts, Whitefield added, "Of course, I pay little heed to denominations when it comes to telling people about the new birth in Jesus Christ. I've come not just for the Anglicans, but for all of Philadelphia, Baptists, Presbyterians, Quakers, Israelites—even Mohammedans!"

"Baptists, Presbyterians, and Quakers, we have aplenty, Mr. Whitefield. We even have a few Hebrews. You will, however, be hard pressed to find any Mohammedans in these parts," Franklin said.

Whitefield smiled. "Ah, but if I did, I would reach out to them as well. God plays no favorites, so I dare do no less." He paused. "Of what persuasion are you, good sir?"

"Anglican, Mr. Whitefield, although I make no pretense about being a good one."

"'Tis better to be a good Christian than a good Anglican."

Whitefield, Seward, and Syms covered the brief distance to the Heath residence while Henry escorted Catherine back to Eleanor Doran's to fetch Margaret. They went from there to the manse, although Catherine would have much preferred to remain in Mr. Whitefield's company. Along the route, she flinched when two High Street Church members averted their heads. She didn't wish to add to Henry's burden and said nothing, although she wondered if he'd noticed the snub. *What's wrong with these people?* They found Margaret in an especially happy mood, and Catherine realized how few opportunities for laughter the child had known lately.

"Father will be so excited to hear about Mr. Whitefield's arrival!" the little girl cried, skipping in the street and kicking up a puff of dust, which Catherine waved away.

"Yes, he will, but we must not burst into his room with the news."

"Would you like me to tell him?" Henry asked. "I plan to visit him when we get to the manse."

Catherine sensed how much this would mean to Henry, but she also wanted to see her father's face when he heard the news. "I think we should both tell him." When Margaret pouted, Catherine added, "Your job is to tell Mother." In her heart, Catherine couldn't predict how her mother would feel about Whitefield, or if she would even care. Maybe, however, God would use the British pastor to reach Ann Harrison.

Ten minutes later, she stood in her father's room with Henry, feeling more than a little self-conscious about her parent's obvious odor. Lena and her mother were doing their best to groom him in his weakened condition, but the smell of illness lingered. That Henry appeared not to notice further endeared him to her.

"Ah, two of my favorite people," Joseph said, rasping.

Catherine knew he must be feeling especially weak or he would have tried to sit up to receive them. Instead, he remained supine.

"Good day, Mr. Harrison."

"You seem excited." He looked hopefully at Henry, then his daughter, and for one terrible moment, Catherine wondered whether he might erroneously assume something about the state of their relationship and say something completely inappropriate. Every sound from the street became pronounced until she seized the reins of the conversation.

"Father, someone you have long awaited has come to Philadelphia." She appealed to Henry with her eyes to continue so he could share the good tidings.

"Mr. Whitefield has just arrived from England and is even now staying with his associates at the magistrate's house."

Catherine saw a spark through her father's dim eyes. "Such happy news! Very happy indeed." He paid for his enthusiasm with a coughing spell and when he recovered, asked for details, listening closely as his daughter and Henry provided them.

"I do so desire to hear him," he said.

"You shall, Father!" Somehow, they would make sure he did.

CHAPTER FOURTEEN

After Whitefield read the Anglican prayers in the evening, he, his companions and hosts relaxed in the parlor over tea and Mrs. Clydesdale's delectable biscuits, which she managed to serve without danger to life or limb.

"My good woman, these are incredible," the pastor told her.

She broke into a grin, curtsied, and bumping into a bust of Homer in the corner, fled from the room.

Whitefield had just come off a long ocean voyage, followed by an overland route to Philadelphia, and he'd been on the go all day. His agenda had included a visit with the Anglican vicar, which Henry arranged. Even after all the activity, the Englishman's face and clothes appeared fresh as the morning dew. Syms and Seward, however, carried heavy bags under their eyes but remained alert and interested in the conversation. In every way, Whitefield lifted Henry's spirits. *Maybe God is using my own ministry in some fashion to prepare the way for a larger work here.* Certainly, the Almighty had used the years of Joseph Harrison's patient toil, and William Tennent had faithfully preached the gospel in Bucks County. The few bumps and bruises Henry had sustained would be well worth any pain, and he knew opposition to the Lord's work often became strongest when and where the impact was greatest.

His thoughts were interrupted when the magistrate's valet appeared in the doorway, subtly clearing his throat. "Gentlemen, Mr. Franklin is here."

The printer, dressed more formally than Henry usually saw him in his occupational garb, came to the parlor bearing a neatly folded wad of newspapers tucked under his right arm.

Edward Heath stood and motioned for him to sit after Francis drew up a chair for him.

"Welcome, Mr. Franklin."

I apologize for coming without warning, Magistrate. I thought, perhaps, Mr. Whitefield might like to see some samples of sermons I've printed." He handed them to the pastor, who accepted them with a smile. As he sat, Franklin said, "I won't stay long."

"Stay as long as you like," Edward said. "We're enjoying tea and conversation with our illustrious guests. Would you care for a cup?" He waved toward the silver service.

"No, thank you very much, although I would enjoy staying for a bit."

"Have you lived in Philadelphia all your life, Mr. Franklin?" Whitefield asked, crossing one leg over the other.

"No, sir. I was born in Boston and came here at a mere seventeen years of age with a wad of clothing stuffed into my pockets and a Dutch dollar to my name."

The minister guffawed. "I would say this city has been kind to you, then, sir."

"Indeed it has," Franklin said.

"And, may I inquire, were you raised in the church in Boston?"

"I was brought up Presbyterian."

Henry was surprised and from the looks of things, so were the Heaths.

"I never knew, Mr. Franklin," Edward said. "I just assumed you were Anglican because you attend Christ Church."

He grinned. "I'm pleased some things about me remain a mystery."

"Why did you change churches, if I may ask?" Henry said.

"If I may be frank, Mr. Sharp, I found the sermons indescribably dull. I believe sermons should make good citizens of people, not good Presbyterians, as my minister was wont to do."

"And have you found the Anglicans more to your liking?" Whitefield's eyes held a glint.

"I would rather not answer, sir, for fear of offending."

The minister laughed again. "Believe me, you wouldn't offend me. I have often spoken out against those in my denomination who preach dead sermons to dead members. In fact, most churches today, at least in England, peddle a form of religion, apart from the power of God. I deplore the deadness of such so-called Christianity."

"These are my sentiments as well, Mr. Whitefield, and I think you'll find conditions somewhat similar here in the colonies." Franklin paused.

"Strange you should inquire after my soul, as I recently had a letter from my parents, who've been anxious for me these many years."

"Anxious?" Whitefield leaned back into his chair. "What, pray tell, is the nature of their disquietude?"

Henry was struck by how interested Whitefield was in other people. There was no trace of putting himself forward.

"I haven't made the kind of commitment to the Lord they believe I must."

The room went quiet. Henry had never heard such an honest confession before.

"I see, Mr. Franklin. What did you tell them?" Whitefield propped his chin on his bent hand.

"I told them how sorry I was they should have any uneasiness on my account. If it were a thing possible for one to alter his opinions in order to please another, I know none whom I ought to more willingly oblige than my beloved parents."

Whitefield nodded.

Franklin continued, "You see, I think vital religion has always suffered when orthodoxy is more regarded than virtue, and the Scriptures assure me at the last day we shall not be examined by what we thought, but what we did. Our recommendation will not be our saying 'Lord! Lord!' but the good we did to our fellow-creatures."

"So, Mr. Franklin, you believe the place of religion is to help people know the difference between right and wrong, then do what's right?"

"Indeed, sir. I think we must do our best to improve ourselves in this life."

Francis spoke up. "Mr. Franklin often places such proverbs in his newspaper. I especially like, 'He that lieth down with dogs shall rise up with fleas.'"

Whitefield laughed. "While I applaud your sense of industry and your pithy wisdom, Mr. Franklin, regarding religion I cannot entirely agree with you."

Henry wondered what approach the minister would take in addressing Franklin's misconceptions. Would he be a diplomat, or would he mince no words? He knew he himself would be tempted to come on strong, perhaps too strong.

"How so?" Franklin asked.

"Well, sir, I contend all people are sinners and cannot by strength of will improve themselves enough to win God's favor, which comes only through confessing one's sins and one's need of the savior, Jesus Christ."

The printer grinned. "I thought you might say something like that."

"And how does this strike you?" Whitefield lifted his chin, awaiting a response.

"To quote King Agrippa in the book of Acts, 'Do you think that in such a short time you can persuade me to be a Christian?'"

Whitefield reared back his head and laughed again, a big, hearty sound which proved contagious. He was obviously enjoying himself. As he wiped a tear from his eyes, he said, "Oh, Mr. Franklin, I can tell you and I are going to become great friends."

Henry had to extricate himself from his bedclothes, unwrapping himself like a mummy after waking from a fitful sleep around midnight. He lay on his back staring at the ceiling on which shadow branches from the bare oak tree swayed, less concerned about his future than he was about Joseph Harrison's determination that his church be a place of spiritual revival. *Maybe Mr. Whitefield's arrival will signal a major change in the church's life.* If a large enough number of people came to true faith in Jesus Christ, they would desire a minister who knew him as well. Then Joseph could truly rest in the knowledge he was leaving his flock in good hands, whether they were Henry's, or some other trustworthy guardian of God's truth.

He slipped from the bed to his knees, resting his head on folded hands. "Lord, I ask you to bless this church and its ministry and to use me in a way honoring to you. May you grant me your wisdom in this treacherous time so I may desire to do nothing offensive or injurious, but only your will. Protect me from harboring malice or bitterness toward my spiritual enemies, knowing they are ignorant of the harm they're causing your Church. I ask you to protect, as well, Joseph Harrison's health, and to pour out your grace and peace upon his wife and children. If your purposes would be best served by healing him, I ask you to return his health. Otherwise, dear Lord," and his voice caught, "I know precious in your sight is the death of your saints."

His thoughts strayed until they rested on Catherine's doorstep, and he prayed the Lord would guard and protect her future as well. Shifting his weight on the cold floor, he prayed for George Whitefield. "Lord, the fields are indeed white unto harvest. I thank and praise you for sending your servant to these shores to proclaim plainly salvation is to be found in none other than yourself. Give him mighty strength of body, mind, and spirit for this awesome task, and bless those who care for his physical needs, including Misters Syms and Seward. Be with the orphans and their caregivers, blessing their stay in Philadelphia and their journey to Georgia, preparing them for a life spent knowing your glorious riches in Christ Jesus."

Henry prayed until dawn broke and it was time to prepare himself to preach. He might have felt exhausted from his nearly-all-night vigil, but his spirit felt refreshed by the promise of a new day.

Catherine got ready for church, and finding her mother confined to bed with a headache, got Margaret up for the breakfast Lena had waiting for them.

"Where is the missus?" the servant asked.

"In bed with a headache."

"Shall I take something up to her?"

"Yes, thank you, Lena."

"And how is the Reverend?"

"Sleeping." Catherine said nothing more, trying to dwell instead on the brightness of George Whitefield's arrival rather than the muted tones of her own life and household.

Lena set bowls of hot porridge before her and Margaret, whose lower lip trembled. "Catherine, is our father going to get well?"

She reached for the small hand. "I pray he will, dear one, but he is weak."

Margaret's eyes filled with tears, and Catherine handed her a linen handkerchief.

"I, I am frightened," she whispered.

Leaving the food on the table, Catherine led her to the parlor where they sat on the couch, and she gently rocked Margaret while the little girl cried. Her own heart squeezed.

"Hush, child. Hush. Why are you so frightened?"

"I, I wonder what will become of us if he, if he ..."

"Now you sound more like Mother than Father." She tried teasing her sister, but a hint of bitterness crept into her voice, which she quickly corrected. Hugging Margaret closer she said, "We have a heavenly Father, who never leaves or forsakes his children. There's nothing to fear, though the earth give way, and the mountains fall into the sea."

"Really?"

"Really."

"Doesn't Mama know this?"

Catherine sighed. "Not yet, darling, but I pray she will. Now, then, dry those pretty eyes and try to eat some breakfast. Mr. Whitefield has come to town, giving us a reason for rejoicing. There is a time to laugh, and a time to weep. It's not yet our time to weep, dear sister, and even when those times come, God's grace is sufficient."

She walked into the church holding Margaret's hand, feeling something wasn't right.

"Where is everyone, Catherine?"

"I don't know." She was in need of as much reassurance as her little sister.

As they stood in the narthex looking into the sparsely occupied sanctuary, Elizabeth came over to them, her face glowing.

"Oh, Catherine, have you heard? Mr. Whitefield has arrived from England!"

"Yes," she said, turning briefly to acknowledge an elderly man's greeting. "Good day, Mr. Amerman."

Margaret exchanged her whisper for a shout. "We met him!"

Elizabeth's mouth fell open. "You have! When?"

Margaret animatedly filled her in on the time they'd spent at Eleanor Doran's house with the orphans. "Mr. Whitefield was there, and he was ever so nice."

Elizabeth's eyes gleamed. "Is he handsome?"

"Not as handsome as Mr. Sharp, right Catherine?" Margaret jabbed her ribs.

A masculine voice interrupted. "I'm glad to hear you say so, Miss Harrison."

Margaret's face turned crimson as Henry came into view, wearing his robe and carrying his Bible. He tousled her hair and laughed. Catherine felt too amused to be embarrassed.

"So, everyone's gone to hear Mr. Whitefield this morning," he said, his voice still light.

"Yes, Mr. Sharp." Elizabeth wasn't looking directly at him.

"I'm glad to see you ladies have stayed behind to worship here, otherwise, I might be preaching to the rafters." He smiled. "I'm looking forward to hearing him myself."

"I wonder what he's like," Elizabeth said.

Other people entered the conversation and before getting totally sidetracked, Henry mentioned to Elizabeth, "Perhaps you and Miss Harrison could stop by one evening so you could meet Mr. Whitefield yourself."

Catherine smiled at his thoughtfulness. She, too, had wanted to sit at Whitefield's feet, but since she and Francis were often talked about in the same breath, she didn't think she would be acting properly to just show up at his house. Because Henry had just given her a perfect excuse to come, however, she planned to take him up on the offer.

CHAPTER FIFTEEN

Ann Harrison's chilliness may have matched the weather, but Henry soldiered on. "Mrs. Harrison, I would like you to meet Mr. George Whitefield, who's recently arrived from England. Mr. Whitefield, this is Mrs. Harrison, our good pastor's wife."

The preacher stepped toward her and bowed. "Mrs. Harrison, I'm very pleased to make your acquaintance."

Her lips tightened. Henry glanced at Catherine, whose eyes were breathing fire. He thought of the brew she was likely mixing in her spirit of embarrassment and indignation. Whitefield had asked if he could accompany Henry on his daily visit to see Joseph, and Henry had been happy to invite him. In recent days, however, the pastor's wife had offered only grunts for conversation and hadn't looked at him directly. He never dreamed she'd be so rude to the renowned British preacher, however, whose every minute this week was accounted for. *Doesn't she realize how Whitefield's extended himself to come here? Maybe I should have warned him. Maybe I should have made sure she wouldn't be here.*

A brittle oak leaf blew in from outdoors and skittered across the floor. Catherine stepped forward, brushing against her mother. "How kind of you to visit my father, Mr. Whitefield. Mother, our guest is much in demand, yet he's taken time to see us."

Henry's chest tightened—the scene was painful to witness. Ann Harrison found the voice she'd seemed to have misplaced among the clutter of her bitterness. "Do come in, Mr. Whitefield. You must know, however, I regard you as a religious enthusiast." Her emphasis on the last word left no doubt about her opinion of him.

He bowed as if she'd just gushed all over his presence. "Thank you for welcoming me to your home."

Henry was amazed there wasn't even a hint of sarcasm in the man's response, although the irony wasn't lost on him.

"Mr. Whitefield!" Margaret broke through, stopping just short of throwing her arms around the minister.

"Good morning to you, Miss Harrison." He bowed and smiled.

"How are the orphans?"

"They are well, indeed, enjoying Philadelphia, though eager to resume their journey to Georgia."

"When will that be?"

"Their ship leaves on Thursday, which I believe is tomorrow."

"Oh, I hate to see them go! May we visit them today, Catherine?"

"Yes, of course. Perhaps we can help them prepare for their journey."

"We could make cakes or biscuits for them to take along." Margaret grew more animated, unaware her mother was slinking out of sight.

"First, however, you must go to school," Catherine said.

"We can go afterwards."

Catherine looked back at Whitefield and Henry, who watched as she graciously seized control of the situation. "Please come in, gentlemen, and I'll take you to my father. Margaret, find Lena—have her help you get ready for school. Also, tell her we need extra baking today."

Her sister went to the kitchen while Henry and Whitefield followed Catherine up the narrow staircase. He'd been visiting daily, but Henry sensed a change from the day before. Joseph's grip on life had become even more tenuous. He wasn't coughing as much, but the pastor's complexion was waxy, his cheek bones sunken. His eyes seemed to have retreated into their sockets. *Does Catherine realize how near his end is?* He looked over at her as she knelt by the pastor's side, stroking his brow.

"Father."

His eyelids fluttered, and he smiled up at her. "Cath-rine."

"I've brought some friends. Mr. Sharp is here."

He raised a hand, and Henry stepped forward to take it, taking care to be gentle.

"Hel-lo, my friend."

"Good day, Mr. Harrison."

"And there is someone else, Father, someone you've longed to meet." She motioned for Whitefield to come closer. "Father, may I present Mr. George Whitefield?"

Harrison's eyelids flew open, his face filling with all the warmth his wife's had lacked, and then some. "Mr. White-field. It—is—a—plea—sure."

The Englishman took the man's hand as Henry stepped aside. Outside, the world of buying and selling went on. Inside, a saint of the Lord was nearing the end of his earthly journey.

"Believe me, sir, the pleasure is all mine. I've heard much of your ministry for the Lord Jesus."

Henry smiled at Catherine, who returned the gesture. *How dear these two are. How dear she is.* He and Catherine stood in the background as the two ministers spoke like old friends. Henry knew from experience whenever he met someone who'd experienced the new birth, they could start talking on a level of intimacy unknown to others. After fifteen minutes, Joseph Harrison's eyes once again retreated. Whitefield behaved himself like a true gentleman. "I must go now," he said, "but I will see you again."

Harrison shook his head. "You—have—other—sheep. Thank—you. All—I—want—now ..." He paused, as if reaching for breath "... to—hear—you—preach."

He was far too weak to be moved, but Catherine's face suddenly beamed. "Mr. Whitefield, I heard you were going to speak from the courthouse steps tonight. Is this true?"

"Indeed."

"Father, I'll open your windows so you can hear him, and we'll listen together."

Harrison promptly fell asleep, a smile on his face. They left the room and returned to the first floor where Ann stood erect, chin lifted. Henry sensed she had something on her mind, but he was unprepared for what came out of her mouth.

Without looking into his eyes, she said with a trembling voice, "Mr. Sharp, given the situation at the church, I don't think you should visit us anymore."

Catherine gasped. "Mother! These are our friends, and Father relies on Mr. Sharp."

Just as unexpected was Ann Harrison's tearful withdrawal. Henry's jaw was an open hinge. Whitefield stepped into the moment, putting a hand on Catherine's shoulder. "She's much grieved by your father's condition." Her lower lip quivered. "If you're able, Miss Harrison, come tonight to the magistrate's after I finish preaching. We can speak freely then. In the meantime, may the peace of Christ be with your spirit, and upon this house."

This house divided, Henry mused.

Grateful Margaret was at school, Catherine stood ramrod straight before her mother in the kitchen, the furthest room in the house from her father's quarters. Lena wisely retreated upstairs. "What has come over you, Mother?"

Ann took a deep breath and seemed to hold on.

"Mother, look at me." The woman turned slightly. "How could you tell Mr. Sharp he's not welcome, or be so rude to Mr. Whitefield?" She actually stamped her foot. "He was our guest, and a very distinguished one."

"They are both enthusiasts." She spoke mechanically, as if she had been coached.

Catherine scowled, her body trembling. "Who told you that?"

"I cannot speak for myself?"

"I feel I no longer know you."

All the fire went out of her mother, leaving her spirit covered in ashes. "You and your father left the faith we used to know."

"For something real and living, not dead and dry. I wish you knew it as well." When she saw tears slip from her mother's eyes, she mistook them as a sign of softening and gently touched Ann's shoulder. "Mother, there is no faith apart from knowing Jesus Christ."

Ann jerked her arm away. "I cannot listen to this, Catherine."

She choked on her voice. "Very well, Mother. Go ahead and listen to Mr. and Mrs. Oldfield. Find your strength in them, but you will not forbid Mr. Sharp from visiting Father."

Her mother's eyes flared. "Is this where your faith leads you, to disobey your mother?"

Catherine hated the way her words were being twisted and started with a sharp comeback. Then she suddenly remembered the evil one had blinded her parent—he was the enemy, not her mother.

"I've been obedient to you and Father my entire life, and at this moment when Father is so ill, I choose to obey him. He needs Mr. Sharp's visits." When Ann opened her mouth, Catherine interrupted. "I'm not yet finished, Mother. Perhaps you won't want to hear this, but you must—Father isn't long for this world."

Ann jerked back as if avoiding a full-on slap across the face.

"You know this is true, and we must prepare. My main concern is to do everything I can to give him peace and joy in his final days, including having Mr. Sharp come—if he'll even return after being flown at today."

"Catherine." Her mother's cold hand clutched her daughter's. "The Oldfields will help us when, when …"

"The Oldfields are helping themselves, Mother. They want to get rid of Mr. Sharp so Mr. Oldfield's brother will take over, something Father doesn't want to happen."

Ann's brows raised as if she hadn't considered such a thing. "What, then, would happen to us?" As if grasping for a branch on her way over a cliff, she asked, "Has Mr. Heath spoken to you yet? You know he means to have you for his wife."

Catherine didn't want to have this discussion now.

"You know, daughter," Ann said perking up, "this could be our answer. The Heaths are wealthy and honorable, and they're good to us. We wouldn't have to worry about being, being, destitute." She seemed to strangle on the last word. Her grip on Catherine's hand tightened. "I'm counting on you. Jacob won't make enough of a living as an apprentice to help us, and Mr. Heath will make a good husband."

Catherine felt like the walls containing all her mother's fears were pressing on her. She shook her hand free, went to the hallway for her cape and bonnet, and opened the door.

"Where are you going?" her mother called.

"I need some air."

"I don't mean to …"

She was out the door, she needed to see Eleanor Doran.

George Whitefield kept pace with Henry's long strides. "You are shaken, sir, by Mrs. Harrison's words."

"I'm aware of the fragile state of her mind since her husband became ill." He looked at his companion. "I'm just sorry she was so discourteous to you."

Stepping aside to avoid a puddle, the minister laughed. "I've been called far worse than 'enthusiast!'"

Morning Glory

They were silent for some moments. Horses clopped, wagons rolled, people milled in the street. Henry appreciated Whitefield wasn't yet so well-known they couldn't walk undisturbed.

"Would you care to talk, Mr. Sharp?"

"You're a busy man, sir, and you have a lot on your mind already."

"If I ever become too busy to listen to a brother in Christ, I'll have failed utterly." He pointed to a bench down the street in a park. "Let's talk over there, unless you prefer to walk."

"Let's sit."

After they settled down, Whitefield said, "In spite of Mr. Harrison's illness, I could feel his strength of spirit. He seems like a good and faithful servant of Christ."

Henry sighed. "He is. When I become discouraged, I remember how Miss Harrison suddenly appeared at Mr. Tennent's door a few months ago when I was contemplating calls from two Bucks County congregations. When she came and said, 'Ask for the German,' I knew this was where I belonged, no matter how temporary or how difficult."

Whitefield laughed. "Ask for the German. I like that."

"Those words have helped me through the challenges."

"I have a feeling other things have helped as well." He winked.

"The joy of the Lord has been my strength," Henry said, not fooling anyone.

"That, my friend, isn't what I meant." He paused. "You and Miss Harrison are close?"

"Uh, yes."

"My question disquiets you. Why?"

A squirrel streaked across the park a few feet away, chased by a small boy whose mother stood talking to a friend.

Henry decided to unwrap his thoughts and emotions and present them to the caring pastor. "What I tell you is in confidence."

"I give you my word."

"You're right about my being close to Miss Harrison. We've worked well together since my arrival, often visiting parishioners. While her mother has stayed by her husband's side, Miss Harrison has been my right hand at the church. Of course, the magistrate has also been helpful, being the clerk of session."

"Helpful, but in a different way." Whitefield grinned.

Henry gave a laugh. "Being in his home has complicated things, although I'm grateful to him beyond words and don't wish to complain in the least." He paused. "You see, Francis Heath has told me he wishes to, well, have Miss Harrison for his wife."

Whitefield pursed his lips. "Oh."

"William! Come here this instant!" The child's mother began clapping her hands to distract her son from chasing a chicken wildly flapping its wings and squawking. A few moments later, when the mother caught her son, the men resumed their conversation.

"Do you know how Miss Harrison feels?"

"I can't be sure. You see, there's a certain way I find her looking at me sometimes, along with how we're so comfortable together. At times, I almost think of us as a couple."

"How is she in Heath's presence?"

"Friendly. Polite. I can tell she enjoys his company, but there doesn't seem to be any spark, if you will. Miss Harrison is deeply devoted to Christ, and Mr. Heath isn't. He's keen on having her, though, and seems to take her friendliness for affection."

"And you can't very well court her while you are living under his roof."

"Exactly." Henry felt relieved to hear someone say this out loud. "And now her mother has banished me from the manse."

"Her bark seems far worse than her bite, poor woman. Well, then, we'll just have to trust the Lord to work all this out so everyone will benefit, and he'll be glorified."

"Oh, I do." Then he laughed. "Most of the time."

CHAPTER SIXTEEN

"Dr. Gilchrist, my daughter insists we open the windows in order to hear Mr. Whitefield." There was no doubt which side of the argument Ann Harrison fell on.

The doctor patted her shoulder as if she were Margaret's age. "At this point, opening a window can't hurt, Mrs. Harrison, and who knows, might even help."

Ann frowned. "Surely a man of your stature doesn't approve of such an … an enthusiast."

There was that word again. Catherine looked away from the conversation taking place just beyond her father's closed door. His wracking coughs overpowered his withered frame, and now drops of blood clung to the phlegm. She wanted to give him every happiness until his time came and decided to stand firm against her mother's erroneous opinion.

Gilchrist laughed. "I've heard Mr. and Mrs. Oldfield use the same term many a time since the preacher set foot on our shores." He leaned closer to her. "Just between us, Mrs. Harrison, the preaching at Christ Church has become insufferably dull. I think we could all use a little enthusiasm." Ann drew her head back and stared at the doctor as if he'd suggested she run naked through the streets.

"Open the windows, Mrs. Harrison. Let some joy into his sickroom."

"Yes, yes, of course," she muttered.

He expanded his chest, grinning. "Truth be told, I would like to hear the man myself, and you, my dear, happen to have the best seats in town."

"You're most welcome to join us," Catherine said, trying not to gloat.

"Why, thank you, my dear. I'll see how my schedule plays out. Of course, being here would allow me to be closer to your father."

As Ann led the doctor down the stairs, her daughter slipped back into Joseph's room, eager to share her news. When he coughed, she handed him a handkerchief to cover his mouth until the paroxysm passed. His pallor had increased.

"Father, I have good news."

Apparently too spent for words, he nodded.

"The crowds gathering to hear Mr. Whitefield have increased to such an extent Christ Church can't accommodate them all, so he is going to preach on the courthouse steps this very evening. Father, all we must do is open your windows, and tonight you will have the most comfortable seat in all of Philadelphia!"

Joseph smiled, picking at his covers. "Very ... pleased. So ... pleased," he muttered through tears. "Have ... Mother ... come ... tonight."

"I will," she promised, although she realized getting her mother to listen to George Whitefield might be as difficult as convincing her sister to wash behind her ears. She watched as her father reached into his dwindling reserves of strength to tell her something further.

"And ... Mr. ... Sharp."

He didn't know what he was asking.

After seeing the orphans onto the ship bound for Georgia and walking her back to the manse, Henry winced when Catherine once again apologized for her mother's behavior. He held up a hand and gave her a tender look.

"Please, Miss Harrison, don't let your heart be troubled. She's suffering. We must pray for her."

"You're very kind." After a momentary pause she switched subjects. "The orphans are so dear. I feel sad never to see them again after this."

"They certainly took to you." Henry smiled at her, realizing he was inviting intimacy, but unwilling to hold his feelings back completely. By the look on her face, he guessed she felt something as well, although he wasn't free to explore.

Across the street, workers scrambled to sweep the courthouse steps clean in preparation for the evening preaching. Several bystanders hovered nearby, gesturing as they spoke.

"I'm very much looking forward to hearing Mr. Whitefield tonight."

"Oh, I am as well, Mr. Sharp, and I'm glad Mrs. Doran will be coming to the manse so she can hear him from there. She would never be able to stand through his presentation, let alone in such a crowd."

He watched as she cleared her throat, placing her gloved hand delicately on her mouth. He could tell something was on her mind.

"I wonder if you might like come to as well, to watch from the windows."

He had a hard time controlling his gape.

"Dr. Gilchrist says Father may have his windows open to hear, and Mother has consented, however reluctantly. Father specifically told me he would like you to be with him tonight, and so I ask you on his—and my—behalf, would you care to join us?"

Henry hardly knew what to say—Mrs. Harrison had just prohibited him from darkening their door.

"Does your mother know?"

"I can't honestly say she does. However, you will be Father's guest, as well as mine. I have an idea to make the situation more comfortable for you." She leaned a little closer, causing his heart to throb. "If you invite the Heaths, there would be safety in numbers." She laughed. "Mother would never dare misbehave in front of them."

Henry bowed. "Then I'll gladly take you up on your offer, and I'll be praying for your mother to have an open mind to Mr. Whitefield's message."

Catherine looked up at him. "Mr. Sharp, I'm concerned for your welfare."

Henry cocked his head, astonished at her directness. "What concerns you, Miss Harrison?"

"I'm upset by the way the Synod is discussing your tenure with us."

"Thank you."

"Do you think they'd actually dismiss you, especially with Father so ill?"

"I wish I could say otherwise, but from what Magistrate Heath tells me, I fear they're considering my dismissal quite seriously."

She gazed somewhere in the distance, then said with obvious distaste, "No doubt Mr. Oldfield's brother is more than ready."

He didn't dare tell her how deeply this distressed him—she had enough to be upset about.

When they made eye contact again, she asked, "If such a terrible thing were to happen, what would you do?"

The question of his future fluttered between them, and he wished he could reassure her. "At this point, I'm trying not to borrow more trouble than has been given to me."

"Forgive me. I'm too impulsive at times. I should not have asked." She put her hand on his forearm, and her tenderness shot a wave of warmth through him.

"You're exactly as you should be, Miss Harrison."

They were staring at each other. He had to push on. "Of one thing I'm completely certain, whatever happens, God will work it together for our good, and his glory."

※

Henry entered the magistrate's home after paying a brief visit to Eleanor Doran, whom he'd be picking up in a carriage at six o'clock. The place was oddly quiet, especially with George Whitefield in residence. The only thing greeting Henry was the clock ticking in the entryway and the muffled sound of the servants at their various duties. He hung up his hat and prepared to go to his room when he heard Francis calling from the parlor.

He found his friend seated at his desk covered with ledgers.

"Good day, Mr. Heath."

"Good day to you, Mr. Sharp. Have the orphans made it to the boat then?"

Henry sat opposite him. "They have."

"What a delightful group of children! Such a credit to Mr. Whitefield and his companions."

"Indeed."

"Are you looking forward to the preaching tonight?"

"Very much. In fact, I've been asked to invite you and your father to the manse to watch from there."

"May I ask, by whom?"

Henry's throat constricted. "Miss Harrison. She's opening the house to yourselves, Mrs. Doran, and Dr. Gilchrist. I believe her friend Elizabeth may be there as well."

"How kind of her. Actually, my father will be entertaining guests here tonight for the same purpose, but I'll gladly accept her offer." He grinned. "Actually, Mr. Sharp, I have a question to ask." He crossed his legs. "You're close to Mr. Harrison, and there's something I need to discuss with him."

Henry sensed in his gut what Francis meant.

"Do you believe he's in a sound state of mind?"

"I do."

"Good. I feel I must do this before he ... before he leaves us. I'd like to have you there, for moral support." His winsome expression told Henry moral support wasn't something Francis needed. *If he only knew what he was asking of me.*

Catherine felt happier than she'd been since her father's illness, with a house filled with friends who were happy to have front row seats to what the *Pennsylvania Gazette* heralded as "The Event of the Year." Henry had brought Eleanor Doran and Sally, having struggled to breach the enormous crowds thronging High Street and all adjoining roads. Gilchrist, the physician, exclaimed over the thousands of people thronging the area. Jacob was outside with Benjamin Franklin covering the story for the paper, and so would not be joining them. Each time Catherine had welcomed a guest, she poked her head out the door, feeling the snap of autumnal air and seeing lanterns illuminating the multitude, crammed shoulder-to-shoulder, creating their own brand of warmth. She realized she and her household were practically barricaded inside their home, people pressing on every side.

Ann Harrison's color seemed less pallid as she rose to the occasion, helping friends find comfortable seats at the windows both upstairs and downstairs, and directing Lena in the serving of refreshments. Catherine was especially relieved when her mother focused on greeting Eleanor Doran, even managing a polite nod to the young minister. She was trying not to think too much about Francis's arrival ahead of everyone else and his desire to speak privately with her father. She had prayed her mother wouldn't suddenly appear to lead the conversation who knew where. When Francis emerged five minutes later, his unfocused eyes and distracted expression left Catherine puzzled about what had taken place.

After everyone had arrived, Eleanor Doran, Sally, and Lena remained downstairs swaddled in capes and not a few quilts to offset cold pouring through the open windows, which also admitted the cacophony of the multitude. Upstairs, Francis, Henry, Catherine, Ann, the doctor, and Margaret had squeezed into Joseph's room where he sat up, barely visible under an avalanche of blankets.

Catherine went over to him and kissed his hollow cheek. "Father, Mr. Whitefield is going to begin any minute now."

He broke into a smile. "I ... have ... waited ... so ... long." She noticed how he was picking at the blankets again, almost vigorously now.

"God has answered your prayers. Are you comfortable?" She pulled a quilt up to his chin.

"Yes."

With his eyes, he indicated the side of his bed, and Catherine sat next to him, leaning against the headboard, careful not to disturb his bedclothes. He wasn't coughing, had actually been quiet for much of the afternoon, providing her a sliver of hope. Her mother perched on the other side in a chair, shivering under a heavy coat in an exaggerated way, frowning at mentions of Whitefield.

At last, Catherine caught a glimpse of George Whitefield striding up the courthouse stairs with his Geneva gown flapping in the breeze. Feathery applause and a sea of uplifted faces greeted him. If she read the audience correctly, Catherine guessed they might not feel right about applauding a minister, yet within minutes, Whitefield was throwing out convention like last night's table scraps.

Clutching a Bible, he struck a compelling pose against the background of the stately building. When he lifted his voice, his words carried over the people's heads and into Joseph Harrison's room, as clearly as if he were standing next to them.

"It is my distinct honor to be standing before you this night, in the name of our Savior Jesus Christ, and for his sake." Whitefield spread his arms. "I speak to all of you Philadelphians, whatever your creed. My text— First Corinthians 6:11. 'But ye are justified. The whole verse is And such were some of you; but ye are washed, but ye are sanctified, but ye are justified in the name of our Lord Jesus Christ, and by the Spirit of our God.'"

He leaned over a pulpit for a few measures, then abandoned the dais, nearly prancing along the platform. "It has been objected by some, who actually are friends to the present ecclesiastical establishment, that the ministers of the Church of England preach themselves, and not Christ Jesus the Lord—that they entertain their people with lectures of mere morality, without declaring to them the glad tidings of salvation by Jesus Christ."

Francis turned from the window and muttered to the room, "He minces no words."

"He certainly doesn't," Henry said.

Catherine felt the throb of her pulse in her temples, having never heard such bluntness from her father when he preached.

"How well grounded such an objection may be is not my business to inquire." Whitefield strode from one end of the stage to the other. "All I shall say at present to the point is that whenever such a grand objection is urged against the whole body of the clergy in general, every honest minister of Jesus Christ should ... declare with all boldness and assurance of faith 'that there is no other name given under heaven, whereby they can be saved, but that of Jesus Christ.' They should be ashamed of this their same confident boasting against us."

"How vulgar!" Ann gasped as she rose. "I cannot stay and listen to this, this, babble!"

Everyone turned from the window in her direction.

"Oh, please do stay, Mother." Catherine looked at her father, whose eyes were closed, his mouth wearing a broad smile. She had to admit the preacher's unorthodox style was outside any parameters she'd ever known, and made even her uncomfortable. She even had a flickering doubt, as if she might have been wrong to support Whitefield, and yet, the substance of his message! He was saying the right thing at the right time, if in a bizarre sort of fashion. Perhaps by hearing the Word in this way, her mother would come to believe. She looked at Ann, who seemed to waver, a sapling caught in a breeze, until Francis got up and steadied her. Then she sat back down.

Whitefield slowed his pace and gazed at the throng. "Who can but delight to talk of that which the blessed angels desire to look into—that induces me to discourse a little on that great and fundamental article of our faith; namely, our being freely justified by the precious blood of Jesus Christ. 'But ye are washed, but ye are sanctified, but ye are justified, in the name of our Lord Jesus Christ, and by the Spirit of our God.'

"Now, then, let me ask you, should we not pay more than just a passing nod on Sunday mornings to this wonderful God?" Whitefield's eyes blazed, his finger pointed like a weapon at the crowd. "Shouldn't you? And you? And you?" Each jab seemed to single out an individual as if he were the only one present. "Of course, you should! And do you think he is more interested in where you go to church than he is with the state of your soul?"

"By golly, he's actually dancing!" Francis gave a nervous laugh as he stood by the window.

"That is quite enough for me." Ann gathered up her skirts and rushed out of the room. This time no one tried to stop her as she left in a major huff.

By now Whitefield was working himself into a proper lather. "Father Abraham! Whom have you in heaven? Any Episcopalians?"

Catherine felt as if she'd lost her balance on a wharf and slipped into the freezing Delaware River. The people in the street, as well as those leaning out of windows shouted back, "No!" She looked at her father, still smiling, his eyes now wide open. She glanced at Henry, whose gaping mouth attested to his own feelings about the uncommon presentation of the gospel.

"Any Presbyterians?"

The people roared. "No!"

"Any Independents or Seceders?"

"No!"

"New Sides or Old Sides?"

His voice and dance moves increased with the naming of each group, his face animated. This was something new, a bringing together of all the denominations, rather than the usual calling of attention to their differences.

Jesus did, after all, pray his followers would be as one as he and his Father were one, Catherine considered. Still, the effect of his words was something like the demolition of an old brick building in which the rubble hadn't quite settled.

The roll call continued. "Any Methodists?"

"No!"

"Whom have you there, then, Father Abraham?" Whitefield answered his own question, peering into the crowd. "We do not know those names here! All who are here are *Christians*—believers in Christ, men who have overcome by the blood of the Lamb and the word of his testimony."

A short time later he concluded, "God help me, God help us all, to forget having names and to become *Christians* in deed and in truth." He moved his right hand across his damp brow as he prayed, then began accepting handshakes from men who pressed up the stairs toward him. Catherine watched until he disappeared from sight.

The crowd didn't disperse until an hour later, the people discussing a sermon unlike any they'd heard before or could ever imagine. Inside the manse, the Harrison's guests had retired to the parlor where they drank apple cider and talked about the unconventional English preacher.

"The way he pranced about like an animal!" Ann Harrison shuddered. "I've never seen anything so shameful."

Henry and Mrs. Doran, though surprised by Whitefield's theatrics, exclaimed over his spiritual gifts.

Francis remained quietly thoughtful, as if he had a lot to consider before speaking his mind.

"He was really noisy," Margaret said with a laugh.

Eleanor Doran smiled at her. "Well, my child, no one ever said God's trumpet would be easy on the ears."

When he left an hour later, Francis paused before Catherine at the door, opened his mouth to say something, then closed it again. "Good night, Miss Harrison, and thank you very much for your hospitality."

"Likewise," Henry added, walking over to them. "Would you care to join us at the house to see Mr. Whitefield, as he invited you earlier?"

She looked from him to Francis. "I would love to, but I feel I should stay with Father tonight."

"Very well," Henry said. "I'll see Mrs. Doran and Sally home now."

"Thank you," she said, assuming the role of hostess. Her mother had gone back upstairs with Margaret, who'd giggled a lot during the melodramatic sermon.

When everyone had gone except the doctor, Catherine followed them upstairs to where her father lay with his eyes closed.

Dr. Gilchrist bent over him and said nothing for such a long time, she began twisting a lock of hair. "He sleeps soundly. This has been a big night for him."

She smiled. "He was so happy."

He touched her shoulder as he headed toward the door. "Send Lena for me if you need anything."

"Doctor Gilchrist, he's not coughing as much. Might he be getting better?"

He addressed her as if she were Margaret's age. "I wish I could say, my dear. Try to get some sleep."

Catherine found his admonition easier said than done as she lay awake for hours filled with the echo of Whitefield's forceful message and her worrying questions about the future. She was almost surprised when she found herself waking up at the break of day.

CHAPTER SEVENTEEN

Catherine found her father's room swathed in half-light, the windows closed, a fire burning low in the grate. She walked to his side to see his eyes open and a peaceful smile on his face. He looked years younger, the way she remembered him from her childhood, and her heart leapt at the thought of a miraculous recovery.

"You're looking wonderful this morning, Father. I think Mr. Whitefield had a good effect on your health." She smiled down at him, then frowned when he failed to answer her. "Father?" Catherine gazed at a face so filled with life yet so still she had to sit down in her confusion. *Is he? Could he be?* His chest didn't rise and fall under the covers. She felt for his pulse, finding the great heart had been stilled sometime during the night. She knew she needed to wake her mother, but not until Catherine took the sacred moment to kneel by her father's bed and pray alone, undisturbed by the grief of others. Before the full impact of her own sorrow could slam against her spirit, she felt a kind of happiness for him knowing the strife was over, the battle won.

Thank you, dearest Lord, for giving me such a father, who was your good and faithful servant. Help me be as kind and honorable, as faithful as he was. She paused. *And Gracious Lord, grant peace to my mother, who will be deeply moved by Father's death. Help her rest in you, rather than give way to fear. Bless Jacob and Margaret, helping them to know you better as well. I love you, Lord. I praise you for my father.*

Along with the hard chill of the floor, Catherine felt an amazing, seeming invincible, peace. When she opened her eyes, she caught her breath. Light flooded into the room and illuminated her father's countenance—more radiant than a thousand suns. She squinted to avoid being blinded, sensing the glory of the Lord was passing by. Then the radiance slowly withdrew until the sunlight glowed like a spent ember through the blinds. She started breathing normally again, transfixed until a knock at the door brought her back to the present.

"Miss Harrison?" Lena opened the door a crack and peeked around the corner.

"He's gone, Lena, gone to glory."

The servant pulled a handkerchief from her apron pocket and wept soundlessly for several moments. "I came in here not two hours ago to tend the fire, and he was alive." She blew her nose. "What should we do?"

"Go for Dr. Gilchrist. I would like him to come right away. I'll waken Mother and Margaret after he comes, if they're not up by then." She paused. "Please stop by Mr. Franklin's after you see the doctor and tell Jacob he's needed at home."

"Yes, miss." She hesitated. "Are you all right?"

Catherine smiled. "Thank you, I am." She couldn't bring herself to speak of what had just happened. Not yet.

Lena was staring at her father's body. "He went out right before dawn."

While the servant fetched the doctor, Catherine dressed, then returned to her father's side where she stayed awaiting Gilchrist's arrival.

"He hasn't been gone long," the doctor concluded after a brief examination, "perhaps an hour. Does your mother know?"

Catherine shook her head. "I thought you should be here when I tell her."

"Good thinking." He expelled a puff of air. "Your father was the most honorable man I ever knew."

Her eyes swam against sudden tears. "Thank you."

When Ann heard the news, she burst into sobs, then she subsided into a silent, numb state, as if she'd retreated deeply into the folds of herself. Catherine knew the arrangements would mostly be falling upon her, but she didn't mind, wanting to do for her beloved father in death as she had in life.

The morning and afternoon were a blur of funeral preparations and the receiving of so many guests the manse seemed more like a tavern. Henry and Francis arrived together, having been informed by Lena of the minister's death, and together they helped receive people, including the Oldfields, who brushed past them to pour out a torrent of sympathy upon the young widow. The magistrate also came, offering to help however he could. Privately, he took Catherine and her mother aside.

"You have much on your minds just now. One thing you needn't concern yourselves with is where you will live. The elders have decided to give you the use of the manse for as long as you need it."

Relief swept through Catherine, another of her prayers answered. "Thank you, Magistrate Heath."

"Please thank them for us," Ann said.

"Tell me," Heath said, "did Mr. Harrison leave instructions regarding his funeral?"

Ann's fingers touched her parted lips, then she slowly shook her head. "We never discussed funeral plans."

He glanced at Catherine. "Nor did we, sir."

"May I suggest we honor him with a service at the church led by Mr. Sharp, who is, after all, still our pastor?"

Ann stiffened. "Some may be offended."

"I have no doubt, Mrs. Harrison, but we must remember even the Lord didn't please everyone."

A smile crept across Catherine's face—her father would have appreciated the humorous comment. "I think Magistrate Heath is right, Mother."

Ann Harrison nodded very slowly, eyes closed as if to the inevitable.

"As for the burial ..." Heath's voice trailed.

Ann spoke up. "At the church yard." Then she began crying, and the magistrate touched her hand.

"Mrs. Harrison, my own heart grieves deeply. Your husband was my closest friend and confidant. I will do everything I can to help your family through this."

Margaret never strayed far from Catherine, occasionally breaking into tears, then collecting herself to converse with visitors, many who brought pies, cakes, meats, and vegetables. When George Whitefield came to the manse to offer his condolences, Catherine thanked God her mother was in her room resting. As Catherine conversed with the minister, she heard a familiar voice.

"Miss Harrison." Benjamin Franklin had come with his wife to pay their respects.

"Good day, Mr. and Mrs. Franklin. I believe you know this man," she said with a note of humor.

"All the town knows him, my dear," Franklin said, "as they did your treasured father. He was a fine man, and he will surely be missed."

"Thank you, sir."

Deborah Franklin hugged her and asked after Ann.

"She's upstairs, resting. You're welcome to pay her a visit."

"Thank you. I believe I will."

Franklin appeared eager to talk with Whitefield, but also reluctant to do so in the presence of grief. "Today, Philadelphians are abuzz with the sad news of Joseph Harrison's death—and George Whitefield's preaching," he remarked.

Jacob came over, steering the direction of the conversation toward the living. "Mr. Whitefield, we estimated a crowd of about six thousand last night."

Now that a family member had introduced the subject, Franklin seemed all in. "We have never seen such a gathering before. I was amazed at how well your voice carried. Still, I can't be sure how many were able to hear you at the great distances at which some were forced to listen."

"I was happy to share God's salvation with so many," Whitefield said. "In England, people aren't pleased to hear preaching outside church walls—here, well, they tolerated it well enough."

Catherine spoke. "You will be doing so again, then, sir?"

"This very day, Miss Harrison, although I deeply regret this should happen on the night of your father's death."

She smiled at the young, white-haired minister. "On the contrary, Mr. Whitefield. My father dedicated his life to bringing lost sheep to the Shepherd. Your preaching tonight will be a kind of tribute to his ministry." She had to clear her throat.

Only Elizabeth Worthington and Francis were on hand in the evening when Whitefield once again preached from the courthouse stairs. Ann Harrison had holed herself up in her room, refusing to participate in such a "vile demonstration," especially while she was in the throes of mourning.

Catherine needed to be uplifted as the heavy veil of grief began descending upon her spirit. She sat with her friends at an open window in the parlor so as not to disturb her mother. She didn't know how this was possible, but more people than the previous night had squeezed into the street—she couldn't see any space between individuals. Stars twinkled in the heavens, lights shone from every High Street window and business. Although the night wasn't cold, Francis insisted Catherine cover herself with two shawls.

As he mounted the courthouse stairs, Whitefield spoke of her father's passing.

"Before I open God's holy word, I wish to give thanks for the life of a dear friend and a faithful shepherd of God's flock. Mr. Joseph Harrison, pastor of the High Street Presbyterian Church, left this world for the next just before daybreak today, and while we rejoice in his heavenly reward, we offer condolences to his dear wife, his children, and all the church members who loved him so much."

Francis reached over and squeezed Catherine's cold hand. With the other, she wiped a tear. She appreciated his close attention, but in her heart, she wished Henry were in his place. Tonight, however, he was assisting Whitefield because both Syms and Seward were sick with colds.

Moments later, she found herself completely caught up in the preacher's rousing message about what he called the "almost Christian." Catherine wondered what Francis would think of the message, believing he was just such a person. *Might God use this to open his eyes?* She considered how her father had prayed for several years for Francis's conversion—perhaps God had meant him to plant and water the seed of faith, then give the growth to George Whitefield on the night of her father's death. If those prayers were at last fulfilled, however, she would have to think differently about Francis because no longer would their faith impede their union. She wondered whether she could learn to love him romantically. For now, she chose to focus on Whitefield's sermon.

"An almost Christian, is one that halts between two opinions; one that wavers between Christ and the world; that would reconcile God and Mammon, light and darkness, Christ and Belial," Whitefield began. "It is true, he has an inclination to religion, but then he is very cautious not to go too far in it: chiefly, he is one that depends much on outward ordinances, and on that account looks upon himself as righteous, and despises others. At the same time, he is as great a stranger to the divine life as any other person whatsoever." He leaned over and spoke as if to one person instead of thousands. "In short, he is fond of the form, but never experiences the power of godliness in his heart."

Catherine felt riveted to her seat, and although she didn't look at Francis, she could hear his sharp intake of breath.

The hard hitting continued.

"If you consider him in respect to his neighbor, he is one that is strictly just to all; but then this does not proceed from any love to God or regard to man, but only through a principal of self-love; because he knows dishonesty will spoil his reputation, and consequently hinder his thriving in the world."

After energetically setting forth the nature of an almost Christian before a completely rapt audience, Whitefield turned to his second point, which was to consider why so many people fell into the category. Francis was leaning against the window sill, his arms folded across his chest, seeming unaware of anything or anyone else except Whitefield and his piercing words.

"And the first reason I shall mention is, because so many set out with false notions of religion. Though they live in a Christian country, yet they know not what Christianity is. This perhaps may be esteemed a hard saying, but experience sadly evinces the truth of it, for some place religion in terms of this or that communion, more in morality, most in a round of duties, and a model of performances, and few, very few acknowledge it to be, what it really is, a thorough inward change of nature." He punched at the air. "A divine life!" Another jab. "A vital participation of Jesus Christ, a union of the soul with God; which the apostle expresses by saying, 'He that is joined to the Lord is one spirit.'"

Catherine wondered when the minister might be coming up for air. How could he possibly go on so long, so strongly, seeming without taking a breath?

"Hence it happens, that so many, even of the most knowing professors, when you come to converse with them concerning the essence, the life, the soul of religion, I mean our new birth in Jesus Christ, confess themselves quite ignorant of the matter, and cry out with Nicodemus, *How can this thing be?*" His arms flung out toward the crowd, Whitefield's crossed eyes wide with disbelief.

Mother would despise the idea of a minister not being saved.

Whitefield wasn't holding back. At all. He was dancing around, speaking of the folly of being an almost Christian as if he were shaking the pointed words out of his very body. "It is true, such men are almost good, but almost to hit the mark, is really to miss it. God requires us 'to love him with all our hearts, with all our souls, and with all our strength.'" The voice rose and fell with great feeling. "He loves us too well to admit any rival; because, so far as our hearts are empty of God, so far must they be unhappy. The devil, indeed, like the false mother that came before Solomon, would have our hearts divided, as she would have had the child. But God, like the true mother, will have all or none. My son, give me thy heart, thy whole heart, is the general call to all; and if this be not done, we never can expect the divine mercy."

Francis had the look of a man being carried downriver by a great flood, casting about in desperation for something to hold onto. Catherine didn't know what to do, torn between helping him and just letting Whitefield, like nature, take his course. She could see many people in the crowd crying, others were trembling, some had even fallen prostrate. She'd never seen the likes of this before.

Whitefield turned venomous words on those ministers he dubbed almost Christians, calling them "one of the most hurtful creatures in the world. They are wolves in sheep's clothing. They are false prophets. These, these are the men that turn the world into a lukewarm Laodicean spirit, that hand out false lights, and so shipwreck unthinking, benighted souls in their voyage to the haven of eternity." He poked the air as if to deflate them. "These are they who are greater enemies to the cross of Christ than infidels themselves, for of an unbeliever everyone will be aware, but an almost Christian, through his subtle hypocrisy, draws away many after him, and therefore must expect to receive the greater condemnation." He let out a huff which carried along the crowd like a mighty thunder.

"To add a word or two of exhortation to you, to excite you to be not only almost, but altogether Christians, O let us scorn all base and treacherous treatment of our King and Savior, of our God and Creator." He flailed his arms, began jumping up and down. "Let us not take some pains all our lives to go to heaven, and yet plunge ourselves into hell ... let us give to God our whole hearts, and no longer halt between two opinions—if the world be God, let us serve that. If pleasure be a God, let us serve that. But, if the Lord, he, be God, let us, O let us serve him alone!" His gaze roamed over the crowd like a hungry lion on the prowl. He was far from finished.

"Or do you think that being only half religious will make you happy, but that going farther will render you miserable and uneasy? Alas! This, my brethren, is delusion all over, for what is this half piety, this wavering between God and the world, that makes so many, that are seemingly well disposed, such utter strangers to the comforts of religion?"

His pace began to slow, and for a moment he seemed to pull into himself. Then he poured forth once again. "Let me therefore, to conclude, exhort you, my brethren, to have always before you the unspeakable happiness of enjoying God. And think of this!" He stopped and stabbed the air. "Every degree of holiness you neglect, every act of piety you omit, is a jewel taken out of your crown, a degree of blessedness lost in the vision of God. On the contrary, be daily endeavoring to give up yourselves more and more unto him. You will be always watching, always praying, always aspiring after farther degrees of purity and love, and consequently always preparing yourselves for a fuller sight and enjoyment of that God, in whose presence there is fullness of joy, and at whose right hand there are pleasures for evermore." He shouted out twice, "Amen! Amen!"

The only sounds breaking the stillness were those of people crying. Catherine watched Henry walk to the top of the courthouse stairs and embrace Whitefield, then they retreated inside where she imagined they'd be praying for the multitudes. She looked over at Francis, standing at the window with moistened eyes.

"Oh, Mr. Heath! How can I help you?"

He gave a short laugh. "It is I who came to comfort you on this sad day."

"I have enough empathy to share with those whose spirits are heavy."

He hung his head. "You're very kind, Miss Harrison. You see, Mr. Whitefield's words seemed to be for me alone. Each one was like an arrow piercing my heart, which I confess, has been hard toward the things of God." He paused. "Now I understand what your dear father has been telling me these many years."

Her eyes widened. "You do?"

"I've been an almost Christian."

She had a feeling of rowing against the tide.

CHAPTER EIGHTEEN

Henry had stayed up late into the night talking with George Whitefield, who displayed no fatigue even after his energetic performance. Several people followed them to the magistrate's house for evening prayers, and Edward Heath welcomed them, appearing to enjoy the lively people and conversation. In his life, Henry had experienced the Divine Presence on a few occasions at his home church, as well as at the so-called Log College, savoring each experience and cherishing them in his heart. Last night when Whitefield spoke on the Courthouse steps, he knew God was there too, filling the twenty-four-year-old preacher with supernatural power to draw men, women, and children to God. As the lights shone in the streets and from the windows, faces in the crowd reflected God's light, which was driving away spiritual darkness and complacency. That this was happening during an unsettled time at High Street Church and in Henry's ministry gave him hope, even a measure of joy.

To top it all off, Francis Heath had returned home pale-faced and barely able to contain his shaking. After visitors finally left, he told Whitefield, Henry, and his father, "I have determined to no longer be an almost Christian."

Whitefield had called out "Hallelujah" and embraced his new brother in Christ. Edward shook his son's hand, murmuring congratulations without looking into the young man's face. Henry, though thrilled about Francis's conversion, refused to consider the consequences regarding his relationship with Catherine, knowing the finding of one lost sheep was far more important.

Henry was in his room preparing a sermon for the Harrison funeral, praying for words of healing and grace for the divided congregation, when the valet knocked on his door. He looked up and called, "Yes, Mr. Henson."

He opened the door a crack. "A gentleman has come to see you, sir."

"Did he give his name?" Henry removed his cloak from the back of the chair.

"Yes. A Mr. Tennent, sir."

"William Tennent! Thank you, Mr. Henson."

The man stepped aside as Henry slipped on his waistcoat and hurried down the stairs. The familiar figure standing just inside the entryway filled Henry with a kind of buoyancy. Tennent beamed up at him.

"Mr. Tennent! How good to see you! Have you come alone?" Henry grabbed his pastor's hands and shook them for several moments.

"I'm very pleased to see you as well, Henry. You are looking just fine, and yes, I came here alone, although some of my students arrived in the city yesterday to hear Mr. Whitefield preach."

He liked hearing someone call him by his first name, something he hadn't experienced since his arrival in Philadelphia. "How is my family?"

"Everyone is well, and they send their love." He leaned closer. "Your mother also sends provisions."

He laughed, although his stomach felt suddenly hollow, his spirit like a boy who's been away from his mother for a very long time. Henson came up to them, taking the minister's hat. "The parlor is available, sirs. May I offer refreshments?"

"You may indeed, my good man," Tennent said, his cheeks rosy from travel. "Although I don't find you changed, Henry, I cannot say the same for Philadelphia."

"How so, Mr. Tennent?"

"As I found my way here, I passed people singing Psalms and hymns on the street!"

Henry smiled as he led the minister to the empty room where they sat across from each other.

"When I got your last letter, I made arrangements to get here today."

"I'm so pleased you're here to see Mr. Whitefield, who is by the way, staying with his traveling companions in this very house."

"What do you know!" He slapped his palms against his thighs.

"He isn't here at this moment, however. He's often away during the day visiting various people in the city, as well as preaching hither and yon. He has an enormous amount of energy. Did you know last night he spoke on the Court house steps before a crowd of several thousand people?"

"Oh, that I could have been here!"

Henry sought to reassure him. "Yes, sir, but he'll be doing so again."

"What was it like?" Tennent rested his hands atop the cane he carried.

"Something I'll never forget, Mr. Tennent. He has the ability to speak compellingly about the gospel and the need for repentance, a simple, direct message delivered with great enthusiasm. Mr. Whitefield is dramatic, I'll give you that, but you couldn't hope to meet a sincerer and humbler person."

"I do hope to meet him! But I also came to see you, son, to hear from your lips how you're faring in the midst of the church's trials. I've been told the Synod is going to decide soon whether or not you may continue."

Henry nodded. "I'm trusting in the grace and strength of our Lord."

Tennant pursed his lips. "I think you should know the people in Bedminster continue to want you to be their pastor. I haven't, on the other hand, heard from the other congregation since you came here."

"I appreciate their kindness toward me." He wondered whether or not God might be leading him to one of those two places after all, then he raised a more immediate issue. "I do have additional news, of a different sort—sad news."

Tennent frowned. "What is it, son?"

"Joseph Harrison passed away early yesterday morning."

The old minister sighed. "He was a good and faithful servant of the gospel. How is his family?"

"They're holding up—even his widow, who's been in an emotionally charged state since my arrival, fearing her husband's death. Now that he has indeed died, she's been very quiet."

"I must pay them a visit. And Miss Harrison? How is she?"

"A pillar of strength, sir. She is her father's daughter."

"Have arrangements been made? I suppose you'll be doing the funeral."

"Yes."

"You sound tentative, son." He tilted his head toward Henry, who told him about his strained relationship with Ann Harrison and some of the congregation.

"Actually, sir, you might consider preaching the service instead of me. You knew Mr. Harrison a lot longer than I, and you're a respected member of presbytery." As soon as those words were out of his mouth, Henry regretted saying them. Rather than apologize for the *faux pas*, he looked at his mentor, and the two of them burst out laughing.

Catherine had never seen this many people at the manse at one time. She would have liked to retreat upstairs and lie down for a spell, but with her mother resting, she must carry on as hostess.

The church had also been so crowded for the funeral that several dozen people had been forced to stand while Mr. Tennent preached powerfully about the glory of knowing Christ and the folly of living apart from him, destined for eternal separation from the Holy One. Henry assisted, leading the congregation in prayer at the beginning and end of the service, then gallantly stood by her and her family in a receiving line. She'd hoped Mr. Whitefield could have been there, but he was obligated to preach in the morning at Christ Church, then in the afternoon at the jail.

Lena and the magistrate's cook had prepared several chickens for guests, and when their numbers swelled to fifty, then sixty and up, Catherine instructed them to put out all of the food people had been bringing. Although she felt wobbly from her own hunger and emotional strain, she couldn't bring herself to eat just yet.

Francis was unhappy with her. "You must keep up your strength," he insisted.

"Yes, I know. Just not yet, Mr. Heath." Pausing, she asked, "Have you seen my sister?"

"No. Would you like me to look for her?"

She shook her head. "No, thank you."

For some reason, she didn't want to be near Francis Heath just then. "If you will excuse me."

She wandered into the dining room where Benjamin Franklin was holding forth in lively fashion about Mr. Whitefield while Margaret sat on the sofa next to Henry, resting against his chest, her face drawn. Catherine made her way to them, stopping a few times to receive expressions of sympathy from two couples from the church, half-listening. She was glad to see Margaret's obvious comfort with Henry. Did she feel the same about Francis? She wasn't sure. Next to her sister's couch stood Elizabeth, who put her hand on Catherine's elbow and smiled sympathetically. Mr. Worthington stood next to her speaking to Benjamin Franklin.

"So, Mr. Franklin, why did you want to measure the strength of Mr. Whitefield's voice?"

The affable printer put down his cup of apple cider. "I've been reading accounts in the British papers of his preaching in the fields to upwards of twenty-five thousand people, which seemed to me an incredible number. I wanted to discover for myself if this could be true."

The corners of the elder's mouth rose. "And how, may I ask, did you endeavor to find this out?"

"Consider this—the courthouse is in the middle of High Street, which is on the west side of Second. I was standing among the crowd at the rear, so I could determine whether I could hear him from that distance, which I could. As Mr. Whitefield preached, I moved further away, until I was at Front Street, almost to the river."

Elizabeth's eyes sparkled, Catherine recognizing this as a sign of mischief. "And could you still hear him there, Mr. Franklin?" she asked.

Noticing her sister, Margaret gave her a grateful, though pained, smile, and Henry nodded at Catherine, sliding over, so she could sit with them.

"Yes, my dear Miss Worthington," Franklin went on, "his voice still rang out." He began gesturing with his perpetually ink-stained hands. "Now then, imagining a semicircle, of which my distance should be the radius, and that the area was filled with listeners to each of whom I allowed two square feet, I computed that Mr. Whitefield might be heard by more than …" He paused for a dramatic effect. "… thirty-thousand people."

Gasps broke out. Catherine herself was astonished to hear the number, although she'd seen the dense crowds outside the manse.

"Leave it to you, Mr. Franklin, to conduct an experiment on a spiritual matter."

All heads turned to William Tennent, who now stood in the doorway.

Franklin laughed. "Not only could I hear him, sir, but his delivery was so improved by frequent repetitions that every accent, every emphasis, every modulation of voice was so perfectly well turned and well placed that without being interested in the subject, one could not help being pleased with the discourse. Such pleasure is the same kind one receives from an excellent piece of music."

"Mr. Franklin," Tennent said, "God has given Mr. Whitefield a powerful voice in order to speak about sin and salvation, to have people exchange head knowledge of Jesus Christ for a heartfelt personal commitment. These are simple doctrines, but they contain more power than even the strength of his voice, which I am looking forward to hearing, if possible, this very evening."

"Yes, yes, I understand what you are saying—"

Tennent cut him off. "Truly, Mr. Franklin?"

Catherine held her breath, hoping her family's dear friend would come to the Savior, along with so many who were daily being converted under George Whitefield's preaching. Franklin, however, sidestepped the question.

"I'm amazed, sir, how people of all sects and denominations turn out to hear him, as well as to observe the extraordinary influence of his oratory upon his hearers. How much they admire and respect him, notwithstanding his common abuse of them by assuring them they are naturally half beasts and half devils!"

The room erupted into laughter, and when the conversation continued, Catherine felt Margaret sigh against her. She spoke softly into her ear. "What is it, sister?"

The eight-year-old looked up at her first, then Henry. "How can people laugh on the day of Father's funeral? Don't they care?" Tears trickled down her face, and Henry reached into a pocket for his handkerchief.

"You know, Margaret, we've all been so sad today. Gathering under Father's roof and sharing a meal and conversation helps ease some of our grief. Think of it this way—Father would want us to laugh and be happy. He was always such a joyful person, so in this way, we can honor his memory."

Margaret sat up straighter, looking into her sister's amber eyes, renewed hope smoothing the lines of grief. "Truly?"

"Truly." She smoothed loose pieces of hair from Margaret's brow, her own words coming back to reassure herself. She glanced at Henry, whose pale blue eyes seemed to penetrate her very soul.

"Mr. Whitefield, I believe you should take some nourishment."

Henry felt some misgivings interrupting the visitors who crowded the magistrate's home to have Whitefield pray with them—many were in tears over their sinful states. The minister had given everything he had, and this after preaching again before thousands from the courthouse stairs. Henry could tell by the slump of Whitefield's shoulders his strength was waning.

Edward Heath cut in, waving to get the visitors' attention. "My friends, you must allow Mr. Whitefield to eat and rest since he's scarcely had time today for either."

The Englishman perked up. "I've enjoyed conversing and praying with you about the Lord, who is the Bread of Life, but now I need to enliven myself with earthly bread."

As the men and women left, William Seward summoned his friend to the magistrate's table where Mrs. Daley and Mrs. Clydesdale busied themselves with much serving.

"What are your plans, Mr. Whitefield?" William Tennent asked over bowls of rabbit stew and warm bread with fresh butter.

The smell of cinnamon filled the room, leaving Henry to conclude Mrs. Daley had also baked an apple pie. He reminded himself to thank her and the rest of the staff for the extra work they'd been doing since George Whitefield's arrival. Now, they also had William Tennent to look after, since he'd accepted the magistrate's invitation to lodge there. Henry was happy to be sharing his room with his pastor.

Whitefield's voice resumed its usual heartiness. "I plan to remain for some time, perhaps up to two years, in order to proclaim Jesus Christ the length and breadth of the colonies. The Lord has shown me how great a need there is for revival here. I also want to firmly establish the orphanage I've begun in Georgia."

"An ambitious goal," Edward Heath said, tenting his hands on the table.

"With the Lord, all things are possible."

"Please consider my home your own whenever you come to Philadelphia."

"I'm most grateful, Magistrate." Whitefield tore a piece of bread from a fresh loaf.

"What are your immediate plans, sir?" Henry asked.

"I need to travel north for a week or so to preach, then, God willing, return to Philadelphia for another course of preaching and ministry."

"For how long will you stay when you come back, Mr. Whitefield?" Francis asked. He waved Mrs. Clydesdale off when she offered more stew.

"I'm not sure, but I must be getting to my orphanage by Christmas and will be preaching all along the way. After staying a spell in the Georgia colony, I plan to come back here once again, then head up into the northern colonies where I'm also expected. I am especially keen to make the acquaintance of Mr. Jonathan Edwards in Massachusetts, who's written about a revival in his congregation."

"I've read his account as well," Tennent said. "We, too, have experienced the purifying flames in my sons' and my churches. The Lord is clearly awakening our people from spiritual slumber."

"I feel called, sir, to use whatever influence or fame I may have among the colonists to preach a living Christ here, so America may be vibrant with faith."

"My dream of such has strengthened me in the face of much opposition."

"How have things been, Mr. Tennent?" Henry asked, leaning back in his chair.

The old man sighed. "I'm afraid I lost my head recently, my dear Henry—I resigned from the presbytery."

Henry gaped.

"Our old friends leveled charges against me."

He had a mental image of the night Catherine Harrison and her brother had found him at the church along with one of Tennent's thorns in the flesh.

"What was the offense, if I may ask?" Whitefield leaned into the conversation.

"I allowed a defrocked pastor to preach at my church."

"Hmm, and why was he defrocked?"

"He was deemed improperly trained yet was licensed by the New Brunswick Presbytery. I myself thought he needed more training before being licensed, but the point is my former student has been made an example.

"What will you do?" Henry asked.

"I'll likely transfer to the New Brunswick Presbytery after having burned my bridges."

There was silence for a few moments, then Whitefield spoke. "We all have our trials in the Lord's work, especially when he's using us most effectively. Don't lose heart, my good sir. My opponents plague me as well." He gave a laugh. "Do you know they've even resorted to personal attacks, finding particular amusement in my crossed-eyes?"

Henry was surprised to hear Whitefield mention his somewhat odd appearance but found the candor as refreshing as the minister himself.

"They like to call me Doctor Squintum." The men shook their heads and chuckled. "As long as I can see Jesus Christ clearly, I'm more than satisfied."

More laughter broke out, then Tennant spoke. "I wonder, will you make time, Mr. Whitefield, to visit my church and school in Neshaminy, just twenty miles north?"

The young Englishman stuck out his hand with a broad smile. "I'll be only too happy to accept your kind invitation, Mr. Tennent."

Henry felt a kind of shifting of the floor beneath him.

CHAPTER NINETEEN

"Your house seems unusually quiet after hosting all those children." Her voice sounded an octave higher in her ears as she attempted small talk. Catherine was finding the entire city strangely empty, almost bereft, since George Whitefield had left the day before, and in the aftermath of her dear father's death. Her temples almost throbbed when she thought about the likelihood of Henry Sharp's soon departure as well. She and Eleanor Doran sipped tea, the rain beating a staccato rhythm against the windows. Had she not felt a great need for the woman's companionship, Catherine would have stayed at home.

Her elderly friend smiled. "I enjoyed every minute of their company, and I intend to keep in touch with them."

"I'm certain they will enjoy hearing from you. I also understand from Mr. Whitefield you've promised to support his orphanage."

She waved in a gesture of dismissal. "We're on this earth to love our God and help orphans in their distress."

Catherine knew the verse she alluded to included "widows." This widow, however, was well-situated financially.

Mrs. Doran put her cup and saucer on a side table. "You're quiet today."

She gulped hard and whispered. "I feel burdened."

"Tell me about it, my dear."

She did, though not with words. Tears flowed from her eyes, and she felt powerless to stop them. Balancing on her cane, Eleanor rose from her chair and sat next to Catherine on the small settee, holding the young woman, murmuring words of comfort. When she had spent the last tear, she withdrew from the comfort of her friend's arms, closed her eyes, and took a deep breath. She was ready to talk. "Most of the time, I feel God's comfort, but then, sadness suddenly overtakes me."

The woman nodded, seemingly in tempo with her thoughts. "Have you read the Psalms lately?"

Catherine shook her head.

"I recommend you do. King David expresses the depths of human emotion in them, and because these words are inspired by God, I know he's comfortable with our cries. You've experienced a great loss, and you will need some time to heal."

She wondered if she should mention another thing weighing her down. Because she feared no condemnation, she forged ahead. "Mrs. Doran, I'm wrestling with resentment."

The faded eyes searched her face, her spirit. "Tell me, my dear."

"My ... my mother." There, she'd spoken the words which had been burning a hole in her, then rushed to douse the fire. "I don't think I should feel this way." More tears rose to the surface, quiet ones she kept in check with her damp hankie. "My mother used to be so strong, but my father's illness and death have turned her into someone frail and needy."

Eleanor took her time to respond. "I fear she's journeyed to the depths of her emotions alone, apart from Jesus Christ, which is never a safe place to be."

Her words rang true to Catherine—they also sent a shiver along her back.

"She's drowning in solitary grief when you need a mother to comfort you."

"Yes! You're right." Catherine paused, looking down. "Am I being sinful?"

The widow placed a fragile, though resilient, hand over Catherine's. "If you would permit me, I will mother you for now."

She smiled as tears watered her lips. "I'd like that very much. Thank you."

"You're to come to me at any time, understand?"

"Yes, ma'am."

"I have faith your mother will come through to the other side of her grief. She became confused a few years ago when you and your father experienced the new birth in Christ. Let's pray for God to blow away the chaff from her spirit."

Catherine entered the door and began shaking the rain from her cape when she noticed a man's cloak hanging from one of the pegs. Lena shuffled into the entryway bearing a pair of house shoes for her.

"My, but you're drenched, Miss Harrison! Better get into dry clothes before …"

She reined in her words, but Catherine could mentally fill in the rest of the sentence—*you catch your death.*

"Oh, I should bite my tongue off!"

Catherine smiled and touched Lena on the shoulder. "You meant no harm. Who's here?"

Lena lifted her hand and held it next to her mouth. "The magistrate, miss."

"I'd like to see him. Please tell him I'll be downstairs as soon as I can change my clothes."

Catherine hurried to her room and moments later joined her mother and the magistrate in the parlor. Empty tea cups cluttered the table between them. Edward Heath stood and bowed. "Good day, Miss Harrison."

"Good day to you, sir." She sat next to her mother.

"I have some news I believed would be best shared immediately and in person."

Her heart started thumping, until she searched her mother's placid expression.

"The session has decided to continue giving your father's salary to your mother for the next four months, to enable you to get back on your feet. You will also have the use of the manse until such time as the new pastor requires it."

Although these were generally good tidings, Catherine shifted uneasily, wondering what might happen in four months or sooner if a new pastor needed the house. She'd always hoped Henry Sharp would be that man in spite of the opposition he'd faced—the majority of the congregation thought highly of him.

"Thank you, Magistrate Heath. Please convey our gratitude to the elders."

They spoke for a short while about the weather, then the subject of George Whitefield came up. Edward told them, "Since he came, I haven't been as busy in court. The manners of the population have improved considerably under his preaching. I've seen some of the most profligate men now walking the streets singing hymns and helping women with their packages instead of drinking their time away in the taverns."

Catherine thought about changes in their church as well. Whitefield and Henry's detractors had remained largely subdued while others in the congregation, including Elizabeth's father and Elder Shipman, had enthusiastically embraced the new birth.

"Nevertheless, I find him difficult to watch," Ann said. "I've never seen a minister cavort like an animal."

Catherine was surprised to hear her mother openly contradict the magistrate, especially since George Whitefield had shared his house. However, her mother had at least been listening. "You must have been paying attention, Mother."

"I find it impossible not to when he shouts so." A slight smile drew up the corners of her mouth, the first Catherine had witnessed in months.

When Edward left shortly thereafter, she and her mother saw him to the door. She disliked bringing up the topic she had on her mind. "Magistrate, you spoke of a new pastor." She paused, as he stood wrapping himself in his cloak. "Might it still be Mr. Sharp?"

The big man exhaled, his breath carrying the scent of a recently smoked pipe. "I expect the synod's decision any day now, and I don't expect it to be in Henry Sharp's favor." Her glance fell along with her spirits. "I sincerely wish I could tell you otherwise."

Henry decided to stop by Franklin's printing establishment after visiting Mr. Worthington's wife, who'd taken to her bed with a severe headache. *There might be a letter from the synod.* While he dreaded such a dispatch, constant uncertainty felt like a relentless dripping in his soul. He reached Franklin's shop and opened the door, careful not to let the wind yank it from his grasp or off the hinges. The stout proprietor greeted him, apologizing for staining Henry's hand with ink.

"I'm grateful the wind has literally blown you into my shop, Mr. Sharp. Life has been fearfully dull since Mr. Whitefield's departure."

He couldn't resist teasing Franklin. "Are you beginning to believe him, then?"

"One doesn't have to subscribe to his doctrines to enjoy the show he puts on, my good man."

"What, then, will it take for you to receive our Lord Jesus?" He maintained a bantering tone in spite of being dead serious about the subject.

Franklin's eyes twinkled, and his lips twitched. "How can you say I haven't, Mr. Sharp?"

He squinted, tilting his head. "So, you have then?"

"Actually, while I thoroughly admire our mutual friend, I don't agree with his particular theology." Resting his thick hands on the counter, he laughed. "I will say he's persuaded me otherwise about his orphanage, though."

"How so?"

"You know I've made no secret of my opinion—I think he's foolhardy to want to build an orphanage in Georgia when Philadelphia could use one and would be much more cost effective because he wouldn't have to transport supplies and men all the way to that godforsaken colony. I told him I would support him if built one here."

Henry recalled the several times Whitefield had told his audiences he wasn't going to take up an offering for himself but would instead use every bit of money he collected for the orphanage—the generosity of wealthy friends took care of his needs. Henry had never before met a man so void of interest in the material aspects of life, who trusted himself entirely to the Lord's bounty.

Franklin continued, "Mr. Whitefield was as stubborn as Mrs. Frankel's mule, however, so I told him he should get nothing from me." He crossed his arms over his chest. "Well, sir, after his last sermon, I had in my pocket a handful of copper money, three or four silver dollars, and five pistoles in gold. As he proceeded, I began to soften and concluded to give the coppers. Wouldn't you know, another stroke of his oratory made me so ashamed I gave the silver."

Laughter rumbled in Henry's chest, sensing what was coming, knowing first-hand Whitefield's powers of persuasion.

"Well, Mr. Sharp, our friend finished so admirably I emptied my pocket wholly into the collector's dish, gold and all!"

He burst out laughing, and Franklin joined in until they sounded like two hyenas. "Oh, Mr. Franklin," he said, swiping at a tear, "there is hope for you yet."

"Funny, Mrs. Franklin often says the same thing."

Following on the heels of his quip, the two men hooted again, until the fit subsided. After leaving the printing shop with his and the Heaths' mail, Henry strode quickly to the magistrate's where he went to the parlor to see if there was any correspondence for himself. Midway through the pile he found one, *the* one. He put the Heath's letters on a table and went to his room where he sat on the bed, still in his overcoat. *Lord, please prepare me for what's inside. Above all, let me glorify you.* His breathing quickened as he began reading, knowing immediately from the tone the synod's decision. According to their Act of 1737, they judged his education substandard, and therefore, disqualified him from preaching within the bounds of their far-reaching authority. Effective immediately.

I can't preach anymore at High Street. He stared, unseeing out of his window at a leafless chestnut tree swaying in the wind. *What's going to happen to the people when Mr. Oldfield's brother surely takes over?* He sighed. *What's going to become of Catherine, who's spirit is so sensitive to truth and falsehood?* He'd harbored a secret hope there might be some legitimate way to her heart, but now he had nothing stable to offer her—he wasn't welcome to preach in any Presbyterian church in any part of the synod. He'd known all along this might happen, but now Henry felt his strength seep as if he were a bucket riddled with holes. Opening his Bible to the Psalms, he began praying. "Save me, O God, for the waters have come unto my soul. I sink in deep mire, where there is no standing: I am come into deep waters where the floods overflow me …"

"I can't say I didn't expect their decision, but I'm no less angry for it." The crease between the magistrate's eyes deepened. "What will you do now?"

"I plan to go home tomorrow, sir. I can appeal to the New Brunswick Presbytery to ordain me."

"It has been a pleasure to have you, son. Any time you find yourself in Philadelphia, I would be honored to have you consider this your second home, just as I've informed Mr. Whitefield and his companions." Seward had stayed behind to secure passage for the trip to Georgia.

When he could speak again, Henry asked Edward Heath to take good care of the Harrisons. "They've become very dear to me."

"I give you my word."

"Mr. Sharp!" Catherine opened the door to admit him.

The earlier storm had abated, but the wind continued prowling around Philadelphia's sturdy buildings.

"Am I welcome?" He looked past her, presumably to see if her mother was around.

"You are always welcome here. Mother and I were just sitting in the parlor."

He turned to go. "Perhaps I should come back in the morning."

"Nonsense. Do come in."

Catherine took his hat and cloak and led him to the parlor. A look darted between Henry and her mother.

"What brings you here this evening?" Ann asked, returning to her needlework. And without waiting for an answer, asked, "Would you like some tea, Mr. Sharp?"

"Uh, no, thank you very much. I, uh, won't be staying but a few minutes. I have news I want you to hear from me."

"Please have a seat." Catherine rested her suddenly trembling hands on her lap, hoping he couldn't see them.

He sat on the very edge of the sofa. "I heard from the synod today—they decided to invoke the 1737 ruling in my case."

She didn't want to hear this, but still the words pierced the roaring in her head. "Does this mean you may not preach here anymore?"

Her mother dropped a stitch, then several more.

He nodded, and when he spoke, his voice was thick. "I've come to love this church deeply. I wanted to honor your late father's desire that I help to shepherd it."

When she could speak, Catherine reassured him. "You have honored him, Mr. Sharp." She wondered what might be going through her mother's mind. Would she be glad, or perhaps remorseful?

"Thank you."

"What will you do?" Ann asked. Catherine and Henry looked at her simultaneously, as if a mute person had found her tongue for the first time.

"I'll leave in the morning for my home in Warminster."

Catherine swallowed twice, struggling to keep her emotions from screaming out of her.

"Thank you for your many kindnesses to me." His voice faltered. "I wonder if you will do me the favor of another."

"Of course, Mr. Sharp." Catherine leaned toward him.

"Please tell the church goodbye for me, especially those members whom I have grown close to—you know who they are, Miss Harrison. I regret deeply I cannot tell them myself."

"You may be assured I will."

"Thank you." He rose and faced Ann. "I've been honored to serve your husband in his hour of need. He was a truly great man of God."

A tear slipped down her cheek. "Mr. Sharp, I …"

Henry bowed. "May God bless you, Mrs. Harrison."

With little else to be said, he went to the door. Catherine followed, neither of them saying anything, although for one moment at once brief and endless, they gazed into each other's eyes. She watched him walk down the street, his cloak whipping in the wind. He was gone. Her father was gone. Her mother was, in a manner of speaking, also gone. Fear beat at her temples.

CHAPTER TWENTY

At dawn, Henry set out for Warminster, stopping once in Germantown out of necessity, not because of actual appetite. The hearty owner frowned at the young minister's half-finished crock of oxtail soup in spite of his generous tip. Henry's heaviness of spirit had tricked his stomach into feeling satiated. He spent most of the time thinking and praying, trying to connect with the God he served while fending off demons of discouragement.

The last time he'd experienced anything remotely similar was after his grandmother's death a few years earlier. Although she'd lingered on her sickbed for several months, when death did come, Henry's grief wrenched him, as if one of his hands had been cut off.

Likewise, a week ago, he would've told anyone who asked that the synod would probably vote to have him removed from the High Street pulpit, but when they did, he suffered. Rising from a slouching position, he reminded himself not even a powerful synod could thwart God's plan for his life, and some way, somehow, this setback would result in God's glory and Henry's good.

He arrived in the late afternoon hours just as the sun slipped over the tree line, staining the horizon. His mother was standing in the kitchen garden gathering what was likely the last of the herbs. Her round face broke into a smile, though her eyes told a different story—he knew she could tell something was wrong.

"*Willkomen daheim!*" She placed her roughened palms on his cheeks when he dismounted, and though she fit neatly within the fold of his arms, he had become a child inside.

"*Danke schon, Mama.* I'm very happy to see you." He tried to inject cheerfulness in his tone, but he'd never been especially good at hiding his feelings.

She pulled away, giving him a thorough once-over. "I am, too, but what brings you here, son?"

He'd been rehearsing his speech, but now words scattered. "I'd like to wait until I can see the whole family."

Mama had never been one to back down. "You would first tell me if you are well."

"I am, mostly."

Her shoulders resumed a more normal sloping as their servant Katarina came out of the house, rattling away in German at the sight of him. Her outcry brought William and his little sister outside where they hugged Henry and slapped him on the back.

"I'll go fetch Christian and Papa," Sarah cried. "Opa is sleeping."

Soon Henry was in the dining room drinking his mother's strong coffee, telling his story to the entire family while Katarina kept refilling his plate with *lebuchken* and dark *brot*. He managed to separate bitterness or anxiety from his account, not wishing to burden them, but to bless the Lord who held his future securely. His mother, however, was not so sanguine.

She brought her hand down on the table, causing utensils to clatter and a cat to flee from the room. "I would like to thrash those men, as well as the ones who keep hounding dear Mr. Tennent."

His father scowled. "And they dare call themselves Christians."

"Our Lord had his enemies as well," Henry said. "He warned us we could expect the same."

"Yes, but pain still hurts," Sarah said in a voice as small as herself.

Henry smiled at her, noticing her willowy figure was beginning to fill out. *This one could break hearts someday. It's a good thing she has a father, grandfather, and four brothers to look out for her, not to mention Mama bear.*

"What does this mean for your ordination?" William, ever-practical, asked.

Henry sighed. "I can't serve any churches within Philadelphia Presbytery."

His older brother Peter spoke up. "There is, of course, the New Brunswick Presbytery."

Henry replied, "And I'm thinking along those lines."

His father added, "Let's not fret, which leads only to evil."

Henry pursed his lips and nodded.

After putting his belongings in his room, Henry told his parents he was going to the Tennents' to let them know what had happened. He decided to walk and in the chill of the night, looked up at the brilliant display of stars, picking out the Great Bear and Orion. Their Maker was his as well. Lights also glowed from within the Tennent house when he arrived.

"Why, Henry Sharp!" The minister's gray eyebrows raised at the sight of his former pupil and neighbor.

"Hello, sir."

"Who is it, William?" Catherine Tennent came to the door as Henry stepped inside. "My goodness! We were just discussing you."

"You were?"

"Yes, yes," Tennent said. "There's someone I want you to see."

Mrs. Tennent took his cloak, and Henry followed her husband to the parlor where, to his amazement, George Whitefield and his companion sat before a vigorous fire. The English preacher jumped out of his chair at the sight of him. There was much backslapping and the shaking of shoulders.

"Have a seat, Henry," Tennent said, motioning to an empty chair when the commotion subsided. "We weren't expecting to see you here." He narrowed his eyes. "Trouble then?"

Henry nodded. "The synod has invoked the 1737 Act. I left High Street just this morning."

"Ah." Tennent dragged out the simple word, glancing sideways at Whitefield.

Henry wasn't sure why, but he had a distinct feeling his pastor knew something he didn't.

"I expected them to do this," Henry said, "but initially, the news unsettled me."

"As well it should!" Catherine Tennent said, reminding Henry of his mother. "I'll fix you a nice cup of hot tea."

"Thank you, madam," he said, rising with the other men as she left the room.

"Does Miss Harrison know?" Whitefield asked.

Henry nodded.

"Henry, as unfortunate as this development is, I believe the Lord has gone ahead of you in ways you could not have anticipated," Tennent said.

"Sir?"

A twig snapped in the fireplace, sending sparks shooting up the chimney.

"Yesterday, Mr. Fretz came from Bedminster asking after you."

Henry's energy returned. This was the man who'd approached him earlier about starting a German Reformed church for their settlement.

"He wondered if you might still be available."

"What did you tell him?" The sound of his heart thumped in his ears.

Tennent leaned back in his chair, folding his arms across his chest. "I said I'd write you to find out, then no sooner did I finish the letter, Mr. Whitefield and his friend arrived, just before dinner."

"Our timing was perfect," Whitefield quipped, and the men laughed. "For some reason, we always tend to show up as meals are being served." Then he grew more serious, but not by much. "You're in demand, Mr. Sharp. You see, I also have need of you."

Henry frowned. "Sir?"

"As you're aware, I need to return briefly to Philadelphia, not just to preach but to see how Mr. Seward is doing."

"I believe he's been coming along well with Mr. Heath's assistance," Henry said. "They've been able to find a suitable sloop for your travels."

"Ah, I'm happy for such news. At any rate, I'm still minus a companion, with only Mr. Syms to accompany me this time. We have need of another."

Henry's scalp prickled, thinking he might know where this was heading.

"I've prayerfully sought the Lord in this matter and believe he's leading me to ask you."

Henry pointed to himself. "You want me to go with you and Mr. Syms, sir?"

"Yes, Mr. Sharp."

Henry had a strange feeling the French called *déjà vu*. Not so long ago, he'd sat in this very parlor while Catherine Harrison uttered her life-changing, "Ask for the German." Once again, the Lord was appointing him to accompany someone in need. Once again, Mr. Fretz would have to wait.

❦

"Come in." Catherine expected to see Margaret at the door, but her mother filled the frame instead. "Did you need something?"

"No, daughter, but I think you may."

"Excuse me?" She sat up, trying to hide the tracks of her tears.

Ann sat on the edge of the bed. "I haven't paid nearly enough attention to you since ..." Her voice caught. "Will you forgive me, Catherine?"

She answered with a tearful embrace.

"I believe your sadness isn't just about Papa," Ann said moments later. Catherine nodded, looking down at her fingernails. "I could see your attachment to Mr. Sharp, though my eyes were almost blinded by my own pain." She paused. "He's a good man."

"Yes, he is. I'm so very glad you see this." Catherine blew her nose then asked, "How is your own spirit, Mother?"

"Wrenched from its moorings, like a ship without an anchor."

"I sometimes feel the same, Mother, but in our Lord Jesus I find hope and consolation."

"Your father would've been pleased to hear you say that." She exhaled and spread her hands in her lap. "I know our Lord cares for those who mourn, yet I fight deep fears about our future. The church will continue Father's compensation for several months, but what will happen next?"

"We must commit this to the Lord." Catherine hoped she could continue taking her own advice.

After visiting Elizabeth late Friday morning, Catherine saw Francis Heath walking away from her house in the direction of the docks. She entered the manse a few minutes later and found her mother sitting by the dining room window smiling, which gladdened her own heart. "You look well this morning," she said.

"Oh, my dear, I have such glad tidings." Ann Harrison clasped her daughter's cold hands, her eyes aglow.

"What?"

She leaned closer, as if she were Elizabeth's age and about to confide in her closest friend. "Mr. Heath was just here."

"I saw him walking toward the docks. Was he looking for me?"

Her mother shook her head. "No, he came to see me." She smiled, but Catherine's body stiffened. "He told me just before your dear father died, Mr. Heath spoke to him about seeking your hand in marriage."

Her throat constricted, her heart seemed to stop. "Wh-what did Father say?"

"He told Mr. Heath to ask you, and he would bless your decision."

Catherine stepped back, bumping into a side table and reaching out to keep the furniture from crashing to the floor. Now the choice really was up to her, but was this really a choice at all? Her father's death had left his family next door to genteel poverty. Henry Sharp was gone, and he'd never spoken to her of love in the first place. If she didn't marry Francis Heath, she had no other prospects.

"He sought my blessing as well, hoping he wasn't being presumptuous in speaking so soon after your father's death." Ann clasped her hands together. "Oh, Catherine! This could be the answer to our prayers!"

She wasn't so sure. Now that Francis had met the Savior, a major barrier to their relationship had come down. Of course, she'd always admired him, and he was handsome. Marrying him would certainly secure her own future, as well as her mother's, and her sister would have better prospects as well. Looking at her mother, Catherine could see what she'd looked like before Joseph's lingering illness, more alive, cheerful. This change was answered prayer. What about her feelings for Henry, though? Would they soon fade like last season's flowers? Had they been simply fleeting fancies for a handsome stranger, such as Elizabeth often had? She was, after all, young and impressionable. Steeling her spine, she told herself feelings such as those could be set aside quickly enough.

Whitefield leaned back in the wing chair, thumbs clasped behind his waistcoat, rocking, apparently deep in thought. The fire popped and crackled, and their stomachs were full, thanks to the ministrations of Catherine Tennent, now sitting among them.

Henry thought Whitefield looked happy to be in the presence of a few friends, rather than surrounded by constant throngs. If he were to go with the minister, he'd have to get used to crowds. How exciting the adventure would be, though—something to remember for the rest of his life. He'd tell his children the stories, then his children's children. A shadow suddenly smeared his happiness. He'd still lost Catherine Harrison. When Whitefield began to speak, Henry turned his focus on him instead.

"I pray, Mr. Sharp, you will not permit the enemy to discourage you after your recent experience." His crossed eyes contradicted each other, at the same time burning and healing. "The Lord Jesus Christ is at work in the colonies in ways I only half understand. I see this everywhere, and I'm sure the enemy despises us."

Henry nodded.

"Tell us, Mr. Whitefield, about your sojourn through New Jersey and New York," William Tennent said.

"We met so many worthy people who've been touched by Jesus. Each time I preached, whether inside meeting houses or in the fields, multitudes came—I don't know how they materialized so quickly."

Syms broke in. "We could arrive in a town in the morning and by afternoon, there were hundreds, frequently thousands, who came to listen."

"Amazing." Tennent shook his head.

"I was especially pleased to have met several pastors, including your son Gilbert," Whitefield said, looking at the Tennents, "men who hold to the teaching about the new birth. Many have labored for years with little outward response, only to find recently men's hearts have melted under their preaching about sin and repentance. Mr. Syms, who was the Dutch minister we met near New Brunswick? I have such difficulty with his name." Whitefield frowned.

"I believe it was Frelinghuysen."

He poked the air with his forefinger. "Yes, thank you! The Lord has used this old man to bring many sons to glory. Oh, what a worthy old soldier of Jesus Christ!"

For a moment, Henry detected a hint of Whitefield's animated preaching voice.

"I know him well," Tennent said. "He's a friend of Gilbert's, who has labored amidst much belittling from carnal ministers."

"Indeed. But, my friend, he fears nothing but the One who can destroy both body and soul in hell."

"How about that fellow, Cross?" Syms asked, puffing on a pipe.

"Him, too! He's also near New Brunswick and told us the Lord has brought about three hundred wonderful and sudden conversions of late, people who've come to him in great distress of soul, who've been marvelously delivered."

"Three hundred!" Henry gave a low whistle.

"Yes, indeed, Mr. Sharp. And to think Mr. Cross, Mr. Freling—whatever-his-name is—, and a Mr. Camel, are accounted by other clergy as enthusiasts and madman!"

"I can imagine you also endured hardships along the way," Catherine Tennent said.

A knowing look passed between Whitefield and his companions.

"There was one fellow especially, a Mr. Vessey, whom I wished had behaved in a more Christian manner. He seemed to be full of anger and resentment, and before I even asked him for the use of his pulpit, he turned me down. He asked to see my Letters of Orders, and when I told him they were left in Philadelphia, he asked me for a license, and so on. Finally, after he accused me of breaking our church's canon, I reminded him of his reputation for frequenting public houses."

Those in the room broke into gales of laughter.

Whitefield looked sheepish. "Naturally, my words only stirred him up more. I assured him my preaching wasn't intended to sow divisions, but to propagate the pure gospel of Jesus Christ. I also told him if he denied the use of his church, I'd gladly preach in the fields, for all places were alike to me."

"I can guess how he responded," Tennent said.

"Mr. Vessey said," and Whitefield lowered his voice, "'Yes, I find you have been used to that.' Then he accused me of censuring my superiors in ministry. I assured him I was no respecter of persons." After a brief pause, he continued. "I pray the Lord will lighten his darkness and grant other carnal priests to be obedient to the faith."

Henry saw an opening to present something weighing on his mind since the synod's decision. "Mr. Tennent, I'm concerned about such a man taking the pulpit of High Street."

"Andrew Oldfield."

"Yes, sir. Do you know him?"

Tennent exhaled and looked up at the ceiling, where shadows of the flames chased each other. "I know him, though not well. He suffered some misfortune two or so years ago when his wife and daughter died of the smallpox."

A light went on in Henry's mind. "I recall hearing about the tragedy."

"He's a nice enough fellow, although quite bland, always trying to please everyone."

Unlike his brother. "Is he an Old Side?"

"Andrew Oldfield does not take any side. One might say he's neither hot nor cold."

Whitefield added a quotation from Revelation. "I know thy works, that thou art neither cold nor hot; I would thou wert cold or hot. So then because thou art lukewarm, and neither cold nor hot, I will spew thee out of my mouth."

CHAPTER TWENTY-ONE

"I wasn't expecting to see so many people today, Mr. Whitefield." William Tennent surveyed the crowd swelling the grounds at his church—men, women, and children squashed together. "Hopefully, my detractors are among them." He grinned, and the two pastors shared a brief laugh as they waited to begin the service.

"If they are, my good Mr. Tennent, I pray they'll have open hearts, rather than open hands—full of rotten tomatoes."

Although Henry was accustomed to great numbers coming to see Whitefield, he hadn't expected so many in the hinterlands, people who'd come from miles around and on short notice. He was pleased his family numbered among them. When he had told them his new plans for traveling with the minister, they had given Henry their blessing. He choked up when his father once again offered financial help so his son could pursue God's call. Henry peered into the faces of the multitude, hoping to see them, but they'd blended in with this host.

"See how the people have tethered their horses to the hedges and are standing for the preaching?" Whitefield asked, pointing with his right forefinger. "In England, they sit astride their animals, which causes a good deal of disorder."

"We are Presbyterians after all," Tennent said wryly. "We do things decently and in order."

Although the weather had turned downright cold, the low temperature didn't prevent Whitefield from speaking for an hour, or hastening afterward to preach at Abington, a village between Warminster and Philadelphia. There, he once again braved the frosty air to address thousands who couldn't fit inside one church building. Many hearts again turned to the Savior, men and women weeping with remorse for their sins, filling the atmosphere with joyful shouts. As they departed, Henry wondered what Magistrate Heath would say when he showed up at his door again in a few hours. More to the point, he considered what Catherine Harrison might think. Her image filled his mind as his party advanced through the gleaming night to Philadelphia.

Elizabeth had come to see Catherine in the afternoon, and when the latter shared her suspicions about Francis Heath's coming to call in a few hours, she made her friend promise secrecy.

"You've certainly landed quite a catch!" Elizabeth exclaimed. "Just think—Mrs. Future Magistrate Heath."

Catherine frowned. "What are you talking about?"

"Naturally, Francis will follow in his illustrious father's footsteps, and you'll have Philadelphia at your feet." She sighed and shook her head. "Too bad Mr. Sharp had to leave. Now that he's free to pursue others, I have no chance with him."

Catherine didn't even try to check her irritation. "You speak nonsense."

"Nonsense, indeed!" She put her hands on her hips. "As if you didn't know Mr. Sharp was sweet on you!"

She couldn't change the subject fast enough. "I must do something with my hair," she said, making the motions of fussing.

Fortunately, Elizabeth dropped the Henry Sharp subject and flew into action, treating her friend like a doll needing special attention. There'd been no time to see Eleanor Doran or seek her advice, and Catherine felt she didn't want to go there until after she'd actually accepted Francis.

Just before he came, she ran her hands down the front of a favorite silk dress to smooth imaginary wrinkles from the glistening blue fabric. Her mother and Margaret had retreated upstairs to read and sew. Only Lena remained to answer the door, and when the familiar knock came—two taps, a short pause, then another two taps—Catherine took a deep breath as she sat in the parlor waiting for her future to unfold.

Lena's voice carried from the entry, sounding higher pitched than normal. "Good evening, Mr. Heath."

"Good evening to you, Lena. I've come to see Miss Harrison."

Catherine's heart fluttered, more so when Francis appeared in the doorway in clothes she'd not seen him in before. Normally, he and his father turned themselves out expensively but without unnecessary flourishes. Tonight, however, Francis appeared more vibrant in a medium blue coat with a waistcoat of a slightly lighter shade underneath. His white shirt was impeccably starched, the black shoes polished to rival any mirror. She'd never quite noticed before how shapely his calves were, which caused heat to rush to her cheeks.

"Hello, Mr. Heath," she managed to say. "It is a pleasure to see you."

He bowed. "The pleasure is mine."

Catherine glanced quickly at Lena, who hustled to the kitchen for refreshments. "May I say how beautiful you appear this evening, Miss Harrison?"

She smiled. "Thank you. You also look well."

Catherine saw his soldier-stiff shoulders relax. "Please, sit down." She waved a hand to indicate the spot next to her, which still provided ample space between them. She could tell by his eager expression he realized she was giving him all the right signals, and she wondered if he would try to make small talk or get right to the obvious point of his visit.

"How are you coming along?"

"Better, thank you. Jacob was here earlier, and he's in good health. Our spirits are beginning to return."

"I'm glad. It takes time to work through loss."

She nodded, knowing he understood.

"I'll always remember the last time I saw your beloved father. I felt awkward in a way because one doesn't lightly bring up delicate subjects at such a time. I did, however, believe it was the most honorable way to say what needed to be said."

"And what was that, Mr. Heath?" Catherine knew, of course, but she wanted to make this easier for him.

He cleared his throat. "I told him I wanted very much to seek his blessing to make you my wife."

Catherine's body tingling, she savored the moment, the soft lighting, the soothing smell of burning beeswax, the muffled voices of her mother and sister upstairs.

"He told me I should ask you, and he would bless your decision. He had great respect for you, as do I. You are a rare and discerning woman."

She looked at her hands, moving independently of her thoughts, as if she were doing needlepoint. "Thank you."

"I also spoke with your mother, sharing my concern about asking too soon, yet emboldened by the thought of giving you something happy to look forward to—a wedding and marriage."

"You're very kind."

"Your good mother has given me permission." He reached for her hands, and she felt their firmness, which sent a quiver through her. Looking into her eyes, he asked, "Miss Harrison, would you do me the honor of becoming my wife?"

Catherine swallowed, unable to answer at first. "Yes, Mr. Heath. Yes, I will."

"Thank you, my dear." He exhaled as if he'd been holding his breath. "You've made me the happiest of men. I'll try to make you the happiest of women."

※

When Henry showed up on the Heaths' doorstep with the Whitefield entourage, Henson's craggy face straightened into an actual smile, and the magistrate pumped his hand.

"Mr. Sharp, I'm happy to welcome you back." He glanced over Henry's shoulder to where Whitefield and Syms stood.

Henry bowed. "Thank you, sir."

"Well, come in, come in, then." He waved them inside. Whitefield draped an arm across Henry's broad shoulders, straining on tip-toes to reach such a great height. "I'm pleased to tell you Mr. Sharp has agreed to go with Mr. Syms and me to Georgia." He looked admiringly at Henry. "He even set aside an invitation to become a pastor to help me."

Heath nodded. "Well, that is good news. I must hear all your reports, and your good Mr. Seward has some to share with you as well, when he returns a bit later. First, you might like to retire to your rooms and let my staff attend to your needs."

Following an hour's rest and a light meal, the men withdrew to the parlor for an unusually quiet conversation, possible only because no one else in Philadelphia knew Whitefield was back in town.

"I say, Seward, I'm happy to see your face again! I hear Mr. Francis Heath has been helping you find a sloop and supplies for our journey."

"Indeed, he has. He appears to know every captain of every ship in Philadelphia's harbor, as well as their states of financial affairs. I believe you'll be pleased with the sloop I've engaged."

"Of course I will." He rubbed his hands together. "Now then, where is our good friend, Francis Heath?"

As if arriving on stage at just the right beat, the son of the house appeared, causing his father and his father's guests to chortle. Henry's laughter died on his lips when he saw the triumphant look on his friend's face.

"Mr. Whitefield. Mr. Syms! How good to see you again!" He came across the room in two strides and shook their hands. "And Mr. Sharp, what a pleasant surprise to find you here!"

Henry noticed his friend's grip wasn't exactly firm. "I'm happy to say I've become one of Mr. Whitefield's traveling companions."

Francis clapped his hands. "Well, I'm glad to hear this. Speaking of good news …"

The magistrate spoke as if there were only two of them present. "How did it go, son?"

"Splendidly, Father. I have the pleasure to tell all of you how God has blessed me tonight." He paused, thrusting out his chest, his stance that of a herald. A town crier. "Miss Catherine Harrison has just agreed to become my wife."

Henry watched the scene unfold in a peculiar state of slow motion while each of the men took turns congratulating Francis. Their lips were forming words, their hands grasping Heath's. So, Catherine did love Francis after all. Only his lack of faith had prevented her accepting him sooner than this. Henry heard himself say, "You'll make a good husband for her."

"Thank you, my friend. Rest assured I will take very good care of her."

With a leaden heart, Henry forced himself to participate in the subsequent conversation, grateful for the mercy of his own room an hour later.

※

He'd been gone less than a week, but Philadelphia's landscape had changed dramatically for him. He was no longer supplying the High Street pulpit. Catherine was now betrothed. Mr. Oldfield's brother Andrew had been quickly rushed to the scene to take the reins of the church. On Sunday morning, he breathed a sigh of relief not to be going back there, although he felt badly about not being able to say a proper goodbye to Joseph Harrison's congregation. Instead, he accompanied Whitefield to Christ Church where he experienced an Anglican service for the first time, one he felt certain would have been considerably more formal had his theatrical friend not been preaching and had there not been a disturbance during the sermon.

A well-dressed man stood and shouted from the back. "Good people of Christ Church, there is no such term as imputed righteousness in Holy Scripture! Such a doctrine puts a stop to all goodness! We are to be judged for our good works and obedience."

Henry's blood ran cold at the outburst, never having witnessed such conduct before, not even in the most trying times between William Tennent and his foes at Neshaminy Presbyterian. People sat transfixed, mouths agape. Henry was in the second row of pews, his head turning first to look at Whitefield, then back to where the disturber of the peace still stood. "Who is that?" he whispered to the man sitting next to him.

The fellow glanced over his shoulder. "Mr. Shaw, a former minister of this denomination. He's now secretary to Mr. Penn, the proprietor."

Henry was disappointed to find a man of such high rank behaving like a common rabble rouser. Whitefield, on the other hand, wore the expression of someone used to this kind of behavior. He stood resting one elbow in the palm of his other hand, his chin perched between his thumb and forefinger while the "gentleman" flung his diatribe at the visiting minister.

Finally, he broke in. "If you are quite finished, my good sir, I must deny your first proposition. Imputed righteousness most certainly does have a scriptural expression. Just look at Jeremiah 23 where we find the words, the Lord our Righteousness. However, I don't believe a worship service is a proper place for such a debate, so I will say no more at the present time."

Henry observed Shaw's face turn blood-red, and he took his seat, muttering to himself. Whitefield continued his message as if nothing strange had happened, and the people also settled back into the captivating rhythm. He voice was a rising and falling tide, his expressions bottomless, as if he were an actor on a stage, but with far greater reverence.

Amazing, how Whitefield manages to combine the holy act of preaching with the far less sanctified business of performing.

He rushed through the midday meal at the Heath's, then told Whitefield he had an important visit to make. "I'll be back in time for the afternoon preaching," he promised.

They were standing next to the dining room table, and the minister beckoned Henry to come aside for a private word. "My good fellow, let's understand something. Don't begin to think I own you or your time. You are my friend, not my servant. Actually, we are fellow servants of the Lord Jesus, and in that spirit, we may be accountable to each other."

"Thank you, Mr. Whitefield. I'm happy to have this understanding between us. I would like to be at the afternoon service, but if I don't meet you here, I'll see you at the church." He winked. "Perhaps our friend from this morning won't be doing us the favor of his presence."

Whitefield smiled. "I don't really mind the disruption so much as the darkness of his spirit. There are so many like him, and I struggle at times to know what I should say to enlighten them." His expression wore a plea. "Above all else, Mr. Sharp, promise me your prayers."

"You have them."

He knocked upon Eleanor Doran's front door and waited for Sally to answer. When she did, her eyes opened wide as she exclaimed, "Mr. Sharp! I thought ... well, I didn't think ..."

He bowed. "Is Mrs. Doran able to receive me?"

"Yes, sir. Please come in." She stepped aside, and he handed his hat to her, followed by his woolen cloak. Henry followed her into the parlor where the lady of the house had been dozing near a sun-spattered window.

Sally bent down and called softly, "Mrs. Doran."

"Huh?" The old woman's eyelids fluttered.

"You have a visitor."

Blinking a few times, she gazed upon Henry, then broke into a grin. "Mr. Sharp!" He went to her side and took her chilly hands in his big, warm ones. "Mrs. Doran."

"I thought you had left town, and without seeing me."

"I beg your forgiveness. I was instructed to leave the church at once, so I went home to Warminster, regretting I hadn't taken the time to see you."

"There is nothing to forgive. A nasty business that. We should be seeking your forgiveness. Are you well?"

"Yes, madam. As soon as I returned home, the Lord showed me what I must do next." He told her about his visit to William Tennent's house and George Whitefield's request.

"I am glad to hear the Lord has redeemed the unpleasant situation in which you found yourself."

"Indeed, he has. Perhaps some meant it for evil," he said, paraphrasing Joseph's words, "but God clearly meant it for good."

"When will you be leaving?"

"Around the end of this week—Thursday, I believe."

"I think you'll have many adventures, Mr. Sharp."

A knock at the door interrupted their conversation, and Sally appeared from the back of the house. Henry heard a woman's voice joining the servant's, a voice he knew. And loved. He was a statue unable to move. The visitor's eyes widened, and the color drained from her face.

"Mr. Sharp!"

"Miss Harrison." He forced himself to rise and bow.

"Wh-what are you doing, I mean, I thought you were ... I thought ..."

He didn't expect her to be so flustered. She was newly betrothed, and he would assume, overflowing with happiness.

"Yes, Miss Harrison, I did leave, but there's been a turn of events. I caught up with Mr. Whitefield in Warminster, and he asked me to become his traveling companion to the Georgia colony. We're stopping in Philadelphia, along the way."

"I see. Well, then, I'm happy for you." She smiled as if expected to do so, without meeting his eyes.

"You are well?"

"Yes."

"And your good mother?"

"She improves daily, I'm happy to say." She shifted from one foot to the next, then straightened, seeming to remember why she had come. "Mrs. Doran, how are you today? I missed seeing you at church."

"I'm well, my dear, but I was unable to come. How was the service?"

Catherine sniffed. "I actually fell asleep."

Henry was tempted to rejoice over Andrew Oldfield's effect on Catherine, but he denied himself the cheap privilege.

"Well, do come and join us, Miss Harrison. Mr. Sharp was just telling me about his upcoming journey."

Catherine sat across from them, and Sally paused at the edge of the room, looking unsure what to do since Catherine remained in her outer garments. When the visitor made no move to take them off, Sally left.

Henry told her about the need to bring supplies to the children and to find a place to build the actual orphanage, how Whitefield planned to preach his way down, as well as back. When he exhausted the topic, he thought he really should say something about her engagement. "I understand you have news of your own, Miss Harrison."

She gave a start. "I do?"

He smiled. "You are betrothed, are you not?"

"Betrothed?" Eleanor stared at Catherine.

"Uh, yes. Francis Heath has asked me to become his wife." She said this in staccato fashion, devoid, Henry thought, of emotion, as if she were describing picking up the mail or going to market.

The widow caught Henry's eye, and he had to turn away.

"Then I congratulate you," she said. "He is a fine young man."

"Y-yes, he is."

"When is this to take place?"

"We, uh, plan to discuss this in the next few days, but we're thinking of right after Easter, in late April."

He tried to sit still, but he couldn't stop his heart from hammering an unsteady rhythm. After some minutes of forced conversation, he declined an offer of refreshments and begged their pardon to leave. "I must go to the preaching this afternoon," he said, rising.

"Will you be able to call again before you leave?" Eleanor asked.

"I give you my word." He bowed over her outstretched hand.

"And, Mr. Sharp, there is one thing more. Would it be possible to have Mr. Whitefield come with you to bring me the Lord's Supper?"

"Indeed, Mrs. Doran." He turned to Catherine. "Good day, Miss Harrison. I wish you and Mr. Heath all the best." He spoke as if he might never see her again, and although the chances were highly unlikely, in one sense they were true. From now on, she belonged to someone else.

CHAPTER TWENTY-TWO

"Sister, would you explain something to me?"

Margaret walked between Catherine and Francis after leaving Christ Church, where George Whitefield had just spoken to a packed audience. Even Ann had gone, at the strong suggestion of the magistrate. While meeting with Catherine and her mother about the upcoming wedding and future plans, he'd mentioned going to hear Whitefield.

"I wish you would also come along, Mrs. Harrison," he'd said. "I believe getting out will do you a lot of good."

Catherine had tried to hide her smile as she thought of her mother's desire to please Edward Heath. The service had gone down pretty well, she thought, though her mother had recoiled a time or two at the minister's dancing, shouting, and waving of arms. If she were honest with herself, Catherine didn't exactly care for some of Whitefield's theatrics, but she accepted them as coming from a pure heart aflame with Christ's love.

A breeze ruffled her skirts, and Catherine let go of her sister's hand, so she could push aside a ribbon from her bonnet flapping in her face. The trio was headed toward the magistrate's home to await Whitefield's arrival, and while Catherine was thrilled to be seeing the minister again, she cowered at the thought of Henry Sharp's presence. She was doing everything she could to put away her feelings for him, like a hat she no longer wore, but being in his presence complicated the effort. At least he wouldn't be in Philadelphia for very long this time, she considered, then she and Francis could plan their future together unimpeded.

"Sister, I have a question."

"Uh, yes, Margaret." She dodged a steaming horse pie on the cobbled street.

"What exactly did Mr. Whitefield mean by 'God is our righteousness?'"

"Father also spoke of this. You see, no matter how hard we may try, we can't do enough to earn God's favor. We've sinned against him in thought, word, and deed, and we can't be made right before him by our own efforts."

"Then, should we even try to be good?"

"Being good is its own reward, but we can't be truly righteous before a holy God apart from Christ's work on the cross. By putting our faith in him and what he's done for us, we become acceptable to God."

Margaret's eyes glistened. "I think I understand, sister! Oh, I want to have such a faith as this, so I may be acceptable to God."

Catherine stopped suddenly, causing Francis to stumble.

"Oh! Do excuse me!" She covered her face, as well as a laugh, with her gloved hand. "I was taken by my sister's comment."

"As well you should be," he said, recovering his dignity. "I think she's just made a declaration of faith."

"Dearest Margaret, do you wish to belong wholly to Jesus Christ?" Catherine asked right in the middle of High Street.

Tears appeared in the girl's brown eyes, and her lips trembling, she nodded.

"We must tell Mr. Whitefield," Francis said.

Their opportunity had to wait, however. The preacher was swarmed by people who had followed him to the house. Among them was his opponent from the morning service, who continued to maintain Jesus couldn't become someone's righteousness. No amount of reasoning would persuade the man, and Whitefield at last threw his hands up and exclaimed, "Art thou a master of Israel, and knowest not these things?"

The man left in high dudgeon. When the crowd began to thin after Whitefield announced his desire to attend the Quaker's meeting, he noticed Catherine and her sister. "Well, good evening, my dear ones! I trust you are well. And your mother?"

"She's coming along rather better than before, Mr. Whitefield. She was encouraged by your message today."

He grinned boyishly. "So, she came after all. I'm glad to hear the Lord is opening her heart and comforting her as well."

Catherine pushed her sister forward. "Actually, Margaret has something to tell you."

He squatted and opened his arms. "Come here, dear child." She came and rested against him. "What good thing has happened to you?"

"Christ has become my righteousness, Mr. Whitefield. I am a Christian."

Whitefield's face broke into a wide smile. Then, he became more serious. "Our Savior has washed away your sins, Miss Harrison. You are a new creation." He paused. "This would have made your dear father very pleased."

Catherine's eyes welled with tears, and encouraged by Margaret's response to Christ, she was heartened to continue praying for her mother and her brother. *Perhaps all of Philadelphia will come to know the Master!*

Henry didn't know how George Whitefield could preach morning, noon, and night, receive guests until the stroke of midnight, and also provide well-thought-out messages. Although he'd always been on the high side of an energetic constitution, just watching the itinerant minister fatigued him. There was barely time for Whitefield to eat and rest before his next round of preaching. Perhaps, Henry considered, the positive response of the masses of hungering souls kept him going, along with the Holy Spirit, of course.

As he lay in his bed, he thought about the journey their entourage had made seven miles north of the city to Germantown earlier in the day where he'd acted as an interpreter. He didn't translate the message while Whitefield preached from a balcony to several thousand people, but afterward he helped the preacher converse with the German occupants of the village. Once he'd laughed out loud in spite of himself when a rosy *frau* came up to them in tears, saying, "That was the best sermon I ever heard, although I did not understand a word of it!"

In fact, there'd been a good deal of weeping as hearts fell under conviction of their sinfulness before a holy and just God. Several people invited them to dine at their homes, and Henry wished they could have obliged each one. Instead, they fellowshipped with a Swiss minister who'd been banished from his country for preaching Christ, who also told them about many souls in Germantown who'd fled to America seeking relief from religious persecution.

Henry stared at the ceiling and smiled upon also remembering the aged hermit they visited late in the afternoon, a man who'd once been very wealthy but who chose to live in voluntary poverty in order to follow Christ more closely.

He and Whitefield's entourage had arrived back in Philadelphia about eight o'clock, finding a large gathering waiting for them at the magistrate's house. Many of the people, including two Quakers who were questioning the principles of their religion, waited to ask Whitefield their questions and be assured of their salvation. Henry watched his fatigued friend give them a word from the Scripture, sing a hymn and pray with them, all before going inside.

Before they retired for the night, Whitefield had said, "I'm convinced God has begun a work in many souls here, which encourages me when I'm too tired to go on."

But go on they would, especially since their journey to Georgia was to begin the day after tomorrow. Henry mentally reviewed all the details needing to be attended to in the meantime, thankful he'd come on board to help Whitefield. His heart fairly sang every time the minister took up a collection for the orphans—when people reached into their pockets and gave generously. A number of women had also contributed blankets and socks. The thought of the orphans turned his mind to Eleanor Doran and his promise to take her communion tomorrow.

The church was packed, and for two hours, Whitefield preached. Afterward he struggled to make his way to the magistrate's for rest and refreshment before going out and delivering his farewell sermon in the afternoon. Because no church was able to hold the crowds, once again he preached from the courthouse steps. Their procession across High Street to the house was painfully slow as people thronged on all sides, each of them wanting a touch or a personal word. Henry did his best to keep them moving, but most would not be deterred, not even by his large frame. He recognized one of the men from the Germantown crowd, and they began to converse in their native tongue.

"*Guten tag*," the man said.

"*Guten tag*."

"I've come today because of my daughter." She smiled up at Henry, and he nodded at her. "When Mr. Whitefield preached, he sowed some good seed in her heart, and she desires to speak with him. Is this possible?"

"Come with me, and if the crowd should separate us, come to the magistrate's house on High Street."

They weren't, however, parted, and when Whitefield saw the man and his daughter a few minutes later, he stopped to address them. Once again, the man told his story, this time in tears, which also flowed from his daughter's green eyes. "She wonders how she might keep this faith and make progress."

"My dear daughter, how greatly the angels in heaven rejoice at your knowing him!" Whitefield said, once again animated, energetic. "There is nothing on earth more important than this. Now you must watch and pray not to fall to temptations designed by the Evil One to tear you from our Lord. Keep close to Christ by faith, and I'll pray for God to water the good seed his own right hand has planted in your heart."

This is the crux of what we're doing. We're pouring ourselves out for the sake of Christ, who is gathering colonial Americans to himself as never before. The faith of their fathers and grandfathers had sustained those people in their most dire straits when they first came to these shores, but the current generation had grown spiritually lazy and needed to be awakened. Henry had never seen anything like their response to the gospel, not even when people fell under conviction of sin under William Tennent's preaching. The fields certainly were white unto harvest, and Henry rejoiced to be among the laborers bringing in the sheaves.

He hoped the magistrate would come to a fullness of his own faith, as well as those in the church he'd been forced to leave. Gazing out among the multitude that night, he'd seen more than a few people from High Street Presbyterian, and he'd even had a few opportunities to greet a handful of them as he and Whitefield walked together. A tepid minister may have been thrust upon them, but there was strength and salvation in the solid food Whitefield was offering, and those who were ready would take and eat. Maybe all wasn't lost at the church after all.

As the weak afternoon light surrendered to lengthening shadows and dropping temperatures, Whitefield began to wind down. "Oh, but I had strength to speak all day of our blessed Lord, I would!" he told the assembly.

"Must you go?" someone cried out. Others just plain cried.

Henry wondered what kind of sermons they'd be hearing in Whitefield's absence, whether those ministers who didn't understand the new birth would continue serving up bland porridge rather than the solid food of the gospel. How would Catherine put up with such preaching? He pulled himself up short. She wasn't his to think about so much.

"Your adversary the devil prowls about like a roaring lion, seeking whom he may devour." Whitefield flung out his warning. "I wonder he hasn't been more active here, but I expect he and his emissaries to rage horribly now you've heard and accepted the Word of the Lord, which has no equal." He thrust his arms outward. "Prepare yourselves, then, against the day of spiritual battle, and I implore you to pray for me, as I pray for you, while we're apart. If God wills, we will be together again next spring." His arms raised. "In the meantime, may God bless you for providing so wonderfully for my dear orphans, whom I plan to see in not too many days."

Henry accompanied Whitefield to a church warden's home for a late meal, then they strode back to the Heaths' where a predictable group had gathered to await the minister's arrival.

Deep shadows fanning underneath his new friend's eyes concerned Henry. "Mr. Whitefield, if you like, I'll address them, telling them you must get some rest."

He grasped his shoulder. "I suppose I should let you, but look at them, my friend—they're like sheep without a shepherd, and I must be about my Father's work. Although I have no message left for tonight, I can pray with them."

Before they retired, Henry and Whitefield slipped quietly out the back of the house to bring the Lord's Supper to Eleanor Doran. A half hour later while he sat holding her wrinkled hand, she pulled Henry close to her face and whispered. "Mr. Sharp, our precious Lord has a way of working all things in our lives, even the very hard ones, for his glory, and our good."

He didn't have to ask what she was referring to.

The magistrate's house was devoid of its usual order and calm. Mrs. Daley and Mrs. Clydesdale pressed the valet into service to help with breakfast, while they scurried to prepare provisions and clean clothes for the departing men. Normally, such a thing would be an unspeakable breach of decorum, but Henson remained unflappable, demonstrating his eagerness to participate in some small way in Whitefield's ministry. Outside of the house, hundreds of people had gathered to see the itinerant off.

"I cannot thank you enough, Mr. Henson," Whitefield told him after the meal. "You have done so much for me and my family." He'd already had special words of appreciation for the females of the household.

The valet smiled, a rare occurrence. "You've done a great deal for my spirit, Mr. Whitefield. The least I can do is serve you who serves our Lord Jesus."

Whitefield grinned. "Mr. Henson! Have you come to the Savior, then?"

The lined face reddened. "Indeed, sir."

"Why, I rejoice with the very angels!"

Henry had noticed the magistrate also seemed softer towards the things of God. While Edward Heath had always demonstrated respect for the Almighty, he didn't seem to have a personal connection. Now he was speaking from less of a distance, more intimately, as though he were drawing closer. Henry would continue to pray for him.

Just before lunch, Whitefield completed his written sermons for Benjamin Franklin to print. "There you go, Mr. Sharp. Please apologize to him for my taking so long."

Henry noticed the tousled hair and some ink splotches tattooing Whitefield's fingers.

"I'll take them to Mr. Franklin straightaway."

Henson slid noiselessly into the room. "If I may, sir, perhaps you should use the back entrance. The crowd is pressing against the front door."

"Thank you, Mr. Henson. Mr. Whitefield, the people of Philadelphia hate to see you go."

"And I hate to leave them, Mr. Sharp. I feel my ministry has just begun here." He sighed. "I will, with God's help, return soon. In the meantime, we must pray for their souls to be nurtured and trust our God to continue the good work He has begun in them."

"Good morning, Mr. Sharp!"

"Indeed it is, Mr. Harrison," he said to Jacob, closing the door to the print shop behind him. "We have an excellent day for traveling, more like spring than late November."

"Yes, sir. And are you ready to leave?" The young man dried his hands on his ink-splotched apron and shook Henry's hand.

"I am."

"Catherine told me you're going with Mr. Whitefield." At the mention of her name, Henry smiled. Jacob leaned across the counter and put a hand to the side of his face. "Mr. Franklin and I think you got the short end of the stick from the synod." Then he straightened. "I never got to thank you for helping my father, Mr. Sharp. I know he would've been pleased."

"Thank you, Jacob. I was honored to assist. As for the rest, God takes care of his own."

Jacob's eyes, the same shape as his sister's, met Henry's. "I'm beginning to understand."

Henry smiled. "Ah, but I'm pleased to know this!"

Henry wanted to say more about the new life in Christ, but Franklin came lumbering down the stairs. "Good day, Mr. Sharp! I hoped Mr. Whitefield would send you today."

They clasped hands. "I have those extra sermons he promised," Henry said. "I also wanted to say farewell."

"Yes, I hear you're going adventuring with the good parson." He scratched his chin and laughed. "I had a few of those in my youth, but somehow I doubt yours will be of the same variety."

Henry grinned. "Perhaps you would sell me a bound blank book, so I can keep a journal."

Franklin lifted a finger. "Coming right up."

"I know of an especially nice one in the back," Jacob said, and he disappeared. Franklin leaned on the counter. "How long will you take getting to Georgia?"

"Mr. Whitefield is hoping to reach the orphans by Christmas."

The printer grumbled, bear-like. "I still think he should build that infernal orphanage here. I would've been only too glad to help."

"Yes, we know." Henry laughed.

"I suppose the Almighty would have it otherwise, and who are we to oppose him?"

"Indeed, Mr. Franklin."

"Well, Mr. Sharp, I'm glad to see you have landed on your feet after the synod's decision." He sniffed. "Blind guides and Pharisees!"

He winked. "Am I to understand you've come to the light yourself, Mr. Franklin?"

"You and your Mr. Whitefield! You don't give up, do you?"

"No, sir."

He moved to his desk. "For now, let's focus on an earthly transaction, Mr. Sharp."

He produced a piece of paper with the terms of agreement for publishing a volume of Whitefield's sermons, which Henry reviewed. "Yes, this is good. He'll be pleased. Thank you."

"I plan to publish them some time in the next few weeks. I'll also be printing some of his messages in the paper." Franklin paused. "Do you have any idea when you'll return?"

"Mr. Whitefield has accepted preaching engagements for the spring in New Jersey, New York, and New England, so we hope to be back in Pennsylvania by April." *Before Catherine's wedding.* Now that was something he didn't want to see.

"And then what will you do?"

"I'm hoping to become the pastor of a new congregation in Bucks County."

Franklin smiled. "You'll make a fine one, Mr. Sharp."

Jacob returned with a leather journal that Henry found to his liking. He paid for the book, signed the agreement on George Whitefield's behalf, and left.

"Good luck to you, Mr. Sharp." Franklin's voice followed him out the door. "Write everything down, and I just might publish your journal when you return!"

CHAPTER TWENTY-THREE

Henry gazed out the front window at the masses at the front of the house blocking the door. *How will we ever be able to make our way through?* He felt Francis's presence just over his shoulder, apparently wondering the same thing.

"I suppose, Mr. Whitefield, you could just go out the back way," Heath proposed.

Henry didn't think his friend would go for such an avoidance tactic and quickly found his suspicions confirmed.

"I must take my leave of them properly, Mr. Heath. I'll say a few words, and we'll pray together." Whitefield turned to Henry, his round face as sanguine as the man's spirit. "Are you ready, Mr. Sharp?"

"I am." Henry breathed a quick prayer. "How about you, Mr. Syms?"

"Indeed."

"Then, we must go." Whitefield strode over to the magistrate and gripped his hand. "Once again, I thank you, my dear friend, for your tremendous hospitality. Words cannot express my gratitude. Thank you as well for allowing Mr. Seward to stay a while longer."

"No thanks are necessary, Mr. Whitefield. God bless you—may you return here safely."

Whitefield shook Seward's hand next. "My dear friend, be well, and I shall see you again, God willing, in Georgia."

Seward's eyes misted. "I look forward to the day."

As Whitefield worked through his farewells to the staff, Henry said his own, echoing his deep gratitude for all the Heaths and their household had done for him. When he reached Francis, the young man told him, "I do hope you make it back in time for the wedding. Such an occasion wouldn't be the same without you."

Henry smiled around the dryness in his mouth and nodded in what he hoped amounted to more than half-hearted ascent.

"Miss Harrison was unable to come this morning to say goodbye, but she sends you her best wishes and promises to pray for you."

"Please thank her for me." He managed not to choke on the words.

"And you will write?" Francis cocked his head to one side.

"I will."

When Henson opened the front door, Henry half expected the masses to thrust their way inside, and he braced for the impact. Instead, the noisy crowd went completely silent when Whitefield appeared and lifted his hands, as if a schoolteacher had just issued a rousing command. Henry and Syms flanked him on either side.

"My dear friends, you are so kind to bid us goodbye. I've come to love you deeply in the time I've spent in this City of Brotherly Love. Until we meet again, let us pray together."

As Whitefield asked a blessing, Henry became attuned to the sound of weeping threading through the people. His own heart felt somehow heavier at the thought of leaving the city, his family, and Catherine, but he wrestled his sadness into submission and willed his attitude into one of praise for God's providence over all things, including the hard ones.

When Whitefield finished the benediction, he exhorted the people to stay close to the Savior. "He never leaves us, my friends. He never forsakes us. He alone is the anchor of our souls, so stay close to him and, God willing, I'll return to you soon to sing his praises with you again!"

Twenty men on horseback accompanied them out of town. Henry didn't look back.

⁂

Catherine was almost grateful when Andrew Oldfield paid an official call later that day—anything to fill the emptiness left by the departure of George Whitefield and Henry Sharp. Of course, she was dubious about the pastor—her father adamantly had not wanted him to serve High Street Presbyterian, and he'd only come now because the synod had dismissed Henry. Although Catherine found his brother and sister-in-law odious, she prayed to have the mind of Christ in the unpleasant situation. With many people having come to the Savior under George Whitefield's preaching, she wondered how her beloved church might change in the aftermath. If many had been truly saved, would they be pleased to have an Old Light in the pulpit? For now, she would try to give the man a chance. Who knew—maybe he'd also heard Whitefield and fallen under conviction.

Oldfield arrived with the magistrate just after noon, the latter in his capacity as clerk of session. Fortunately for Catherine, Robert and Mrs. Oldfield, who constantly fawned over Andrew as if they could take personal credit for his being a minister, had not come. The pastor reminded her only a little of Robert Oldfield—the brother had more bulk and less hair. He greeted her mother with a bow over her proffered hand. "Mrs. Harrison, please accept my sincerest sympathy upon your husband's passing. I didn't know him well, but I knew of his excellent ministry and have always respected him."

"Thank you," Ann said.

"It is an honor to be preaching from his pulpit, and I shall do my best."

"I understand you also have lost a spouse, Mr. Oldfield," Catherine's mother said.

"Yes, madam. Both my dear wife and our child."

After a long pause, Ann said so low Catherine strained to hear her, "Sometimes our lots in life are difficult."

"Indeed, they can be. The Lord gives, and the Lord takes away, according to his plans."

Catherine waited for him to complete the verse, but he didn't. While he was saying some of the right things about God, she wondered why they didn't sound the same as when George Whitefield, Henry Sharp, or her father had uttered them. After they'd sat in the parlor and made small talk, she asked, "Where are you staying, Mr. Oldfield?" She knew she was treading on sinking sand.

"I'm with my brother and his dear wife." He looked at Ann. "I assure you I'm in no hurry to occupy the manse, Mrs. Harrison."

The magistrate stepped into the conversation. "You may be aware, Mr. Oldfield, my son and Miss Harrison are planning to be married."

The minister looked surprised. "I was not. May I offer congratulations, Miss Harrison?"

Catherine thanked him, although she couldn't understand how the news of her engagement hadn't reached him before this. She looked at Edward Heath, waiting for him to reveal information he'd discussed with her, her mother, and Francis two days earlier.

"After they're married in April, my son and new daughter-in-law will reside at my home, while Mrs. Harrison and her daughter Margaret will occupy a home I own nearby."

Oldfield nodded. "I shall be happy for you to stay here until then, Mrs. Harrison."

"That is very kind of you, Mr. Oldfield."

This one isn't like his brother. He strikes me as sincerely caring at least.

"Mr. Oldfield, if you don't wish to stay with your brother and his family until then," Edward continued, "I'll help you find lodgings elsewhere."

"Thank you, Magistrate. Allow me to consider this." After a pause he addressed Catherine. "Miss Harrison, I understand you have a gift for visitation. Would you consider going on as you've been while I'm pastor at High Street?"

Catherine's mouth fell slightly open. Clearly, he didn't feel in any way threatened by the daughter of the manse and, for her part, she was glad to maintain the ministry in which she found such purpose and joy.

George Whitefield may have left Philadelphia, but Philadelphia hadn't exactly left him. When he and his company were seven miles out of town, a large group was waiting for them at a crossroads.

"We've come to see you off, sir," called a man from atop his horse. With him were at least two hundred others, who, Henry could see, judging from their attire and their mounts, were from disparate backgrounds. In Christ, there were among them no Jew or Greek, slave nor free, but all of them had found a common identity in Jesus Christ.

"Then please do join us!" Whitefield called out. "We'll be happy for your company."

They rode about fifteen miles until they reached the town of Chester, and since the noonday meal had come and gone, they stopped just beyond the busy town square, dismounted, and sat along the road to eat. Henry was especially glad to find one of Mrs. Clydesdale's apple pies in a hamper, along with copious amounts of ham and fresh bread. Most of their fellow travelers had brought their own sustenance, and Whitefield shared with those who had none.

Henry surveyed the crowd as he ate. *I wonder why they follow us. Maybe because Whitefield is such a luminary, the latest thing to come from England?* Henry looked from one face to another as his companions carried on a conversation with a father and his son. Like other people in the crowd, their faces reflected years of hard, outdoor work. In the creases and shadows, Henry also saw hunger, although their bodies appeared to be well fed. He surveyed others among them and witnessed the same attitude as they leaned closer to catch every word Whitefield said. Spiritual hunger—that was it. These men and boys were reluctant to let the young minister go before they could be fed once again. He thought of the verse, "The word of the Lord was rare in those days," and here was Whitefield, God's mouthpiece in America to preach the Word. Multitudes were listening. Of course, other men, like the Tennents, Mr. Edwards, and Mr. Frelinghuysen were just as faithful, and as result, the Lord was reaping a rich harvest of souls. *When this trip ends, I'll give my life to preaching the whole testimony of God's Word to the hungry souls in Bucks County. If only Catherine could be there with me ...*

After he'd tossed aside a chicken bone, Whitefield motioned for Henry to come closer. "These fellows have given us their valuable time to be with us. I must give them a word before they go. I know we didn't plan to do so, but we must ever be aware of God's agenda. We mustn't just ask him to bless our plans, but to preach and teach whenever he opens doors."

Henry smiled. This was going to be an interesting journey.

"Welcome to the wonderful world of Whitefield," Syms said, and they all laughed.

A portly man ran up to them, panting. "Good sirs, I am a minister in this village. Today is court day, and the square is full of people, about five thousand, far too many for my humble church. The justices have decided to defer their meeting, so you may preach, and I've secured a balcony for you to use."

Whitefield clapped the man on the back. "Indeed, my friend! Thank you for arranging this. Our God does all things well. These are my companions, Mr. Syms and Mr. Sharp."

"I'm happy to make your acquaintances. My son, Nathaniel,"—he indicated a brawny young man—"will see to your horses and belongings."

They followed him to the manse where they met the rest of his family, then Whitefield began to preach from the balcony. Henry once again marveled how so many people could keep quiet for such a long time, but they just didn't seem to want to miss a single, life-giving word. Not until six in the evening was their work in Chester done, at least for the time being.

"With God's help, I will return to you," Whitefield said. "Stay close to our Lord Jesus and tell me all he has done for you when I come back. May it be far beyond all you can ask or imagine."

They traveled for three more hours in the moonlit evening, refreshing themselves with lively conversation about God's present mighty work and their past experiences of his faithfulness. The time seemed to Henry to be more like three minutes. They at last stopped for the night in the town of Wilmington in Delaware, at the home of an older Quaker couple who had met Whitefield in Philadelphia and invited him to stay. Their home was plain but elegant in its simplicity, and the hearty food the woman of the house served, abundant and satisfying.

While they feasted on ham and potatoes, Whitefield managed to converse about the Lord with several people who'd gathered in the home to meet with him. Judging from their dress, Henry thought some of them were definitely not Quakers. *God really doesn't have favorites among the denominations. All of them are now hungering and thirsting after him.*

Following the meal, Whitefield shared a shortened version of the message he'd given in Chester. Afterward, he led them in decidedly Anglican prayers, although no one seemed to mind.

Whitefield can be all things to all people in order to win some, but I think he's unafraid to be who he is as well.

Their hosts led them to an upstairs room with three small beds. "This is where our children slept when they were at home," the wife said. "I hope you find the accommodations comfortable."

"Indeed," Whitefield said. "You're very kind to open your home to us."

"You are kind, sir, to bring the light of Jesus Christ to us."

As they settled in, Henry lay awake in the dark, talking with his friends.

"What do you think about your first journey with our little band?" Syms asked.

"Exhilarating. I never expected all those people to follow us out of Philadelphia, and then to see the response of those you preached to, well ..."

"I marvel at the great work God has begun in these parts," Whitefield said in the dark. "I haven't seen greater things, even in England." He sighed. "I deeply desire, my friends, to return here in the Lord's good time. I very much hope to see some substantial fruits of our present, weak endeavors."

"I'm surprised to hear you speak of your ministry as a 'weak endeavor,' so powerful is your preaching and the response." Henry spoke in the direction of Whitefield's voice.

The minister started to object, but Syms interrupted. "My friend, you've been used mightily of Jesus Christ to bring people into fullness of faith in him."

"While this may be true, Syms, I pray to our Redeemer to make me humble. Whenever he sees me in danger of being exalted above measure, I want him to graciously send me a thorn in the flesh so his blessings upon me may not prove my ruin."

CHAPTER TWENTY-FOUR

Catherine considered the size of the dining room windows and the woodwork, deciding the Oriental rug with its dominant burgundy and dark blue tones would be staying—she'd work around those colors for new wallpaper and drapes. She smiled when she recalled the magistrate's offer to redecorate his home in preparation for her marriage saying, "After all these years, the place needs a woman's touch." The home was already so fine a residence she didn't wish to remake everything, however.

She stepped back from a window as if examining a painting. "What do you think, Mother? Should we work with a different pattern and try to compliment the rug, or use solid colors?"

"What if you try solids with an interesting fabric?"

"What a good idea!" She smiled at Ann, pleased the wedding preparations were helping move her beyond the narrow boundaries of grief. In fact, her mother seemed almost happy these days, leaving Catherine to think maybe the worst of the ordeal for her had been her husband's illness and the anticipation of his demise. With Joseph gone and her daughter engaged to one of the city's finest young men, Ann Harrison could head into the future without the sword of Damocles hanging over her. Ann had even become more open to the ministry of George Whitefield, the effects of which continued to be felt in Philadelphia on all levels of the social scale. Many had come to faith in Jesus Christ, while those already in the household of believers had been deeply enriched. Catherine relished the frequent conversations she and Francis had with their parents about what being an all-out Christian meant. Her father's and her prayers for Ann were being answered, just as they had been for Margaret. *As for Jacob ...* He was left alone in his unbelief.

And yet—Catherine grieved the loss of her father, often crying herself to sleep at night when the void he had left sucked her in. She'd asked Francis if he had felt similarly after his mother died, feeling odd at first confiding in him rather than Eleanor Doran about something so intimate. She wasn't, however, visiting the widow as frequently these days. Catherine told herself she was so busy with wedding preparations she no longer had as much time as she once had. If she were entirely honest with herself, though, she would've been forced to admit she was staying away because Mrs. Doran was the one person who knew the depths of Catherine's feelings for Henry Sharp.

Fortunately, Francis had proven to be a trustworthy confidant. "I believe women experience emotions more deeply than men," he'd said. "However, I can tell you for many months after my dear mother passed away, I felt the same kind of emptiness you describe. Give yourself time, dear heart. At first, you will think about him constantly, then after a while, the hot poker of grief will mellow into a gentle flame."

Halfway through his encouraging speech, Catherine began to think Francis's words could apply just as much to her feelings about Henry Sharp. She didn't want to carry a torch for him the rest of her life.

Beside the happy busyness of preparing for her nuptials and redecorating her new home, Catherine found solace in her relationship with the magistrate. She'd always had a high regard for him, seeing him more as her father's loyal clerk of session than the formidable force he was to the rest of Philadelphia society. Now that he was going to be her father-in-law, Catherine continued to see him benevolently, especially when he'd invited her to beautify her new home in any way she desired. And when he made an offer of a different sort, her heart was forever sealed to his as a daughter to a father.

The conversation had taken place one evening after dinner while he was smoking his pipe, and Francis was holed up in his office. While the magistrate puffed contentedly, a man comfortable in his own skin, Catherine knitted stockings for Margaret, feeling as if she were living there already.

"I've been thinking about something, Catherine," he said. "Although I've had only a son, I believe when a young lady is preparing for her wedding, she must select a dress for the occasion."

Catherine's heart raced. She and her mother had just been wondering what kind of dress she should wear—more to the point, what kind they could afford.

"I think your frock will have to be modest," Ann had said, which was her way of communicating, "We don't have much money."

In fact, they didn't have money for a new dress, period—not when they were living on her father's limited pension. She wouldn't dream of asking Jacob to contribute when his own pay was so constrained by the terms of his apprenticeship. Her father and mother had created a small dowry for her, but Catherine was loathe to use the funds for a dress when her mother and sister might have greater need of the money in the future. While the magistrate would provide a home for them, no one really knew whether there would also be a stipend and if so, how much.

There was yet another consideration—while she had a certain station in Philadelphia society as a pastor's daughter, Catherine knew any show of the slightest ostentation, real or perceived, would be met by criticism. She'd learned over the years that a pastor's session and congregation held his family to be examples of holy living, which included not reaching beyond one's means. A Presbyterian minister was not to appear wealthy or poor, rather a denizen of the educated middle class. That she was marrying into the upper class complicated the issue—she was a bride between stations.

Returning to the present, she took up the conversation. "Yes, Mr. Heath, I will need to order a dress."

"So, you have not yet?" His eyebrows raised, pipe smoke encircled his head.

Catherine squirmed, looking hard at her knitting. "No, sir."

He became quiet for a few moments. "I'm not sure if I'm breaking with any sort of etiquette, not having raised a daughter, but might I make a present of a dress for you?"

She dropped the stockings in her lap. "Oh, how kind of you!"

"You're not offended, then?"

She swallowed before she could speak. "Not at all." She noticed a rare look of vulnerability in Heath's brown eyes. "My own dear father would have provided a wedding dress for me were he here."

He looked into her eyes. "My dear, may I do this, then, on his behalf?"

"Yes, thank you," she whispered.

When Francis walked her home, Catherine told him about the unexpected gift.

"My father is a good and kind man, and I'm pleased he's doing this. He's almost as happy as I am to have you join our family."

As they reached her house, and he saw her inside, Catherine noticed him frowning. "What's the matter?" She wondered what could have changed his mood so quickly.

"Forgive me, dear one. Mention of the dress has me thinking about the wedding."

She couldn't help but tease him. "Which makes you grimace."

"Only because I'm thinking about who will probably be performing the ceremony."

Now her emotions took a dive. Andrew Oldfield was, to put the matter bluntly, a mind-numbing preacher. He would read a Bible passage then expound his way around the text, veering off into any available ditch. He seemed to prefer stories and examples from his own life, rather than the essence of the gospel. More than once Catherine had dropped off during the sermons only to be awakened by her mother's gentle prods. Judging from the looks on other's faces, they were also restless with the pabulum he constantly dished up, especially after her father, Henry, and Whitefield had given them solid food. She wondered how someone so close to religion could be so far from the Lord. Were it not for the sermons of George Whitefield, which she read over and over in the paper, Catherine's spirit would starve.

Francis took to speculating. "Perhaps he'll no longer be with us next April. He is, after all, a supply pastor."

Catherine sighed. "You know how hard Mr. Oldfield is pushing for his brother to be called permanently."

"Indeed I do, and heaven help us. I'm not certain the rest of the congregation wants him, not after Mr. Whitefield's influence." The sun rose on Francis's face. "Perhaps our friend Mr. Sharp will have returned by then, and he or Mr. Whitefield could marry us!"

His words, like sharpened knives, sliced her spirit. "Mr. Whitefield would be a delightful choice," she said quickly. She didn't want to go anywhere near the topic of Henry Sharp performing her wedding.

On Christmas Eve, after crossing the miles-wide Pamplico River in South Carolina the previous day and trekking thirty-two more miles to Newborn Town, Henry and his companions had found room at the local inn by six o'clock. Their room felt like a lap of luxury to Henry after their grueling, gritty travels. He and his friends sat before a generous fire in the common room where they were by themselves drinking hot tea and reflecting on the holiday.

"I can just see my dear friends back in England," Whitefield said, gazing into the fire. "As they celebrate the nativity of our Savior, they'll be praying fervently, then singing hymns and spiritual songs with joyful hearts."

Having become better acquainted with the preacher during the last month, Henry thought he was likely referring to the Wesley brothers, Charles and John, whom Whitefield counted among his closest friends.

The minister sighed. "I was with them twelve months ago, but still I feel I'm not absent—my soul is closely united with them and all God's children, by the Spirit of his dear Son."

Henry pictured his own family gathered at the Warminster farmstead. They had become Presbyterian because there'd been no Lutheran congregations when they first settled in the area, but at Christmas, they harkened back to the old ways. Presbyterians considered celebrating Christmas to be popish, preferring to observe Easter instead. Germans, on the other hand, including Henry, happened to like the Nativity. He reminisced about the special foods his mother and grandmother had always prepared—sweet and sour cauliflower, pears simmered in red wine, pickles and cheese, stuffed pig's stomach, and mincemeat pie. His mouth watered as he imagined the faces of his beloved family gathered at the table, but his spirit turned suddenly gray, longing for their company.

Whitefield was on a roll. "However separated we are from our loved ones, my comfort is that neither men nor devils can keep us from meeting and dwelling together eternally hereafter." He sipped his drink, then smiled. "As the hart pants after the water brooks, so does my soul long for that time when I shall be summoned to go forth to meet him."

Henry had never spent as much time as his friend pondering the glories of heaven, but rather than finding Whitefield to be morose, the fellow was as cheerful as anyone he'd ever known. They conversed for a while longer, then Henry excused himself. "If you'll excuse me," he said rising, "I'd like to write to my family and some friends back in Pennsylvania."

"I imagine you must miss them a good deal," Syms said.

"Yes, but I wouldn't want to miss this spiritual adventure with you, my dear friends."

Henry went upstairs to the room he was sharing with Whitefield and Syms, and finding paper in his satchel, he sat at a table near a window and began writing to his family. He'd been sending letters to them along the way in an attempt not only to stay connected, but also to relieve any anxiety they might have about his welfare.

> My dear father and mother, grandfather, brothers, and sister,
>
> I greet you in the blessed name of our Lord and Savior Jesus Christ on this eve of His birth. May all of you be well and enjoying this celebration. Would that I could be there with you! It has pleased our Lord, however, to send me on an incredible journey with my brothers in the faith, Misters Whitefield and Syms, whose company I cherish more each day. Never did a man have such stimulating fellowship!

He filled three pages with details of his recent adventures, then signed and sealed the envelope. Refreshing a goose quill, he began a new letter.

> To My Dear Friends, Magistrate and Mr. Francis Heath.

While he believed they'd share his message with Catherine, he decided not to address her individually since she wasn't yet part of their family.

> I trust this finds you and your household well on this eve of our Savior's birth. Tonight, my friends and I are stopping in Newborn Town in the colony of South Carolina at a public ordinary. I thought you might be interested to hear about some of our adventures thus far. I assure you I have experienced more in these past few weeks than most souls know in a lifetime, and I am grateful to our Lord Jesus Christ for favoring me in such a way to witness firsthand His mighty works.
>
> Mr. Whitefield has had many wonderful opportunities to share the gospel with those who are unaware of the spiritual darkness in which they live, as well as those hungering and thirsting after righteousness. After we left Delaware, the crowds became less numerous, in part because there are fewer people here than in the north and spiritual apathy is more apparent here. The people of the southern colonies are eager to acquire and enjoy the things of this world, and therefore, are deader to God. While we stopped in Maryland, some people we met considered Mr. Whitefield a harsh man for his opposition to their entertainments in which they frequently indulge and which they consider to be innocent diversions—things such as dancing and card playing—but which he believes are in opposition to pursuing God's glory,

which should be our single goal. In his view, any activity set upon self-seeking, pomps, and vanities, as Mr. Whitefield calls them, rather than seeking after God, will cause us to become ensnared by the devil. He is a fine example to me in this. While he is far from dour or in any way a killjoy, he finds his greatest happiness in serving our Lord and enjoying His many benefits.

In addition, in the early going, we met many others who have been affected by the spirit of Deism and do not have much understanding about a proper fear of the Lord. When Mr. Whitefield spoke to them frankly about the new birth, I sensed some of the hearers had come under conviction. Who knows what the Lord Jesus may be doing in their hearts?

One woman who generously opened her home to us listened attentively to our talk of the new birth, but when she responded, I could tell she had not properly understood my friend. She said she believed people are to be born again, but not in this life. Rather, at death God shows His mercy to those He has created. We have consistently met people who fall into one of two theological ditches—they either believe God is all merciful and there is no judgment, or He is all justice and there is no mercy. We perceive in these colonies a famine of God's Word and pray we might be used of Him to feed His sheep.

Outside the tavern horses nickered, and a cow lowed, reminding Henry of the circumstances of his Savior's birth in a Bethlehem barn. Feeling the coolness of the wooden table under his hand, he continued writing.

We travel great distances, usually between 25-40 miles per day, often over streams and rivers, on horseback and ferries, without knowing where we will lay our heads at night. Our precious Lord Jesus has faithfully led us to many kind souls who have opened their homes to us, although they had little else but their hospitality to offer. In the early going, we stayed with families who had been recommended to Mr. Whitefield earlier. At one of those places, I had the joy of conversing with some German families in our native tongue about the new birth in Christ. Since Mr. Whitefield does not speak German, he was grateful for my intervention.

Although some of the newspapers have carried negative and false reports about his ministry, people are even more curious to see him and some to offer hospitality. To paraphrase the patriarch Joseph's words, Satan may have meant this for evil, but God meant it for good and for the saving of many souls.

Along the way, we have slept in people's barns and even their kitchens when there have not been public ordinaries. There are, indeed, far fewer taverns in these colonies because the population is smaller, and because people are known for their hospitality. We were invited to stay at the home of one planter, but when we arrived, he was not at home, and his overseer would not admit us. He seemed to be doing battle within himself, however, and concluded we might stop there after all. Since the day had been especially tiring for Mr. Whitefield, the accommodations were very much appreciated. He pushes himself relentlessly in his zeal to speak of God's saving grace to those living in darkness, and as happened in Philadelphia, people come to him at night to converse and pray with him privately. In those hours, we frequently see inquirers receive the new birth.

While there are fewer people here, there seem to be a good deal many more wild animals, especially wolves. One night as we made our way to a settlement where we hoped to find an inn, we heard the howling of a pack, which was particularly alarming since we were not exactly sure where we were or how to get to the town. In His mercy, God sent us a guide to show us the way. Once we were safely inside, Mr. Whitefield said he couldn't help but think how dreadful it must be for a natural man to be placed in such a howling wilderness, surrounded with those many wolves and bears which come out at night roaring upon them. Yet, how infinitely more dreadful to be cast into hell and surrounded continually with the howling of damned spirits!

Henry dipped his quill into the ink and paused before continuing, praying for several people he'd met who walked in such darkness.

> Along the way south, we have encountered many natural challenges as well. During the second week of December, we attempted to cross the exceedingly wide Potomac River into Virginia, but the wind was so much against us and nightfall nearly at hand that we rowed back to shore and stayed at the small home of the ferryman. The wind and snow blew all night, leading us to conclude we and our horses might have been lost

> had we tried to push forward. I agree with Mr. Whitefield about avoiding two extremes in our relationship with the Almighty—either distrusting Him or tempting Him foolishly.
>
> Lest you think all around us is backwoods, there was the delightful town of Williamsburg, Virginia's capital. We had opportunity to dine with the governor at his magnificent palace, along with the Rev. Mr. Blair, who is in charge of an impressive college there whose teachers all hail from Oxford University. Mr. Whitefield knew some of them from his own days at Oxford, which was a cause for joy.

Voices and laughter from the common room drifted upwards, and he guessed some people had come to see Whitefield. He examined what he'd written and decided to bring the letter to a close.

> Mr. Whitefield hopes to reach Georgia around the New Year and be with his orphans shortly afterwards. Mr. Seward will be joining us again as well, God willing. Once he finds a plot of land to build the orphanage on and puts those plans into motion, we will begin the journey back to Pennsylvania. We still hope to arrive in the early spring, perhaps April. I trust all of you are in good health as you celebrate the advent of our Lord. Please greet everyone for me. I will try to write again before long. I welcome news from home.
>
> Your obedient servant,
>
> Henry Sharp

He waved a hand over the letter to dry the ink, thinking about Catherine and her family. Hopefully, their grief was healing. His own had not.

CHAPTER TWENTY-FIVE

Catherine fought leaden drowsiness with flailing determination, first opening her eyes wider, then licking the roof of her mouth. She might have been embarrassed to be nodding off in church, but she was in the best of company—those parishioners who weren't actually asleep wore the same glazed expressions. As far as she could tell, the only people who enjoyed hearing Andrew Oldfield were his brother and sister-in-law, a few elderly members of the congregation who had difficulty hearing in the first place, and Elizabeth, who'd set her cap for the widowed minister. Catherine glanced at her friend, feeling disappointed—the only effect Whitefield seemed to have had on her was to make Elizabeth's heart flutter.

She wrestled an outburst of laughter upon surveying the condition of her small family—Francis's head was practically attached to his chest, her mother's mouth was open, and her eyes closed, and Margaret was unabashedly asleep, leaning against Francis. Andrew Oldfield seemed oblivious as he poured forth high-sounding words, devoid of passion or persuasion. She frequently thought of him in terms of 2 Timothy 3:5. "Having a form of godliness, but denying the power thereof." Paul had further admonished Timothy in his letter "from such turn away." Catherine had a dilemma. *I do want to turn away, but how?* As the daughter of the manse, she couldn't very well join another church. She hoped and prayed fervently the session wouldn't call Oldfield to be the permanent pastor. Maybe they would choose a New Side pastor after all, though finding one who'd been educated according to the synod's mandate was going to be difficult, if not impossible.

She willed herself to sit up straight. Never had she felt so lifeless. Listening to Oldfield's preaching for nearly three months had left her soul famished, and not even the prospect of her upcoming marriage was enough to drive away such hunger. This was a weary land in which there was no food, no Bread of Life. Even in her father's last illness when the situation from a human standpoint was desperate, Catherine felt close to God, but now he seemed to have withdrawn his presence from her. She'd dared mention her spiritual state to Francis, who said he was also missing the life-giving words he'd come to expect from her father, then Henry Sharp, and George Whitefield.

"Those men knew how to preach. They were so connected to the Lord God when they delivered his Word, a person's spirit was fed and could grow. This fellow ..." Francis shook his head. "Dry as dust." In order to bide their time, Francis had purchased all the sermons Benjamin Franklin had been given to publish by George Whitefield, and he and Catherine read them aloud in the evenings. Those times, along with her private devotions, kept her afloat. Except for Francis, no one else would have guessed she was trudging through a spiritual desert, but not even he knew the reason for the rest of her emptiness. Catherine put on a happy face for everyone, hoping by so doing, her inward emotions might catch up with the outward show.

"How are you this morning, Mr. Whitefield?" Henry placed a cup of hot tea and a plate of buttered toast on a table near his friend's bed. The minister sat up and smiled—his hair rumpled, the bags under his eyes giving him the appearance of a man much older than his twenty-five years. "Thank you, my good friend. I'm feeling well, thanks be to God. I'm happy to sleep in my bed after our sojourn throughout Doboy and Darien. How good the Lord was to us, to spare us many sorrows in our travels."

Henry thought back to their recent journey which included a broken rudder, contrary winds, and Whitefield's fever. Throughout the ordeals, however, the preacher had insisted upon delivering sermons twice a day whenever possible, along with buying land for the orphanage in Savannah and overseeing its building, not to mention developing plans for new schools in Georgia. As the windows were open to the cool morning air, Henry listened to the sound of the children running about in the yard, their laughter as pleasant as birdsong. He had been surprised at the warm temperatures in Georgia, realizing his family back in Pennsylvania were likely dealing with heavy wind and snowdrifts.

"Sit down, Mr. Sharp, and let's have a leisurely talk. Have you breakfasted?"

"Indeed I have, thank you." He sat across from his friend on a roughhewn chair.

Whitefield sat up and rearranged his bedclothes. "I'm eager to know how this journey has been for you."

Henry decided to be honest. "I'm grateful to God to be in your company, and although my life hasn't been turning out as I once imagined, God does all things well."

Whitefield cocked his head. "Tell me more."

"I thought there'd be a straight path from Mr. Tennent's school to pastoring a new congregation in Bucks County. Then, I was abruptly called to Mr. Harrison's church in Philadelphia, where I guessed I might stay until my ministry among them was completed."

When Henry paused and looked down at his lap, Whitefield spoke. "Sometimes we don't understand God's ways, but we can be certain they are always for his glory and our benefit. Consider Joseph, who spoke of the ill treatment of his brothers as something God used for the saving of many lives."

"I've often thought of the story," Henry said, smiling.

Just then an orphan burst into the room, one of three German children who'd recently arrived in a condition of desperation, having lost their parents to illness and with nowhere else to go. Henry was especially fond of them, and they'd taken to the big man who spoke their native tongue. The little boy started talking excitedly in German to Whitefield, who held up his hands and cried, "Whoa, there, lad!" He pointed to Henry, who reached out for the boy.

"*Komm hier.*"

The dark-haired boy went over to him and began speaking quickly again, Henry nodding in understanding. When he finished, Henry interpreted. "Johann says Samuel will not let him use the plow, something he considers himself good at, although his brother thinks Johann is too small."

The boy appeared on the verge of tears. Whitefield motioned for him, and Johann drew close, the preacher putting his arms on the boy's bony shoulders. Looking at Henry, he said, "Will you kindly translate for me?"

"Of course."

"You tell Samuel I said he should give you a turn."

Henry repeated Whitefield's message in German, and the sun rose on the boy's face.

"*Ach! Danke! Danke!*"

The boy gave Whitefield an awkward hug and raced out of the room and down the stairs of their temporary quarters.

"You're good with the children," Henry said.

"So are you! I love them dearly." He picked up the cup and drained the tea.

He wondered if he might get more personal with his friend. "Do you think about getting married and having your own family?"

"I do indeed, Mr. Sharp! These are things I hope to have and which I've committed into the hands of our Lord. I'm confident in his way and in his best time, he'll bring a woman into my life who can share my work." He laughed. "Not every woman would be kindly disposed to my particular lifestyle."

Although Henry trusted God's providence, at times he fended off arrows of doubt. He wondered whether God had wanted Catherine and he to be together, but circumstances might have thwarted his will. Though his spirit chafed at the idea of God's will being trampled upon, Henry wished the Lord would just barge in sometimes and make his people do as he desired.

"I suppose you also wish for these things?" Whitefield asked.

"I do."

"I think I understand," he said when Henry failed to elaborate. "You know, Mr. Sharp, in his omniscience, God sees far beyond our limited scope and understanding. I pray this will become clear to you in the matter at hand."

"Thank you. I know these things to be true, but at times I struggle."

"Perhaps you should know I have my own inward battles."

Henry stared at the pastor. "You?"

"Oh my, yes, my friend. At times I can't understand why God would want to use someone like me."

Henry didn't know what to say, having considered George Whitefield the epitome of a godly man. Then again, some of God's most honored servants in the Bible wrestled the deepest with sin and doubt. "How do you overcome your struggles?"

Whitefield lowered his voice, seeming to talk mostly to himself. "By prayer and repentance. I lay myself bare before our Lord Jesus Christ, and when I'm utterly spent before him, he lifts me up, as he has done over and over."

Henry didn't trust himself to speak for a long moment. Then he simply said, "Thank you."

"I don't think we need to struggle alone, to believe no one else understands how wretchedly we can fool ourselves. Satan would have us isolated while God would lift us up within the body of believers."

Feeling relieved, he ventured to move the conversation in a different, far safer, direction. For once, his friend didn't appear to be in a hurry to get out of bed.

"I'm wondering, sir, what you think of the colonies after being here for so many months and having had such fascinating experiences here."

Whitefield put his tray on a nightstand, his face animated. "Oh, what a fascinating place these American colonies are! I'm convinced God intends to use them as a beacon to the rest of the darkened world. For all that, my friend, the colonists appear to be asleep to God. The first generation of settlers who came in search of religious freedom and opportunities to evangelize seem to have given way to a people indifferent to our Lord. Then again, this is not true of all the colonies in the same way."

"How do you mean?" Henry leaned back in his chair.

"You may be pleased to know I believe Pennsylvania is the garden of America. People work hard and complain little. What is best, I believe they have the Lord for their God, something I infer from having so many faithful ministers among them—you and dear Mr. Tennent are examples, as well as our departed friend, Mr. Harrison."

Seeing his birthplace for the first time from someone else's perspective, Henry liked the image.

"I haven't seen the work of conversion carried on with so much power in any other part of America. I like Pennsylvania so well that, God willing, I hope to take up some land to erect a school for Negroes there. I'd also like to settle some of my English friends, whose hearts God will either stir, or the fury of their enemies shall oblige them to depart from their native land." He smiled somewhat grimly. "Your city of Philadelphia is well named—a place of brotherly love, for by its charter all are permitted to worship God their own way, without being branded as schismatics, dissenters, or disturbers. I saw much less of the pride of life in Pennsylvania than elsewhere, my dear friend."

"I'm pleased to hear you say these things about my home," Henry said.

"Yes, but I'm disturbed my own Church of England isn't as strong as it should be."

After a moment Henry asked, "What of the other places you've been?"

"Let me see … I wasn't in New York very long, but some of its more serious inhabitants told me a work of God had never been carried on there since its first settlement. The heads of the Church of England seem resolved to shut out the Kingdom of God from amongst them, but our Lord Jesus has been pleased to get himself the victory. I was mostly opposed there, but since then I have heard much good has been done in a short period of time."

"I'm guessing you're encouraged then?"

"To be sure!" Whitefield put his right forefinger to his lower lip. "Let me see … in Maryland, I believe religion is at a particularly low ebb. There are a number of Church of England ministers and were they found more faithful, the colony would certainly flourish. I believe the situation in Virginia is a little further along because the ministers have better leadership there, but I find almost all are quite settled upon their lees. I think the main cause of irreligion in both Virginia and Maryland is the lack of incorporation of their towns."

"How so?"

"People live at such a distance from the churches, they're more apt to make every little thing serve as an excuse to keep them from public worship. While such remains the case, religious societies can't well be settled, and without control, wicked men may more easily revel and get drunk. Ministers have a harder time visiting from house to house, and schools for the education of children can't be so conveniently erected when the houses are so far apart."

Henry gazed out the window. "What about North Carolina?"

"Ah, sadly there's scarcely so much as the form of religion there. They started two churches a while back, but neither is finished, although there are several dancing masters. The situation grieves me."

"I remember the town we visited in South Carolina on New Year's Eve." Whitefield gave a small laugh and shook his head. "I believe the people of the house we stayed at wished we hadn't come on the very night they met together with neighbors to divert themselves with their country dances."

Henry grinned. "You told one woman how well pleased the devil was at her every step."

"She and her companions had so many arguments to support their wantonness and to prove me wrong! Oh, Mr. Sharp, their attitude made me look back upon my own past follies with shame, for I was just like them. I pray to God he'll draw them away from feeding upon such husks and know instead what it is to feast upon the fatted calf." He gave a low huff. "For now, I hear no stirring among the dry bones. As for Georgia, at least there's strict outward discipline of the Church here, although many of the inhabitants have left the fellowship since I was here last. I hope all who remain will acquaint themselves with God and be at peace with him."

Henry sat silently, listening to his own thoughts intertwine with the children's laughter outside. "Many souls have come to our Savior through your ministry, Mr. Whitefield," he said after some minutes. "I can't help but rejoice greatly."

"Praise and thanks be to God!"

"As for your influence on my life, well, let me just say our Lord Jesus Christ has impressed upon me the importance of single-minded living for him. I've known such joy in my soul as a result. Like you, I want to be poured out as a thank offering to him."

Whitefield reached across the gap between them and gripped Henry's hand. "And so you shall be, my friend. He's given you fine gifts of the Spirit and a passion for the Church. The people you'll minister to will be blessed indeed." He laughed, then sighed. "I wish I were able to do the work of two or even three men, there's just so much to be done."

"I believe, Mr. Whitefield, you already do."

CHAPTER TWENTY-SIX

"I want to know who put those windows up!"

Margaret lifted her hands. "Not I, sister."

"Well, Mother likes them down, and so do I. This room is freezing." Catherine flew to the offending windows and jerked them down.

Lena entered wearing a shawl and a happy expression which quickly went south when she heard Catherine's tirade. "You dislike the fresh air, Miss Catherine?"

"Right now, I do."

"Let me help you." The servant hurried to close the remaining open windows. "I put them up, but I meant no harm. You've always enjoyed a nice breeze when the weather starts to turn."

"A nice breeze, yes, not a typhoon, Lena."

"I am sorry."

She skidded to a stop. "As am I."

Margaret's brightness had not been impeded. "Today feels so like spring."

"Just think, Miss Catherine, in two weeks you'll be a married lady," Lena added. She didn't hear her mistress's sigh. "I just came from the dressmaker, and your frock is ready now. You can go for the final fitting any time."

"Thank you, Lena." Catherine plodded toward the stairs.

"Uh, I thought you might want to go now."

"Maybe later."

Lena and Margaret looked at each other. "She's probably having jitters," the older woman whispered. "Brides often do."

Catherine went to her father's empty room—her mother had remained in the other bedroom since his death—and stood in the doorway, picturing him lying there. If only she hadn't had the same dream again, the one she'd had at least twice a week for a month now. Without variation, she was always sitting in church while her father preached, his presence and voice robust, the way he'd been before sickness came. Then he suddenly disappeared, and Henry Sharp was at the front of the church by the communion table. He gazed at Catherine and smiled as if he wanted her to come to him, expected her to come. She would begin walking toward him but never get closer. The more she walked, the further away he was. Then she'd wake up.

The first time she had the dream, Catherine wept into her pillow. The second time, she wondered why in the world she should have the same dream. After several repeat performances, her pillow took the brunt of her aggravation. That her father came to her at night was one thing. Having Henry Sharp invade her sleep was entirely another.

Maybe she did have pre-wedding jitters after all. Lena may not have realized Catherine had overheard her remark. Then again, Francis had been acting strangely too. For about the length of time she'd been having the recurring dream, Catherine had found him frequently distracted. She'd ask him a question, and he would fail to respond without being prompted, or he'd simply stare out of the windows, silent as stone, while Catherine knitted. One night, he'd begged off reading Whitefield's sermons, then praying as they'd become accustomed.

"I just feel like being quiet with you tonight," he'd said.

When they'd read a sermon the next night, Francis had the sound of a schoolboy reciting the alphabet, and he'd asked Catherine to pray. She stopped suggesting they read together, and the nightly visits grew quieter when she gave up trying to engage him in conversation.

She wandered into her room, closed the door, and sat on the side of her bed thinking about Francis. *How strange to be pursuing him when he was so clearly the pursuer at first.* Both of them seemed to understand and accept he loved her more intensely, but now she was wondering whether she actually might be more in love with him than he with her. *No, I don't think so. I feel for Francis the same as I ever have, a peaceful fondness.* She considered what might have happened to cause his sullenness and dismissed the idea of nervousness about the wedding as being out of character with his personality. Francis Heath was not the kind of person given to nerves. She decided to seek Eleanor Doran's company, not wanting to cause her mother anxiety or try to explain her feelings to Elizabeth. Her friend was not a deep person.

"So, my dear, what's on your mind today?"

Catherine decided to forego her cheerful façade and tell Eleanor about the dream and Francis's unnerving quietness, hoping her dear friend would overlook the way she'd recently put distance between them. The widow listened with her eyes half closed and her fingertips to her lips, as if she were also praying. Although Catherine was in a muddled state, being here brought a measure of peace.

"Dreaming about a departed loved one is quite common," she said. "This happened to me when Mr. Doran died years ago. To this day, I sometimes see him in my sleep."

"I can understand this, but what disturbs me is, well," she fumbled for words and said in a low voice, "the way Mr. Sharp remains in my mind."

Eleanor inhaled slowly. "And you about to marry someone else."

"What should I do?" Catherine's voice sounded to her like a creaking door.

"Are you in prayer?"

"I think so, but Mrs. Doran, my spirit is dried up. God seems far away. I tell you in confidence the present preaching at our church has left me so spiritually starved I'm frightened. Francis and I used to read Mr. Whitefield's sermons together to encourage one another, but he's stopped wanting to, for what reason I don't know." Her head was so heavy she dropped it into her hands.

The elderly woman labored to get up and walk over to Catherine, putting an arm about her trembling shoulders, her shawl covering them. "Then we will pray now, together, and we'll ask God to draw near, to break through all of this confusion and sorrow, just as you have broken through your reticence and come to me."

Catherine looked up at her. "My reticence?"

"Yes, my dear one. You haven't been yourself with me for many months, and now I recognize you again."

She reached for the woman's wrinkled hand. "I'm so sorry—and so thankful for you."

After they prayed, Eleanor advised Catherine to speak to Francis as soon as she could.

"I will," she said. "This very day if possible."

She went straight home, avoiding the dressmaker's shop.

Catherine was in the kitchen with Lena preparing the midday meal when they heard a knock on the front door. Since the servant's hands were sticky with biscuit dough and her mother and sister had gone to market at Head House Square, Catherine answered. Francis stood on the other side of the threshold wearing misery on his handsome face.

A shock wave pulsed through her. She'd never seen him like this before, as if all the unhappiness he'd ever known had gathered in his eyes.

"Is anyone at home?"

"Just Lena."

"Good. I need to talk to you."

She opened the door to admit him, and he walked past her to the parlor without taking off his cloak or hat or kissing her cheek. They usually sat on the couch, but this time Francis took the chair opposite her. Only then did he seem to realize he still wore the hat, which he removed, working it over in his restless hands.

"Whatever is the matter?" Catherine felt as if she'd just climbed the stairs to the steeple at Christ Church.

Lena came into the doorway. "Good day to you, Mr. Heath! May I offer refreshment?"

"No, thank you," Catherine said. "We would prefer some privacy."

The servant slipped back down the hall.

"I hardly know where or how to begin."

She wondered if she should say something or wait. Being a woman of action, she spoke. "I've been noticing a certain distance."

He looked directly into her eyes. "This is true, and for that, I apologize, my dear."

"I, too, have been restless."

The sudden flashing of his eyes singed her. She decided to be quiet and let Francis speak his mind.

"I have had a great uneasiness of spirit." A vein twitched at the corner of his left eye.

"In what way?"

"When I responded to Mr. Whitefield's call to become an altogether Christian, I didn't fully understand the extent of my wretchedness before our holy God. Reading his sermons and searching the Scriptures with you have shown me what a miserable sinner I've been." He looked at her, then toward the back wall.

"God doesn't require us to be good to know him, just repentant, as you have been. Mr. Whitefield cautions us not to fall for the Devil's lies—that we are either good enough or not good enough for God."

"Yes, yes, I know." Francis waved the air in front of him. "I've had to come to terms with a certain sin from my past, something I've never told anyone before."

Catherine waited for his next words, feeling their future together wobbling.

"The Lord has convicted me I must confess this to you, or I am no kind of man, let alone a Christian."

Her heart was skipping beats. She folded her hands on her lap as a way of maintaining her composure as she waited and prayed for him.

"Years ago, when I was at Yale College, I saw being away from home as an opportunity to free myself from my family's rules and expectations. You might say I was something of a prodigal son." He spoke toward the window. "I studied hard, but I also played hard, and I was well-known at the local taverns. Shortly before graduation, I met a girl in one of them, an indentured servant."

Catherine gripped her hands tighter. Francis took several moments before continuing.

"It's difficult to tell someone as pure as you about a shameful deed." He glanced at her, sighed, looked away again. "I became intimate with her, and not long afterward, she told me she was with child."

Catherine gasped, her hand flying to her mouth.

"I know how hard this must be for you, dearest, but I must tell the whole story, if you can possibly bear me out." She nodded, mute, forcing back tears. "I went to her owner and arranged to buy her freedom, then I married her quietly two months before graduation."

Catherine's stomach roiled. She looked at Francis as if she'd never seen him before.

"My plan was to come home, break the news to my parents, then send for her. When I left New Haven, I gave her money to live and to come to Philadelphia in a month's time." He got up and started pacing. "I arrived back home to find my mother dying and no time to tell her or my father what I'd done. A day later, my dear mother passed away. My father and I were so torn up by grief that we spoke of little else. I didn't know how to tell him I had a wife and a child on the way."

When he said, "a wife," the words struck Catherine like a blow. Francis was becoming less familiar to her by the minute.

He exhaled. "When a month came and went, and she hadn't arrived, I began to worry. Two weeks later, I had a letter from her former owner who told me she'd miscarried and bled to death."

This was too much. She began weeping from emotions she couldn't contain. Francis moved closer, covering her hand, but she felt only a cold chill, unable to stop trembling.

Francis couldn't seem to stop the flow of his story. "I felt the judgment of God upon me, but rather than repent, I buried my shame. I figured no one ever needed to know. I could take up my life as if I'd never violated her." He sighed. "A few weeks ago, the Holy Spirit convicted me of my sin. I've felt very much like King David, pouring out my heart before God, begging his forgiveness."

He looked into her eyes. "Although God has forgiven me, I knew you must be made aware of this, and"—he choked—"given an opportunity to change your mind about our marriage." She felt as cold as if the windows were still open in the heart of a gale. What other surprises might life be holding, what other secrets? She couldn't bring herself to speak.

"I'll go now, Catherine, so you can consider and pray over these things. My deepest wish is for God to have you accept me in spite of this, but I'll honor your wishes, whatever they may be. Know I love you more than life itself, and what grieves me the most in all this is how I've surely wounded and offended you."

Francis started to walk away, but she put a hand on his arm to stop him. "Before you go—what was her name?"

"Jane."

He saw himself to the door. She sat on the couch motionless.

CHAPTER TWENTY-SEVEN

Catherine slipped out of the house at dawn, tripping her way over cobblestones to Eleanor Doran's before she had to face anyone else, before she could face anyone else. Through chattering teeth and a trembling frame, she related what had happened as her elderly mentor listened, still in her dressing gown. After the initial outburst, the woman spoke.

"Mr. Heath's confession is an important landmark in his relationship with Christ." She paused. "His relationship with you is another matter."

Catherine looked up at the ceiling and breathed out. "I have always enjoyed his company and loved him as a dear friend. I didn't agree to marry him because I love him in any romantic sense. I thought when he experienced the new birth, I would love him in such a way, but I don't. Especially now."

Eleanor smiled. "I believe you do have such feelings, but for another."

The words hit their mark. A fresh flood of tears surged down Catherine's cheeks.

"Mr. Heath has given you an opportunity to back out of your agreement to marry him. Tell me, my dear, were it not for these other affections, would you still have him?"

She half wondered what words would come out of her mouth, considered herself pathetic when she finally said, "I believe I would because my mother is so pleased about my impending marriage." She was relieved when her friend failed to comment. "Sometimes, I think God may be giving me a second chance at, well, the person I would most like to be with." Henry Sharp's unspoken name hung in the air, an invisible effigy. A wagon rolled along the street outside. "I don't wish you to think me frivolous. I not only have strong feelings for another because I happen to be full of romantic notions, but because we served God so well together."

"I would never consider you frivolous, my dear."

"I'm afraid, Mrs. Doran."

"Of what, Catherine?"

"What if I'm wrong, and Mr. Sharp doesn't actually share my affections?"

"Is this your only fear?"

"No. How will Francis get along if I ... if I break our engagement. And what about my mother? She's been so peaceful, almost happy again. She and Margaret will be taken care of if I marry him. If I don't, what will happen to them?" She didn't have to add, "Or me."

Eleanor took Catherine's hands and moved each word she spoke to the beat of her heart. "My dear girl, you are a wonderful daughter, but you are not God."

Startled, she pulled back.

"Perhaps, just perhaps, he has other plans for all of you."

After Catherine had a chance to collect her thoughts, Eleanor's next words caused the young woman's temples to throb.

"My dear, I've just had a letter from Henry Sharp which I'd like you to read." She reached over to a small pile of envelopes on her side table and shuffled through them until she found the one from Henry, handing the missive to Catherine, who eagerly pulled out the letter written in his careful hand.

Saturday, March 16, 1740

Dear Mrs. Doran,

Greetings in the Name of our Lord and Savior Jesus Christ! It is my fervent prayer you are well as you partake of the marvelous blessings available to those whom he calls his own. I'm happy to report I am once again healthy after lying sick for several days with a fever my other friends also suffered with here. Three German orphans who came to us in January ministered to me with great tenderness while I was indisposed. They have become dear to me, and I am enjoying teaching them English.

Mr. Whitefield continues to preach to his own congregation here. Every Sunday we celebrate the Lord's Supper, and he leads public prayers and gives sermons twice each day during the week. Last month when he suffered from illness, he still insisted upon preaching, but all of his friends firmly suggested he rest, and I had the privilege to stand in for him. I believe there was more than a little disappointment upon the faces of those who saw me rise to address them instead of their beloved pastor. Nevertheless, they received me kindly. How I love to preach the Word of our Lord! I'm looking forward to leading the flock awaiting me at Bedminster, but for now, I am daily grateful for the opportunity the Lord has given me to see the southern colonies and witness first-hand His mighty works here.

Mr. Whitefield and our "little family" as he calls us have been cheered by letters from Philadelphia, New Jersey, and New York telling us of changed lives in Christ. Even Mr. Franklin is pleasantly astonished by the general feeling of true brotherly concern for neighbors, as well as a worshipful attitude bound up with the things of everyday life, particularly the open singing of hymns and saying of prayers in public places. We've also had a letter from a pastor near Philadelphia, who after hearing Mr. Whitefield's message, became convinced that while he was preaching grace, he had not actually experienced grace in his own life. Oh, I wish all the clergy would know Him as they ought! With ministers alive to the Lord Jesus, more people would experience His saving grace. As for us, we are eager to return to see His wondrous works for ourselves, and to witness what the Holy Spirit will accomplish next.

Catherine lifted her eyes from the page and watched the sun's rays cast a small rainbow on the wood floor. She couldn't help but smile.

In addition to preaching here and in the surrounding area, Mr. Whitefield oversees about thirty workers who've been busy constructing the orphan house and out buildings since the end of January. He is keenly involved in the details and has specified the house be sixty feet long and forty feet wide, have a brick foundation, and be two stories high. He's planning for twenty large rooms to accommodate the staff and children. There will also be two small houses nearby—one for an infirmary, the other, a workhouse. The endeavor is expensive, but he trusts the Lord Jesus to supply all the orphanage's needs according to His glorious riches in Christ Jesus.

We had some sadness a few days ago when one of the women who accompanied Mr. Whitefield and the children from England, and who stayed with you in Philadelphia, died. The orphans sang beautifully at her funeral, Mr. Whitefield preached the sermon, and then he gave an additional word of exhortation at the grave. In spite of the terrible solemnity, the Lord's Word came with power, and we rest assured our friend died in the Lord's grace.

Catherine wondered which of the women she'd met had died and whether she had any family back in England. She didn't wish to linger around the subject of death, however, and continued reading.

> On a happier note, we were all much cheered by the recent arrival of Mr. Whitefield's brother from England. This visit has come at a good time because the Church of England Delegate, who once supported our friend's work, now charges Mr. Whitefield with being an enthusiast full of spiritual pride. He says such things because he objects to Mr. Whitefield's frank assessment about the pitiful state of the clergy here, which has caused many people to be indifferent toward the things of God. Even so, we've seen changes among even some of those once-cold ministers. God has clearly broken through bars of iron that had kept those souls imprisoned and has released them to the light of his life.
>
> Mr. Whitefield and some of those clergy had a sharp disagreement about the many balls and assemblies taking place here when there are not enough pastors to serve the people. Many take exception to this aspect of Mr. Whitefield's teaching, although I understand better now than I did at first. When we allow ourselves to be dazzled and overtaken by anything other than the Lord Jesus Christ, we're in danger of missing his abiding presence in our lives, and so, many have gone to ruin and regret. I believe the Lord wants us to enjoy life, but the only way this can happen is when we live and move and have our being in him.
>
> Through Mr. Whitefield, I've learned daily to follow him more closely and love him with all I am and have, blessed be his Name! I have loved the Lord Jesus since my youth but am now filled with a wonder about him and also find myself looking forward to being with him in heaven.
>
> I hope to be back in Pennsylvania soon, perhaps by this time next month. I look forward to all God has ahead for me to do there. I will miss the orphans terribly, though. Being with them has kindled a longing in me to begin my own family, whenever our Lord sees fit to bless me with a godly wife. I would be the happiest of men to find someone like yourself.

Please remember me to all our dear friends there and forgive me for going on so about myself. If you can, perhaps you'll write and give me all the news of yourself and my beloved friends in Philadelphia. I pray for you, and them, daily.

Your obedient servant,

Henry Sharp

After enduring an awkward conversation with her mother over wedding preparations, Catherine spoke to Francis alone in the candlelit parlor. She felt certain his teeth must have been on edge the whole time Ann Harrison prattled, but Catherine admired his demonstration of patience. He looked so handsome in profile, handsome and vulnerable.

"That was difficult," she said after her mother retired.

"I've had more peaceful evenings."

She got straight to the point. "I've made a decision, Francis." She watched his face as he nodded, folding and unfolding his hands. "I also have kept something to myself I believe you should know."

Her fiancé cocked his head. "You have?"

"While I don't have a past, there is a present."

"I don't understand."

Bubbles of anxiety gathered in her shoulders and stomach. She prayed the words wouldn't come out wrong. "First, I'm exceedingly fond of you and want you to know your confession hasn't changed my affections."

He looked down and whispered, "Thank you."

"I think you showed a lot of courage to tell me what happened long ago and how God is working in your spirit. If anything, I admire you more than before you told me." She was shaking again but pushed on, resolute. "My own confession is there's someone dearer to me even than yourself, someone I thought I might be able to forget. I think God may be giving me an opportunity to find out if my affections are returned." She raised her hands and let them fall gently into her lap.

Francis looked away for a few seconds, then into her amber eyes. "Henry Sharp."

She flinched.

"I think I've always known of the feelings you shared for one another, but I purposely blinded myself because I have loved you so very much." He sighed. "Mr. Sharp is a gentleman and a fine man of God."

Catherine began crying softly, and he moved closer, putting his arm around her shoulders.

"Here is what I suggest, my dear. He'll be returning soon. When he does, you must find out whether or not God means you for each other."

She dabbed at her tears. "I can't be certain he feels as I do."

Francis smiled. "I don't believe you need to worry along those lines, Catherine. Even if he does turn you away, I'll gladly take you for my wife, if you'll have me."

She closed her eyes and smiled. "You're a prince among men."

"I'm a man who loves you, and therefore, wants what's best for you."

They agreed to share what had happened only with her mother and his father, and to continue seeing each other as friends in order to protect their mutual confidences until the situation could be settled. Catherine hoped for a quick resolution.

She spoke to her mother the next morning after Margaret had gone off to school and Lena to the market. Her stomach wrenched as her mother's tranquil expression transformed into the anguished mien she'd worn throughout Joseph's final illness. Nevertheless, she clung to her belief somehow, some way, God would provide her mother's deepest needs. In spite of Ann's obvious distress, Catherine maintained a core of peace, a place guarded by God where no anguish could penetrate.

In the evening, she sat in the parlor absently knitting while her mother darned socks and Margaret read her primer. There was little conversation, each keeping to her own thoughts. Catherine's revolved around George Whitefield's return trip and seeing Henry again—would he be much changed by the excursion—and how might they approach the subject of her availability? She considered what she would tell him about her suspended engagement to Francis and imagined how Henry would respond. She was picturing his face when a knock at the front door brought her back to the present. She rose and placed her knitting on the chair. When she opened the door, Catherine's eyes opened wider at the sight of Francis and his father, who seemed taller than usual— and not exactly friendly.

"Good evening, Magistrate. Please come in." They passed by her, and she tried unsuccessfully to make eye contact with Francis. "May I have your cloaks?"

Wordlessly, they removed their outer garments. She took them and hung them up, then led them into the parlor. Her mother quickly laid aside the socks she'd been mending.

"Good evening, gentlemen."

Catherine admired the way she was keeping her cool.

The men muttered greetings as they entered the room and sat on the couch opposite the ladies.

"Good evening, Magistrate," Margaret said, her face shining with happiness. "I wondered why you hadn't come tonight, Mr. Heath. I was missing you." In her innocence, the little girl's words contrasted with the overall demeanor of their guests. Francis offered a weak smile but said nothing.

"Margaret, my dear, run to the back of the house and see if Lena will prepare tea for us."

"Yes, Mama."

After the little girl left, Edward took charge, addressing Catherine's mother. "I've come to discuss the engagement."

Although the familiar joviality they'd enjoyed in the past few months was lacking, Catherine was glad her mother didn't try to offer explanations or excuses. A glance at Francis told her he, too, was uncertain about his father's intentions. *Dear Jesus, please be with us, and may we glorify you no matter what happens.*

"My son has made a full confession to me of what happened many years ago," he began. "I'm pleased his religious renewal has enabled him to come to terms with such an unhappy episode." He didn't look pleased though. Following a heavy silence, Edward slapped his hands to his knees, startling the others. "I have long been of the opinion there should be a marriage between the Heaths and the Harrisons. Therefore, I have come with my son tonight to see that my wishes are fulfilled."

Catherine gasped at his determination, qualities he no doubt employed in the court room but which he'd never displayed to her and her family. He may have been an important man, but something inside her rose to fight. Her mother's mouth had fallen open, but Edward spoke first.

"Ann Harrison, will you do me the honor of becoming my wife?"

CHAPTER TWENTY-EIGHT

Henry leaned over and seeing the closed eyes and slow, steady rise and fall of his chest, concluded his friend Whitefield was asleep. He set a bowl of hot chicken soup on the table next to the cot and was about to leave the room when the minister stirred. "Is that you, Mr. Sharp?" His powerful voice had been reduced to a whisper.

"Yes, Mr. Whitefield. How are you feeling?"

He pushed himself up on his hands and arranged his thin frame against an object doing a poor imitation of a pillow. "My head pounds less."

"I brought you something to eat." Henry handed the bowl to his companion.

"Thank you." He bowed his head and prayed aloud in a mere croak. "We thank Thee, Lord Jesus Christ, for thy bountiful blessings, especially nourishment for our souls, as well as our bodies. I am grateful for Thy provision, and I thank Thee mightily for my little family. Praise and thanks be to Thee, O God. Amen."

"Amen. Would you like me to stay with you?" The ship pitched underneath his feet, and Henry planted them more firmly under his big frame. At the midpoint of their journey to Philadelphia, he had, at last, developed sea legs.

"Please do, my friend. I desire your company." Henry pulled up the only chair in their cramped cabin. "I've been wrestling spiritually, Mr. Sharp."

In the time he'd come to know the English pastor, Henry had developed an appreciation for the man's honesty. Like Nathaniel in the New Testament, there was no guile in him.

"I always have difficulty leaving my flock in Savannah. I love them so, especially my dear orphans. Like a father, I'm always concerned for their welfare and pray especially the Evil One won't have his terrible way with them." He paused, took a sip from the bowl, and continued, his voice beginning to clear through the muck of a severe sore throat. "You drew close to them as well."

"I've developed an attachment to some in particular. I agree with you—leaving them is wrenching."

"What dear urchins they are! Many have put their faith in Jesus Christ, along with several in the colony." His face shone, not just from fever. "Oh, when they tell me of their changed lives ... I cannot wait to see what our Lord will continue doing in Philadelphia and the northern colonies." Losing his voice again, he paused to eat, and continued. "This brings me to touch upon an important matter with you."

"Yes?"

"You plan to shepherd a flock in Bucks County." Henry nodded. "I don't blame you for wanting to settle down. The life I lead is not for everyone." The two men laughed. "Nevertheless, may I dare you to consider, after spending time at home, joining me in New England?"

Henry felt confused by what seemed like an embarrassment of riches. "I ... I don't quite know what to say, Mr. Whitefield."

"Just tuck the idea away for now and pray on it. Oh, Mr. Sharp, the fields are white unto harvest!" In his excitement, Whitefield sloshed a fair amount of soup onto the bed covers and began sopping up the mess with his napkin, laughing over his clumsiness.

Henry smiled as well, although his recurring thought of seeing Catherine Harrison married to Francis Heath, like a thief, stole his joy.

"Mr. Tennent!" Catherine exclaimed when she saw the pastor at her front door. "Oh, do come in. How wonderful to see you again!"

"I'm happy to see you too, my dear." The pastor with his full head of white hair entered the hallway, spilling his native Irish brogue as well as droplets of rain. "I am heartily sorry to be watering your floor in such a fashion."

"You may water my home any time." She reached for his hat and cloak. "Are you alone?"

"Mrs. Tennent is at the market and will soon join me."

"My mother is there as well." She led him into the parlor where they sat by the fireplace.

"Ah, the warmth feels good. While I love early spring, the days can still get mighty chilly."

"I'll be right back. Our Lena is in the kitchen, and I'll have her prepare tea. Please, make yourself at home."

She was gone and back in less than a minute, feeling her face break into a huge grin. This man provided a happy connection with her father, as well as to dear Henry Sharp. She sat across from him. "So, what brings you to town?"

"We're on our way to visit our son Charles, who pastors a church in Delaware." He leaned forward and spoke in a confidential whisper. "I'm also hoping to see Mr. Whitefield as he makes his way northward, so impatient am I to hear him again."

Her voice caught in her throat. "Do you know when he will arrive?"

He shook his head. "I received a brief letter from Mr. Sharp a week ago in which he said they were on their way back—sailing—which, of course, is much quicker than riding."

At the mention of Henry's name, her hands shook.

"So, my dear, I see you have not wed Mr., uh, what's his name? The magistrate's son, I believe. When is the wedding, anyway?"

"Francis Heath." She took a deep breath before offering more information. "We recently called off the wedding, but very few people know."

He cocked his head, concern written in the lines on his face. "Would you care to tell me more?"

Warming to his fatherly concern, she told the story, concluding with her mother's surprise engagement to the magistrate. She trusted William Tennent to maintain discretion about everything she'd shared. He sat for a few moments, tapping his fingers on his lap. Then his face brightened. "Would you like to accompany my wife and me to Delaware? Perhaps, away from Philadelphia, you might find the necessary privacy to see Mr. Sharp and discover what our Lord may have in mind."

Possibilities flashed through her mind, sparking a new light in her eyes. "Thank you, Mr. Tennent. I would love to."

"Mr. Grafton, please accept my gratitude for taking on my little family and me once again," Whitefield said, entering the familiar abode.

"Believe me, we enjoy serving you." The tall, stooped man led the party into his home. "So, have you had your breakfast yet?"

While Henry didn't wish to put out the kind man or his wife, his stomach rumbled at the thought of a home-cooked meal after being on ship's provisions for ten days. He was relieved to the core when Whitefield said, "In all honesty, we have had quite a small meal."

"Then you must allow me to fix something hot and nourishing." Mrs. Grafton flew into action at once as the men settled in their parlor and began speaking of God's activity in Newcastle since Whitefield's departure in the late fall.

"I've seen notorious drinkers forsake their cups in order to follow Christ," Grafton said. "Then they go out and tell others about him, and so it goes. Their family and friends begin to listen, and before you know it, their lives have been turned right side up."

"This is very good." Whitefield broke into a smile.

"Many who've considered themselves to be Christians have come to understand they haven't known the Master at all. Then they are saved." He slapped his knees with his hands.

Henry's whole being swelled with joy to hear of these things.

"Tell me, Mr. Grafton, how is Mr. Hamilton?"

"He has preached the gospel faithfully, Mr. Whitefield. I think even he is surprised at the work of the Lord in our midst." He paused. "I regret to say, however, he's indisposed. Nothing serious, mind you, but he took to his bed three days ago, and to my knowledge, won't be able to preach this morning."

"Then I must preach for him!" Whitefield exclaimed. "I'll go to him just as soon as we have enjoyed your wife's fine cooking."

The morning service was three-quarters full, but once word spread about Whitefield being back, people packed the church cheek-by-jowl in the afternoon. Henry sat along with the choir in the area behind the pulpit, freeing up space in the regular pews. This also gave him the opportunity to lend his voice to the tenors. Buoyed by the warm reception and news of God's work in Pennsylvania, Whitefield preached with even more power and energy than before, his voice once again a force of nature. Toward the middle of the sermon, Henry's gaze wandered among the pews, until he noticed an elderly man with gleaming white hair. *He reminds me of dear Mr. Tennent.* Then he did a double-take—this *was* dear Mr. Tennent and sitting beside him, Mrs. Tennent. Just behind them sat their youngest son, Charles, whom Henry knew pastored a church in Delaware. William Tennent caught his eye, and the men smiled at each other, the elder looking particularly pleased, Henry thought. He wondered who the woman sitting on his other side was, trying to discern her identity under a ruffled sort of bonnet. A moment later, she looked up and made eye contact with him.

Catherine Harrison! His heart thudded. *Or is it Catherine Heath? What is she doing here, and where is Francis?* He returned her smile, detecting a flush in her cheeks. Although normally he could listen to George Whitefield for hours on end, he suddenly felt impatient for the service to be over. When the pastor finally closed with a prayer and a benediction forty minutes later, Henry hurried to the pews where he greeted his friends with much back slapping and embracing.

"Welcome back, Henry!" William was shouting above the din. "How we've missed you!"

"Welcome, my dear," his wife said, hugging Henry as if he were her son.

Charles shook his hand. "It's good to see you again, Sharp,"

"Same here." Henry struggled to be civil, to focus on what they were saying—something about William and Mrs. Tennent visiting their son, and Charles bringing half of his church to hear Whitefield. Yes, yes, how nice. What he really wanted was to see Catherine. And suddenly there she was, pushing gently through the crowd, smiling at him, causing droplets of sweat to break out on his brow at the very sight of those amber eyes framed by a mob of hair under her spring bonnet. She'd grown even lovelier since November, but maybe marriage had done this to her.

"Miss Harrison." He almost choked on her name. "Uh, I mean, Mrs. Heath."

She frowned and laughed nervously. "Mr. Sharp. I'm so very happy to see you."

"Yes, I am. Uh, I mean, I'm glad to see you as well." The sound of conversation humming like locusts died away. There was only her. "Where is Mr. Heath?"

"In Philadelphia," she said, looking as if something inside was bursting to break out of her, but holding back like the lady she was.

"He is not unwell, then?"

"He is quite well."

Henry's blonde brow puckered. "He is quite well?" he said, flustered.

Charles broke into the conversation, gesturing as if he were on a stage. "Ah, Father and Mother! There are so many of my flock I want you to meet. Come over, Mr. Thorp! This is my good mother, Catherine Tennent."

Henry watched Charles divert his parents and congregants, enabling Henry to focus on Miss Harrison, or rather, Mrs. Heath. "I would love some fresh air. Would you like to accompany me outside?" He gingerly offered his arm, and his heart hammered at her touch.

"Yes, I would as well."

He guided her through the crowd into the brilliant afternoon of the early spring day, robins crooning in the church courtyard's chestnut trees. While Henry had grown fond of the mellow Georgia weather, seeing his home region in the resplendent throes of a world skipping back to life after the dead of winter, he felt happy—almost.

"I'm delighted to see you."

"And I'm delighted to welcome you back," she said.

He could listen to her lilting voice forever.

"I trust you had a pleasant journey."

He nodded. "Yes, thank you." Gone were memories of seasickness.

"And your sojourn in the southern colonies, well, I'm sure you have many stories to tell. Your letters were so full of adventures, and of many lives changed by our Lord Jesus."

The full exposure of her face paralyzed him. Finally, he found his voice. "I imagine I'll be telling stories for years to come." He paused. Did he dare? "I'm curious—why isn't Mr. Heath with you?"

She raised her eyebrows and sighed. "Our engagement is on hold."

He squinted, unable to believe at first what he'd heard. "On hold?"

"Yes, Mr. Sharp. Because of his deepening relationship with the Lord Jesus, he confessed something he did long ago at Yale. While this alone would not cause me to sever our engagement, I also had a confession to make."

Could his heart pound any harder and not pop right out of his chest, he wondered? "May I ask about the nature of this confession?"

She nodded. "I'm terribly fond of Mr. Heath and always have been, but you see, I love someone else."

"You love someone else." He once again repeated her words, dumb as a doorpost.

"I'm hoping to find out soon whether my affections are returned." She offered him a mixed expression of coyness, forthrightness, and fear.

He was surprised to find himself suddenly lighthearted, as if the weight of Atlas had been lifted from his shoulders. He shifted his weight onto his right foot. "How do you expect to get your answer?"

"I suppose by telling this story."

They seemed to have reached an impasse, and he needed to say something, even if not particularly clever. *God, help me.* He took the icy plunge. "Please know, Miss Harrison, as sure as I'm standing before you, I have such affections for you."

Her eyes pooled with tears. "Then, Mr. Sharp, my cup overflows."

"Catherine."

"Henry."

They embraced just as the Tennents reappeared in the courtyard, the old man breaking into an uncontrollable grin.

CHAPTER TWENTY-NINE

She stood in the Heath's parlor in twilight's last glow letting Francis down as gently as she knew how. After she'd somehow managed to say what needed to be said, he took the news like the man he was. Catherine stood and went to the door with a relieved weightlessness, accompanied by sadness for disappointing Francis. Before she stepped outside, his hand reached for her arm. "One thing more. I'd like you to keep the dress—that is, if you want to."

Tears stung her eyes. "How very kind of you."

His smile was soothing, his brown eyes tender. "The dress was meant for you, and you were meant for another."

She glanced around the room and gave a wry laugh. "My decorating handiwork will remain with you, however."

"I stand to correct you, my dear. This place bears not only your stamp, but your mother's, who will soon become my stepmother." He grinned. "So there, stepsister."

She laughed, a little louder than necessary.

After a brief silence, he asked, "Have you set the date, then?"

Catherine noticed Mrs. Clydesdale peering around the corner, then disappear when she was discovered. "We have. We'll be married on April 23rd in Warminster."

She and Henry had chosen to get married at Neshaminy Presbyterian Church for a few reasons—they didn't want Andrew Oldfield to officiate, and asking William Tennent or George Whitefield to do the ceremony at High Street instead of the supply pastor could prove sticky. In addition, they didn't wish to cause Francis further discomfort by getting married in his back yard. Francis seemed to understand, and he bowed. "You are very kind."

Catherine surprised herself by taking hold of his hands. "As are you. I pray at the right time, in God's wonderful way, he'll bless you with a woman who will bring you every possible happiness."

On April 23rd, she didn't attend Whitefield's preaching in the church courtyard, but nearly five thousand other people did. Nor did she discover until the next day he'd been so sick that morning, he'd considered not speaking. Instead, she had toiled in her snug new home on the Sharp farmstead, arranging her belongings. Her mother held up an exquisitely carved object. "I assume you'd like this above the fireplace?"

"Yes, Mother. Wasn't Francis terribly kind to give us the clock?" She looked at her slender mother, then glanced at Mrs. Sharp. Everyone seemed to be getting along well, including Margaret and Henry's sister Sarah, who'd immediately bonded over their dolls and lacework. Henry's father, grandfather, and brothers had earlier showed Jacob and Edward Heath around the farmstead's grounds and buildings, the men engrossed in companionable conversation about business, the provincial government, blacksmithing, and farming. Lena and Katarina also worked harmoniously as they prepared the wedding feast.

At five o'clock, Lena entered the cottage with bread and cheese while Ann struggled to untangle her daughter's unruly waves. "You need to eat something before the ceremony, Miss Catherine."

"Oh, Lena, I couldn't." Her stomach was already so full, of butterflies.

"You don't want to go fainting in front of your intended."

Elizabeth nodded. "She's right, you know."

With such a terrible image planted in her mind, Catherine accepted two small pieces of bread and cheese and began nibbling without tasting the food. "Oh, Mother, this hair is the bane of my existence!"

"*Deine Haare sind so hübsch.*"

"I beg your pardon, Mrs. Sharp?"

"I beg *your* pardon. I think your hair is pretty. And, please, do call me Mama." She aimed a furtive glance at Ann. "This is all right?"

Ann smiled in return. "By all means, Mrs. Sharp."

Catherine grinned at the woman. "*Danke*, Mama."

"You are the German already!"

Everyone laughed, relieving some of Catherine's twitchiness. An hour later, her sister and Sarah entered the little house shining from their shoes to their gleaming hair, the product of Catherine Tennent's attention.

"Are you ready?" the minister's wife asked.

Catherine stood and adjusted her dress. "Yes."

"You look lovely, my dear." The elderly woman's face shone with admiration.

The carriage ride from the farm to the church led past the Little Neshaminy Creek. Catherine imbibed the pungent, but pleasant, scent of the soil, admiring the trees and meadow flowers on their way toward full blossom. Early evening birdsong accompanied them to the church.

"What a glorious day!" Elizabeth exclaimed. "I never expected to like the country as much as I do."

"You must visit me whenever you can," Catherine said. She began quoting from the Song of Solomon. "For, lo, the winter is past, the rain is over and gone; the flowers appear on the earth; the time of the singing of birds has come." She thought, but didn't say, *Arise my love, my fair one, and come away.* The thought of her and Henry about to become one flesh filled her with a warming glow.

The church was full when Catherine arrived, and at first, she felt distracted by all the well-wishers, many whom she'd never seen before, figuring they must be members. When she went to Henry at the altar, however, everyone else faded. Even Mr. Tennent's short wedding sermon failed to hold her attention. She'd never seen Henry look so handsome, dressed in a dark blue coat, waistcoat, and breeches, with a perfectly starched white shirt. His blonde hair was pulled back into a neat queue. Not until George Whitefield began the exchanging of the vows was she able to concentrate on anyone else. Judging from the intense look in Henry's blue eyes, he was feeling the same. The winter was, indeed, past.

Before they received well-wishers outside in the courtyard, Whitefield took them aside for a private word, which wasn't easily accomplished with people clamoring to either wish the newlyweds God's blessings or converse with the famous evangelist. William Seward and John Syms engaged a few of the latter in small talk so Whitefield could have a private moment.

He grasped their hands in his. "I want to wish you the richest of God's blessings."

"Oh, Mr. Whitefield, the ceremony was lovely. Thank you for doing the vows for us."

"Yes, thank you, my friend." Henry added, "You seem to be preparing to leave."

He nodded. "I won't be staying for the meal."

"But why?" Catherine asked.

"I'm afraid my presence might be disruptive. The two of you should be the center of attention this evening." He smiled sheepishly. "I tend to be the bride at every wedding and the corpse at every funeral." They shared a good laugh. "To apprise you of my plans, I'll be going to New Jersey and New York for a brief preaching tour, then heading back to Savannah where I hope to remain for the summer. Come September, I'll travel on my sloop to New England where I hope to meet Jonathan Edwards. All of this, of course, is dependent upon the will of the Lord." He looked from one to the other. "Have the two of you discussed coming with me to New England?"

"Indeed we have," Henry said. "This spring and summer, we'll be helping my parents on the farm while ministering to the people in Bedminster. In September, we'll visit Mr. Gilbert Tennent on the way up to join you. I'll be talking with him about transferring to his presbytery, so I can be ordained."

Whitefield nodded. "I'm confident this will meet with success. I'm so very glad you'll be coming with me, especially since Mr. Seward will be returning to England soon." He looked at Catherine. "I'm so pleased my dear friend has chosen a wife who desires to share in his work. I hope to be blessed in such a way myself before long."

Catherine spoke her surprise. "Mr. Whitefield! Do you have a prospect of marriage?"

"No, my dear. I know, however, when my Lord arranges a bride for me, I'll be ready."

The crowd began pressing toward Whitefield, having grown tired of Seward and Syms. Glancing over his shoulder for a moment, he addressed the couple one last time. "I look forward to seeing you both again soon." He looked at Catherine. "Unless, of course, you have other considerations by then." Henry chortled when Whitefield winked at her, and her face flushed. "I wish you Godspeed. Count on my prayers."

The day before Catherine's family and friends left for Philadelphia, her mother came to her outside where the young bride sat on the bank of the barn taking in birdsong and the bleating of sheep. Ann sat beside her, radiant with health and hope. "How is my married daughter?"

Catherine's smile mingled with the sunshine. "Oh, Mother, how happy God has made me!"

Ann patted her arm. "Henry Sharp is a fine man—I've come to love him dearly." She was quiet for a few moments. "You and Father were right about him. I hope you don't bear any resentment over the way I once treated him."

"I never think about those things, Mother."

"Thank you." She paused. "He certainly comes from a good family." She leaned closer and lowered her voice. "I can't understand half of what they say, but I like them very much."

"Neither can I, but Henry has promised to teach me German, and I'm eager to learn."

"Perhaps Mrs. Sharp can teach you something about their cuisine—I find their food delicious."

She sighed. "I do too, but I must be careful not to overindulge."

They were silent for a few minutes.

"My dear, I have something to ask of you and Henry." Ann twisted her fingers, reminding Catherine of days past when her mother had been anguished over her father's health. Maybe she would give up the old habit in time. "Mr. Tennent spoke with Edward and me at length about something last night."

Catherine was still getting used to hearing her mother refer to the magistrate by his first name.

Ann continued, haltingly. "We would like to be married here—tonight if possible—by Mr. Tennent."

Catherine sprang to her feet. "Why, Mother, what a wonderful idea!"

She clasped her hand to her breast. "Oh, I'm so relieved. So, you really are fine with me marrying Edward?"

"Of course, Mother. Why wouldn't I be?"

Ann looked down. "Well, the very fact of him, I mean, after your father and all."

"I think Father would be happy—he had a high regard for Mr. Heath." She smiled. "I'll need to get used to calling him Father Heath." After a pause, "I think having the ceremony here will be a good thing. Somehow, I can't picture you marrying at High Street."

"Indeed. We'd like to exchange our vows at the Tennent's, and Mrs. Tennent said she would have a reception for us there."

"What do Margaret and Jacob think?"

"Jacob is pleased, you know how easygoing he is. Margaret is mostly happy. She adores Edward and Francis, of course. Still, she misses her father, though, and is sad about leaving the manse."

"I suppose Mr. Oldfield will be moving in."

"Perhaps not. As you know, there's been no little displeasure with his preaching, and I have a feeling the session might not call him to be our permanent minister."

Catherine held back on sharing her full opinion. "I'm going to pray for the presbytery to be open to a man who truly knows Jesus Christ."

A look at her mother told her Ann was beginning to understand. "Well, then, I must tell Henry! And my in-laws. And Elizabeth! We have a lot to do, Mother!"

September 2, 1740

Dear Mrs. Doran,

It is my fervent wish that this letter finds you well again. Elizabeth Worthington tells me you have been infirm for several weeks, and I have been praying for your recovery. You've often told me the Lord is close to those who suffer, and I trust you have known Him intimately on your sickbed.

Life at the Sharp farmstead goes well for my family and me. Daily, I thank God for my husband, who is the fulfillment of many girlish dreams. To have a steady man of God as my spouse is a source of great joy, and I have come to love his family as my own. I've learned a good deal of German, and Mrs. Sharp has taught me how to make sauerkraut, chow-chow, apple butter, and the lightest dumplings and noodles imaginable. Needless to say, this pleases my husband!

Henry has been busy assisting his father and brothers on the farm and at the blacksmith shop they operate. On most Saturdays, I accompany him on horseback to Bedminster, which is a little less than twenty miles away. We stay with Mr. Fretz and his family, who are kind and considerate of us. In the morning, Henry preaches in the open when the weather is good and in Mr. Fretz's barn when it is not. Normally, a hundred or so people gather, although at times, we've counted twice that many. There are hungry hearts here, eager for the meat of God's Word, and Henry feeds them well. In just the past three weeks, upwards of a dozen people have repented of their sins and received Jesus Christ! Henry and those dear people pray the day will soon come when they can afford to build a church, and we can live nearby. Then there can be at least two services on Sunday, and they will always have their pastor at hand.

Correspondence between Henry and Mr. Gilbert Tennent indicates the New Brunswick Presbytery will ordain him to the ministry of the Word and Sacrament. How much we look forward to the day! Perhaps the ordination might happen soon, when we travel to join Mr. Whitefield. More about that later ...

She sat quietly for a long moment, considering whether to add the part about Henry not being paid most of the time for preaching, or at least being paid very little. She tried not to fuss, but her spirit rebelled when those who came to hear him took so much, without giving back when Mr. Fretz passed around the weekly collection. He often mentioned how sorry he was not to be providing a living wage, and she wondered what would happen when they actually started serving the church full time. Surely then, she hoped, they would have a more formal agreement about wages. For now, she decided not to say anything to Mrs. Doran.

I am so glad my mother visits you often. She is content now, as a wife in a stable home. Although we both miss my father, we believe he would have wanted us to follow our Lord to our present situations. I know he would be especially pleased about my marriage to Henry!

Elizabeth tells me Mr. Oldfield will be pastoring a church in Delaware soon. I have reason to believe he will ask her to become his bride. I know she hopes so. While I'm happy she has found someone, I pray most of all the two of them will come to know Christ intimately, and Mr. Oldfield will become a living conduit of God's Word. I'm eager for my father's place to be filled by someone like he was, who knew Jesus and loved His people. I often pray for this.

As for Mr. Whitefield, he has written us of his ministry throughout the southern colonies, telling us of dramatic instances of entire congregations weeping before the Lord in repentance, then receiving His grace with gladness. Henry regales me with stories of his travels with Mr. Whitefield and the amazing work of the Holy Spirit through this humble man, who frequently struggles with illness. We are very much looking forward to joining him soon in New England. For a while, last month, I thought Henry might need to go without me, but I was mistaken and will be able to go after all. I very much look forward to the day when I'll become a mother, but I also am happy for the opportunity to be part of God's incredible movement through the colonies, by means of His servant. I will write again, updating you on our ministry and always, I keep you in my heart, in prayer.

Love from your obedient servant,

Catherine Harrison Sharp

CHAPTER THIRTY

Henry glanced sideways at his wife's profile as their cart bumped along what passed for roads in central New Jersey. "How are you faring, dear one?"

"I'm we-u-ll!" Her voice hiccoughed, and she held on to her hat when the vehicle struck a pot hole. "I'm excited to be seeing a different colony."

"Aren't you glad we took the cart?"

She laughed. "Yes, husband, you were right after all."

Originally, Catherine wanted to ride on horseback to meet Whitefield in Rhode Island, but Henry suggested a horse-drawn carriage would be more in order for such a distance. He could get one of the Log College students to drive for them, a young man who'd jump at the chance to see the burgeoning revivals firsthand. His bride, however, insisted she'd be fine on a horse.

He didn't want to insult her intelligence, but he knew the grueling conditions such a journey would present. Catherine had grown up in the city and wasn't used to primitive travel. When she relented, he was greatly relieved.

They'd set off from Warminster at dawn to traverse across Bucks County to the Delaware River where they hired a ferry to New Jersey. From there, they went another twenty miles before the sun flung vivid streaks of azure and scarlet across the western sky. Henry had guessed correctly they wouldn't make New Brunswick in one day and would need to stay at an inn or a friendly household.

The following day they'd set out early for Gilbert Tennent's home in the northeastern part of the colony, where a committee of the New Brunswick Presbytery would examine Henry, and if they found him satisfactory, ordain him then and there. In a letter, William Tennent's oldest son had assured Henry his papers all appeared to be in order and no problems were anticipated.

Next, he and Catherine would travel to Rhode Island where they'd join George Whitefield. Henry tried not to think about all the things that could go wrong on the trip, focusing instead on his bride and the excitement of all God had planned for them to do.

A few miles later along the jarring road, they spotted a red brick tavern, and Henry offered a silent prayer for their first night on the road to be peaceful—not all such places were desirable. He saw the look of happy anticipation on Catherine's face, and his heart filled with gratitude over the blessing of such an amiable companion. Henry hopped off the cart and hitched their horse to a post before helping her down.

The front door of the tavern opened, and a plump man emerged, greeting them with a tip of his hat. "Good evening! Have you come from afar?"

"Hello! We're from Bucks County in Pennsylvania."

"I know the area well." He shook Henry's hand and bowed to Catherine. "I'm a merchant who often passes through that fine area. You've chosen a good place to stay." He gestured toward the tavern with his thumb. "The Vosses are fine people, and the Mrs. is an excellent cook." He patted his ample stomach.

"Thank you, sir. Are you staying then tonight?"

The man shook his head. "No sir, I'm heading home down the road apiece. Well, then, good night to you."

They went inside where a fire provided immediate cheer, and the lady of the house welcomed them, asking the same questions as the merchant. She was quickly joined by her husband, both of them appearing to be in their late twenties. A handful of men, mostly of the middling sort, sat around the hearth with pewter mugs and clay pipes, conversing.

"Well, then, come in and make yourself to home," Mr. Voss said. "My good wife will bring you victuals, and I'll fetch drinks. What will you have, some good beer? Port? Madeira?"

"Cider, if you please," Henry said, "and not of the hard variety."

Voss scratched his chin. "Well, then, you're either a teetotaler or man of the cloth."

Henry smiled. "The latter, my friend."

The man inquired as to his business, and when Henry told him they were going to travel with George Whitefield, the tavern keeper's face seemed to ignite. "You must preach for us in the morning! We haven't had a minister this way in some time. I may feed bellies, but there are starving souls in these parts."

Henry regretted he had to refuse. "I'm so sorry, but we have to leave early." Seeing the man's jaw go slack, he had an idea. "I'll be happy to speak after we've eaten."

Voss's eyes brightened. "Thank you, sir! I must get the word out."

Catherine touched her husband's hand, resting on the table. "I'm thankful you agreed to preach. No doubt there's great spiritual hunger here."

As he waited for their food, Henry noticed Mrs. Voss was expecting a child. He peeked at Catherine, who also appeared to have detected the woman's condition, and pressed her hand. They were hoping for at least four children, six if the Lord so desired.

After supper, Henry preached to a group of twenty men and women, the tavern keeper having somehow sent out a message of a minister's presence, and not just any minister—one who knew Whitefield. Henry never ceased to be amazed at how in the most remote places, word could spread so quickly, but by the end of his discourse, there were some fifty souls crowding the tavern. He spoke of the work of the Holy Spirit he'd witnessed in Philadelphia and the southern colonies.

"The Holy Spirit is our direct link to the Lord Jesus Christ. He compels us to know the Savior and be empowered to live as true Christians, not just those who profess the faith but live as if they're strangers to God. Each of us has to decide which way we'll follow, our own path or the way of the One who made us, redeemed us, and sustains us." Henry's eyes bore into the crowd. "Do you know Him? If not, I urge you to repent of your sins and be saved this very night."

In a corner of the packed tavern, someone started weeping. Another person groaned. Henry spoke to as many as he could individually after ending with a prayer, gratified to see Catherine ministering among the ladies. They didn't get to bed until two in the morning. When they left the next day, Henry made a promise as he shook Voss's hand. "If at all possible, we'll visit again on our way back from New England." Once on the road he looked at Catherine and laughed. "Just think, our tour has only just begun."

They came to New Brunswick in time for the noonday meal, and the committee on ministry's examination of Henry took place at three o'clock. Catherine prayed fervently while he answered penetrating questions about the nature of God, the work and ministry of Jesus Christ, the Trinity, Church history, and Reformed theology. He impressed her with not only the scope of his knowledge—William Tennent had taught him well—but the height and depth of his relationship with the Lord. When the men finally approved Henry's ordination, she wiped away a tear, thinking of how happy her father would've been to see this day.

The service of ordination occurred an hour later and included one pastor who wasn't actually a Presbyterian. She wondered who the man with the vibrant white hair was, having met all the other pastors earlier, her opportunity coming when she and Henry stood in a receiving line in the narthex. After greeting several pastors and a few of their wives, Catherine smiled at Gilbert Tennent, who introduced the stranger.

"Mrs. Sharp, I would like you to meet one of my dearest friends, the Reverend Mr. Theodore Frelinghuysen."

Frelinghuysen! Father often spoke of him. "I'm very pleased to make your acquaintance, sir," she said as he bowed over her hand. "My father, who was also a pastor, spoke highly of you." Catherine knew a great work of God had begun in this area about twenty years earlier, in no small part due to this man's bold preaching.

"Oh, but the pleasure is mine, dear lady. I'm always honored to meet those who labor for the Lord Jesus Christ beside their husbands. May he bless you abundantly."

"Thank you, Mr. Frelinghuysen." She felt as if he'd handed her a rare gift.

Mrs. Gilbert Tennent came over. "Mr. and Mrs. Sharp are going to meet Mr. Whitefield in Rhode Island and accompany him on his journey through New England."

The Dutch minister's faded eyes shone. "What a splendid opportunity!"

Henry completed a conversation with another minister and joined his wife's circle. "Yes, sir. I was blessed to go with him to Georgia these last several months."

Frelinghuysen clapped his hands. "Marvelous! Marvelous, indeed! Our good Lord Jesus has worked among the people up and down the colonies through this man. Just this last April, he preached to a throng outside my church because there were too many to fit inside. Oh, the lives being changed because of God's work in him! Please tell Mr. Whitefield an old Dutchman in New Jersey prays for him to be used mightily to wake our sleeping colonists."

"I shall, sir," Henry said. "I know he looks up to you. You've also done so much."

The old man, as vigorous as any twenty-year-old, batted the air with his right hand. "In his strength, I've been preaching the simple message of repentance unto salvation. He does the rest."

"I so appreciate how Mr. Whitefield stresses the importance of a converted clergy," Gilbert Tennent said.

Another pastor walked over just then and elbowed Tennent in the ribs. "You could pay for that diatribe."

Henry sighed. "Prophetic voices are rarely appreciated."

She studied the resolute expressions of the clergymen, reading in them the aftermath of oppression caused by those who misunderstood the true nature of faith and the Church. *Thank God for them, for this presbytery, for the fulfillment of Henry's calling to ordination.*

Henry and Catherine left early the next morning in order to reach Rhode Island by September 13th, the day Whitefield's sloop was set to arrive. The trip went faster than Henry had anticipated due to favorable weather, and therefore, better road conditions. They reached their destination a day ahead of schedule. "I think we should rest today," he told Catherine. "Once Mr. Whitefield gets here, our lives will be go, go, go."

She reached up to touch his bristly cheek. "You take such good care of me."

"And I always will."

When they met Whitefield at the docks, Henry took immediate notice of his friend's physical state. "I'm afraid you look a bit thinner than at our last meeting."

Whitefield placed his hand to the side of his face and spoke to Catherine. "He's always fussing after me." Then he addressed Henry. "Actually, Mr. Sharp, I admit I felt quite unwell during my stay in the southern colonies. The heat alone is enough to convince a person to avoid hell at all costs." He chuckled at his own joke. "The sea air did me much good, though—

so refreshing! Now I'm ready to preach wherever and whenever the Holy Spirit leads."

Henry whispered in his wife's ear, "Here we go!"

"Are you unwell, Catherine?" Henry asked, bending over her side and stroking loose hairs off her brow.

"I'm fine. What of yourself?"

He sat on the side of the bed and swung his frame into a reclining position. They'd come into Boston after ministering morning, noon, and night in Newport and Bristol for several days in a row. The schedule was bruising, but the people's spiritual needs were so great Whitefield pushed himself until his last reserves of strength had been tapped out.

"I can handle this for now, but I want you to understand, dear one, I don't expect you to keep the same pace. If, at any time, you need to stop, you must tell me." He looked into her amber eyes. "There's no need for you to drive yourself as relentlessly as our friend. In fact, you can serve as a voice of reason when we're out of our own minds." He grinned. "These people have been so long like sheep without shepherds, and their needs are great."

"Please don't worry about me. I promise I'll rest if I can't keep up." She paused. "You know, somehow I expected more of the ministers up here to oppose Mr. Whitefield's ministry. Of course, I'm thankful they aren't."

Henry yawned and stretched his legs—these beds were never long enough to accommodate him. "There are ministers who hold him in high esteem, grateful for his persuasive preaching, even if they don't have the desire to call people to repentance as he does. There's always jealousy, though, because he gets so much attention. In fact, Mr. Whitefield is the last person to want any glory." He rolled over on his side to face her. "I think, too, there is bigotry."

"How do you mean?"

"Some ministers think nothing good can come from those in other churches. They don't understand Christ's call for unity in him."

"I'm learning a great deal, Henry—so grateful for these opportunities." She examined the covers on the bed, relieved they were clean. Tiny critters at the last place they'd stayed had kept her awake all night with their diligent labors.

"You're wonderful."

"Thank you. I think you are, too." Then she frowned. "I'm uneasy for Mr. Whitefield. His color is so pale when he's not preaching."

Henry knew what she meant. When his friend was expounding upon God's Word to the masses, he was dynamic, full of zest. When he rested, which was rarely, he seemed a spent candle, sometimes barely able to lift a fork to eat.

"I know we mustn't hinder the work of the Spirit in his life, but I think he needs to be still from time to time."

"Then I will do my best to take care of him, like a mother hen. And you, too, Henry." She playfully poked his arm.

"I welcome your attentions," he said, taking her in his arms.

As a young girl, Catherine's dreams had never taken her beyond Philadelphia, but here she was traveling in the company of the renowned George Whitefield, who'd just preached to fifteen thousand people on Boston Common and dined with His Excellency, Jonathan Belcher, the royal governor of Massachusetts and a staunch supporter of the evangelist. Catherine, however, resisted being charmed by what Whitefield called "human grandeur," which he considered a trial and a snare. Had Governor Belcher's heart not been toward the things of God, Catherine might have choked on the glorious trappings of his mansion— gilded portraits, polished silver, gold-rimmed plates, posh Oriental rugs, and expensive furniture. What impressed her most about her husband and Whitefield was how they behaved the same toward the governor as they had Mr. Clap, an elderly minister whose deep love for Jesus Christ seemed to transform his rather threadbare clothes into garments of praise. How she'd enjoyed his presence as they wandered about Rhode Island with Whitefield! Clap's energy amazed her. One of his parishioners said being with George Whitefield had made old Mr. Clap young again.

She stepped into the sunshine, welcoming its warming rays on such a blustery September morning. The meeting house had been so packed she could barely tell what the weather was outside. She'd heard someone say about six thousand people had jammed the place, with many more crowding about the windows and doors, straining to hear. Whitefield's voice was known to carry, but when he'd started his sermon, Catherine detected his hoarseness and immediately began praying for him. Thanks be to God, he was able to finish his message, and hundreds stood weeping afterward with repentant and joyful hearts.

She found Henry on the church lawn a little while later, Whitefield in the near distance talking to a crowd gathered around him. Suddenly, Catherine was struck with a powerful urge, as if God were commanding her to pray right now for her friend. *What is it, Lord?* Her entire body was trembling.

"Catherine. Catherine!"

Henry's voice chipped through her deep thoughts until she could see him clearly. "Yes?"

He gripped her shoulder and asked, "Are you well?"

"Henry, I must speak with you. Alone." She looked about herself for some opening in the thicket of trees and people and felt her husband lead her toward the back of the church where fewer people clamored for a glimpse of George Whitefield.

"Whatever is wrong, my dear?"

"I just had an overwhelming urgency to pray for Mr. Whitefield." She read the puzzlement on his face. "I know we pray for him almost without ceasing, but this is different."

CHAPTER THIRTY-ONE

Although Henry admired George Whitefield for treating all people exactly the same, at times he wished the minister wouldn't spend so much of himself on those who drained him. There were folks who'd pour out every trial and tribulation they'd experienced from birth until the present without seeming to consider how they were wearing him out. Just such a fellow was bending Whitefield's ear while as tactfully as possible, Henry nudged the preacher toward a meeting house where he was scheduled to speak.

"And then she says to me, says she, 'Thomas, you old scoundrel, hand that money over to me at once!' I tell you, honestly, Rev'rund, I had no money to give."

The man had repeated this part of the story three times already, and Henry didn't see a conclusion on the horizon. Spotting Catherine across a lawn wearing the hat she kept for rainy days, he motioned for her. When she slid beside him, he murmured in her left ear, "Will you please distract this man? I must get Mr. Whitefield inside."

She'd run interference on three other occasions with similar people and now immediately took charge of the situation. "Excuse me, gentlemen—if you will allow me to interrupt—Mr. Whitefield, you're needed inside."

The minister hesitated until Catherine introduced herself to the loquacious man. "Hello, sir. I'm Mrs. Sharp, a friend of Mr. Whitefield's. Would you be kind enough to accompany me inside to hear him preach?"

The rumpled chap stood speechless, if that were possible, then his face broke into a toothless grin over his sudden good fortune. Henry wondered if he'd done the right thing but when she nodded in his direction, he began walking toward the church with Whitefield. They hadn't taken more than a few steps before an unearthly roar erupted from inside as if the very furies had been unleashed. Before he could make sense out of the clamor, Henry gasped when a man flung himself out of a window, landing with a horrific thump. His immediate thought was to run over to the man, but then another fellow surged through the window, followed by another and another as if the window were a dam which had burst under great pressure. He saw Catherine several steps ahead of him gaping at the scene like Lot's wife. *I must get to her!*

The doors of the church flung open, a horde screaming and groaning as if Satan himself were on their heels.

"Has everyone gone mad?" Whitefield exclaimed.

Henry had never seen the likes of what was unfolding and hardly knew how to respond, until he saw Catherine running toward the mob, no doubt hoping to be of service. He ran after her, throwing out his arm and thumping her across the chest to stop her.

"Henry! I must go to them!" She looked at him without focusing.

"No! You will wait right here," he said in a totally unfamiliar voice.

Even the talkative man had stopped, his mouth at half-staff.

"What has happened?" Whitefield cried out.

People continued pouring from the church, a human rock slide, tumbling over one another in their haste. Children and elderly people had fallen and were being trampled. A man with disheveled hair and a torn cloak fled onto the lawn carrying a woman with a blood-streaked face.

O, Lord, what is this? What do you want us to do? Henry's heart pounded as he remembered Catherine's presentiment to pray for Whitefield the day before. Had God used talkative Thomas to detain them from entering the church?

Whitefield's knife-like voice rose above the din, cutting through the panic. His eyes flashing and arms waving, he was a colossus. "My friends! Those who have been injured require assistance. If you can help, please go to them at once. The rest of us will go into the fields where I will preach. Come! Let's go immediately!"

Henry went up to Whitefield, nervous about his leading this group at this particular time. "Mr. Whitefield, do you think the time is right for you to speak?" Doubt clouded his voice.

The cast of his eyes was pure resolution. "My dear, Mr. Sharp, I must address these people. The gates of hell must not prevail on this of all days."

Henry's jaw dropped at the sight of people leaving the church as orderly as they'd been taking flight moments earlier.

Rebecca Price Janney

Saturday, October 18, 1740

Northampton, Massachusetts

My Dear Mother and Father Heath,

I pray this finds you in the best of health and good spirits. Henry and I are well, as is Mr. Whitefield, at least on this particular day. Since I last wrote, we have traveled some two hundred miles, and he's preached about two dozen times. In addition to morning, afternoon, and evening sermons, he frequently gives a discourse to those who crowd in wherever we happen to spend the night. Many is the time he awakens with practically no voice or with headache or a stomach malady that would render me useless for an entire week, and I think, "He surely cannot preach today." Then he goes to the meeting house or common and as soon as he begins to speak, God bestows a special measure of health upon him. He says in those moments he simply forgets himself and thinks only of the Lord and His mercies. As you know, he frequently cries during sermons about the great sacrifice of Jesus on our behalf. At first, I could not understand and even felt uncomfortable. Now, however, I have also developed a more tender heart towards those who are eternally lost apart from our Savior.

Today we are at the home of Mr. Jonathan Edwards and his dear wife, Sarah, with whom I have felt an immediate bond. You will recall how Father read many of his books and admired him greatly. He and his wife are not only intellectually vigorous, but also kindhearted. They inspire me with their quiet, abiding love for each other, their brood of children (I confess I don't remember just how many there are or all of their names), and their deep devotion to Jesus Christ. I have been warmed by their hospitality, in spite of their heavy duties at home and church. I can't believe they were willing to put up our little party in their full house! I hope to learn from Mrs. Edwards how better to be a pastor's wife, so I may serve Henry just as well.

Although Mr. Edwards and Mr. Whitefield could not differ more in their temperaments, they have taken warmly to each other. Mr. Edwards is a tall, contemplative man whose style is as placid as Mr. Whitefield's is boisterous, and I must strain at

> times to hear him when he preaches. I continue to learn that in Christ, there is no Jew or Greek, slave or free, male or female, but all are one in Christ, who gives us new life.
>
> There is a servant here, a Miss Crider, who has been especially attentive to Henry and me, and who has become as one of their family members. She says five years ago, she was a shiftless and vain lass of questionable character, when she decided on a whim to attend the Sunday service. "Mr. Edwards, he preaches soft and quiet-like, but his message struck me as a hammer blow," she told me. "He made it clear that the likes of me would never see heaven unless I let Jesus take away my sins." Fearing for her eternal soul, she cried out to God to be merciful to her, a sinner, and since then, she has become a changed woman. Indeed, many hundreds of people called upon the name of Jesus and were saved then. I hope Mr. and Mrs. Edwards will tell us more about those days while we are here. I'm constantly astonished at how God has been working in various parts of the colonies through His faithful servants the past several years and how the revival is spreading!

She lifted the quill from the page, quivering at the sudden apparition in her mind's eye of that nightmarish day when many had been trampled, and five people had died. She wished she could banish the images, but she could still see the chaos and hear the shrieks. No one knew exactly what had caused the gathering to panic, but Mr. Whitefield sensed the Enemy had stirred up fear among the people. Catherine was grateful to her core God had spared her husband and the great minister, but since then she'd developed a nagging dread of losing Henry. Hadn't God put a hedge of protection around him when he was in actual danger? Why, then, the fear? She looked out the window, biting her lower lip, deciding not to mention any of these things in the letter.

> I must go now and prepare for the evening service. I smell wonderful aromas coming from the kitchen downstairs, and my mouth waters with anticipation. I've been almost embarrassed at my hearty appetite on this journey and am enjoying the bounties of autumn fare in New England, especially the seafood stews, which they call chowder.
>
> Please remember me to Margaret and Jacob, Francis, Lena, and my dear friends, Mrs. Doran and Elizabeth, whom I have

neglected terribly on my sojourn. Like Mr. Whitefield, I'm keeping a journal, but I'm often too busy or spent at night to record what happened. We plan to stay here a few days, and I believe we will begin heading back to Pennsylvania in early November. I long to see all of you again. Henry sends his best wishes, and we pray for all of you daily.

Your obedient daughter,

Catherine Harrison Sharp

"Mr. Edwards, you have listened to my accounts of revival the length and breadth of the colonies," Whitefield said after the last visitor had finally gone home. "Would you please tell us how it began in Northampton? I know long before I came to the colonies, God was at work in various and sundry places. I'm merely reaping what men like you, the Tennents, and Mr. Frelinghuysen of New Jersey have been sowing, as well as reaping. I've read your *Faithful Narrative of the Surprising Work of God*, but I would like to hear the story from your lips."

They sat before a congenial fire, the women working their needlepoint, the children having long gone to bed. Henry yawned discreetly. No matter how long these two spiritual giants chose to stay awake, he would fight sleep in order to listen. He glanced at Catherine across the room sitting next to the lovely Sarah Edwards, and his wife caught his eye, smiling.

Edwards leaned back in his chair, casting an elegant image. "You see, Mr. Whitefield, for some time before God's glorious work among us, there was a period of extraordinary dullness in religion. Licentiousness for some years greatly prevailed among the youth of the town."

"How so?"

"Many of them were very much addicted to night walking, frequenting the taverns, and lewd practices." He shook his head. "There was so much corruption. It was their manner very frequently to get together in assemblies of both sexes for mirth and jollity, which they called frolics, and they would often spend the greater part of the night in them, without any regard for their families. Then a change began to occur in which I sensed an unusual flexibleness and yielding to advice in the young people." He leaned forward. "There also took place in a nearby town the deaths of two young people, one of whom was a married woman who was considerably worried about the state of her soul. She was able to find consolation in God's saving grace, and she died full of comfort. As she lay dying, she counseled and warned others about their need to know God's mercy and forgiveness for their sins. Many were deeply touched."

Henry was riveted by Edwards' face, which reflected not only fire's glow, but a kind of holy blaze.

"Then, in the latter part of December, the Spirit of God began extraordinarily to set in and wonderfully to work among us. There were, very suddenly, one after another, five or six persons, who were to all appearances converted, some of them in a remarkable manner, among them, our Miss Crider. When she came to me, full of repentance for her notorious lifestyle, I could see God had given her a new heart, truly broken and sanctified."

Sarah Edwards took up the remainder of the story. Henry admired their mutual respect for one another.

"Many young people were awakened in their spirits to the things of God. An amazing change came to our town, and although people continued their daily affairs, everything was conducted with a mind toward Jesus Christ, whose name was frequently spoken and praised."

"They seemed to follow their worldly business more as a part of their duty than from any disposition," her husband added. "Religion was with all classes the great concern—the only thing in their view was to get to the kingdom of heaven."

Whitefield was resting his arms on his lap, apparently catching every word.

"The number of true saints multiplied, and soon there was a glorious alteration in the town. In the spring and summer following, that was in 1735, the town seemed to be full of the presence of God. It never was so full of love nor so full of joy, and yet so full of distress as it was then, because people were coming to terms with their sinful state before a holy God. Parents rejoiced over their children, husbands over their wives, and wives over their husbands. Our public assemblies were beautiful, the congregation alive in God's service, everyone earnestly intent on the public worship."

The fire snapped in the grate, the great clock in the hallway chimed eleven, and they all sat in silence. Then Sarah Edwards spoke again, pausing in her needlework.

"There also came a very hard time. When the Spirit of God was gradually withdrawing, Satan seemed to be more let loose and raged dreadfully. We even lost some who took their own lives and others, who were led astray by strange delusions."

"How awful!" Catherine exclaimed. No ghost story from her youth had ever produced the chill she felt now.

Edwards nodded. "There was considerable opposition to the work God had done."

"I'm not surprised," Whitefield said. "Satan will do all in his power to oppose our Lord. I know this full well, my friend. How wonderful not even the very gates of Hell can prevail against His church!"

"Indeed. The work God had done among the people has continued in their lives since then, albeit quieter. We have not seen so many conversions as during the period I just described, but for the most part, the converted have remained faithful."

Henry spoke up. "I've been privileged to see God's Spirit working powerfully across the colonies these many months. Do you suppose he might be using Mr. Whitefield to bring about a movement to unite the colonies in the cause of Christ?"

Edwards nodded, thoughtful. "This could very well be so as we see these colonies awakening spiritually after a deep sleep. I'm so very happy for your ministry, Mr. Whitefield."

Sarah added, "America was envisioned by the Puritans to be a city upon a hill for all the world to see. There seems to be some great purpose for this nation, a godly purpose."

Normally, Catherine preferred to do her crying in private, but on this day in Mr. Edwards's church, she let tears flow as freely as everyone else's while Mr. Whitefield exhorted the people to consider the great things God had done for them in the recent past.

"Do not forsake your first love!" he said, tears filling his own eyes. "I pray my own soul will be refreshed with the joyful news that Northampton has recovered its first love, and the Lord has revived his work in your souls, causing many more to come to repentance!"

She saw even Mr. Edwards had been deeply affected, weeping quietly along with his congregation. How powerfully she sensed the Lord's presence; even time seemed to be holding its breath.

Morning Glory

Oh, Lord, let me live only for you. Let your spirit chase away everything keeping me from closeness to you and your will. Including the fears dogging her steps.

CHAPTER THIRTY-TWO

The Edwards children frolicked on the lawn while their father and Whitefield's party prepared to depart for Connecticut. Catherine wondered how in the world Sarah Edwards retained her serenity.

"You are a wonderful helpmeet to your husband," the woman said, holding Catherine's hands.

"Thank you, Mrs. Edwards. You've been such an inspiration to me." Not only did she want to serve Henry in the same way, she hoped to be a mother like Sarah Edwards as well. She absently fingered the ribbons on her bonnet, wondering if she dared ask what had been on her mind for days, what she most yearned to ask this godly woman yet feared, because she might seem foolish, even faithless. "I must ask, are you ever, well, ever afraid for him?"

Sarah cocked her head. "In what way, my dear?"

"I sometimes fear my husband may, uh, die." She lowered her voice, "I know how unworthy those words sound."

Her sister in Christ lifted Catherine's chin and gazed into the younger woman's eyes. "We are frail creatures, my dear, one day waxing hot in our faith, another day waning. The only reason for shame is if you nurture these fears and let them consume you." She paused. "I understand your own father left this world not so long ago."

Catherine nodded, sniffing back tears. "Less than a year ago."

"Having such fears is understandable, especially since we live in such close proximity to death. When the Enemy assails me with them, I remind myself our God not only holds the universe together, he holds me and all my loved ones in the palms of his hands." She stretched out her own hands. "He will never leave you or forsake you."

"Thank you. Being with you has been a high point of this journey."

A tow-headed boy wandered over to them, pouting. "Mama, I fell and scraped my knee."

"Yes, I see, darling. I'll take you inside in a moment." She turned to Catherine. "Mrs. Sharp, you are a much-loved child of the living God. Go with our blessing."

"You see the hunger, the emptiness, my friends." Whitefield spread his hands out, employing his mannerisms and voice to their best effect. "Lost souls are finding the Lord Jesus. They're being rescued from the very pit of hell." He was clearly in preaching mode.

Henry looked at Syms, Syms looked at Henry. Catherine took charge. She stood to her feet and positioned herself squarely in front of the pastor. "You are spreading yourself far too thinly, Mr. Whitefield. Just look at you! Your clothes are beginning to wear you, and your asthma has kept you in bed whenever you're not preaching."

"I have decided to let myself be poured out for my Lord, who gave his all for me."

She squared her shoulders and stated, "My dear friend, even our Lord told his disciples to come away by themselves and rest. If you don't heed his voice, yours will be lost entirely. I say we should keep to our original plan to head back to New York, then through New Jersey and onto Pennsylvania. There are people in those colonies who need to hear you as well."

Henry gazed at her open-mouthed, wishing he'd had the courage to say what she was now telling Whitefield. But would he listen? Even with his robust constitution, Henry was beginning to feel the effects of his friend's punishing schedule as they traveled on the high seas of human need. Catherine had been such a inspiration throughout the journey in spite of rough weather, lack of privacy, primitive accommodations, and inferior food. More than once she'd taken to bed with stomach upsets and headaches, but she soldiered on. If anything, he wanted to get her back to a more normal life before they all collapsed.

For the next ten days, Whitefield preached his way southward, stopping at Yale College in New Haven, then Stratford and Rye in New York Province. Upon reaching New York City, their host showed them a pamphlet some Presbyterians were circulating, charging him with being an undisciplined, dangerous enthusiast. In addition, two volumes of his purported sermons had been published in London and sent over to the colonies. The problem was, Whitefield told his friends, "I've never preached on most of those texts!"

Catherine glanced at the bound books, looking so authoritative in their impressive bindings. "What will you do?"

"I shall answer their charges, asking God for a spirit of meekness."

Henry saw at once the gravity of the situation. Someone had put words in Whitefield's mouth—false, damning words.

"Ah, my dear, friend, the Lord will make me more than conqueror through his love. Satan must try all ways to bring the work of God into contempt, but blessed be God, who enables me abundantly to rejoice in all things that befall me. These things serve to humble my soul."

The slump of his shoulders, however, wasn't lost on Henry. He was more than glad when their old friend, the Rev. Mr. Noble, came to them with good news. "I cannot wait to tell you, Mr. Whitefield, of the amazing ways God has been moving in New York since you were last here!" This was balm to their souls.

In the evening, the Englishman began his sermon tentatively. As Whitefield picked up momentum, however, Henry once again sensed the Spirit of the Lord giving his friend a sense of spiritual power and freedom until a mighty, rushing wind brought men and women to tears. Some wailed and keened, beating their breasts, others swooned. He witnessed a half dozen people falling into the arms of their neighbors. He looked at Catherine just as the woman standing next to her suddenly collapsed into his wife's arms. Frowning, she laid the woman on the floor, then ran from the church, pushing through the crowd. He had to get to her and quickly. Whitefield was winding down, his voice giving out. When Henry found Catherine outside, she was leaning against a tree, shaking her head.

"I've come to accept Mr. Whitefield's style and the energy of the audiences who come to hear him, but *that* ..." She pointed toward the church. "What I saw in there felt like hysteria. I'm beginning to understand some of the objections there are to this kind of preaching."

Henry pushed back a desire to defend Whitefield, who'd once told him, "When I consider the depths of my sinfulness and the degree of God's grace and mercy toward the likes of myself, I become emotional, and it carries into the audiences who come to hear me preach." There was such a thing as genuine displays of passion. Were all of them genuine, though?

"I saw that woman fall on you." He started rubbing her neck.

"All I could think of was there might be another stampede like the other one," she choked out, "and I had to get out of there." She leaned against his broad chest, and he put his arms around her. They needed to be going home.

Catherine bounced from one foot to the next. "Mr. Tennent! How good to see you here!"

"And you as well, my dear." Then Gilbert Tennent grasped Henry's shoulders and laughed. In the background, Whitefield was just winding down his sermon from atop a wagon.

"When I heard our friend was in Staten Island, I came with Mr. Cross to see all of you. You remember Mr. Cross?" They nodded and greeted him. "I am glad to find you in this crowd.

"I must say, you appear to be thinner, Mr. Sharp."

"These have been vigorous days."

Catherine had noticed not only her husband's leanness, but a certain pastiness, which did nothing to allay her niggling fears. Some days, she triumphed over them, trusting him completely to the Lord—the next day they resurfaced. "How is Mrs. Tennent?" Henry asked.

Sadness crept into the older pastor's eyes. "I've lost her, my friends."

At first, Catherine wondered what he meant, then she understood. "I am so very sorry. And we saw her just a few weeks ago!"

"Yes, I know. The Lord enabled me with great calmness to conduct her funeral and since then, I've spent my time preaching in the West Jerseys and Maryland. How remarkably God has worked in these places!"

I'm not sure I could be so peaceful if anything happened to Henry.

They stayed with Gilbert Tennent in New Brunswick, a house bereft of its mistress's presence, then continued the next day to Trenton. Whitefield had received some letters and was bringing everyone up to date regarding news he had heard from various places, including Savannah, where a great many people had taken ill and died in the town.

"Fortunately, the orphans are safe and healthy," he said. "I'm also rejoicing because a minister is going to supply my place there. Managing a parish and the orphan house together are just too much for me, especially from a distance."

Henry was glad to hear his friend admit there was something he couldn't do, but he felt like he was hearing the rest of the conversation through a tunnel.

"God seems to be showing me my duty is to evangelize and not fix myself in any particular place. Speaking of evangelizing—Mr. Tennent, I do believe you should go to Boston and continue the work there."

Gilbert hedged. "I'm not so sure."

"What do you think, Mr. Sharp?" Whitefield asked playfully.

How strange. I know Mr. Whitefield said something, but I can't make out the words. Why are both of his eyes crossed?

"Henry? Henry!"

I know her voice, but her face is so white. I never want to distress her. His feet weighed a hundred pounds each.

"He is burning with fever," someone said through the fog in his brain.

"I don't think you should continue just now, beloved," Catherine said as Henry buttoned his shirt. In spite of trembling hands, he persisted.

"The fever broke last night, and now I'm just a little tired." He finished the job and touched her cheek. "I want to go home, just a day's journey. Then, I promise, I'll rest."

They left in soggy conditions, and as they ventured from Trenton to Warminster, they encountered a creek so swollen they had to go off their route to search for a different way across. The detour deprived Henry of what little strength he had. Nevertheless, he was a man on a mission, determined to get home, picturing the scene in the farmhouse so vividly he could almost smell his mother's sticky buns.

Sometime later, they found a place to cross, when there suddenly came an unexpected shout from the other side. "Sirs! I beg you come no further!"

What was this? Who's calling out? I don't know her voice. He felt someone, maybe Whitefield, yank his right arm.

"Stop, my friend!"

"Henry! Stay with us."

Catherine's voice. What's happened?

"You can't cross here—you'll surely drown!" called the woman.

"What should we do?" Catherine was speaking again. "Oh, Mr. Whitefield, we must get Henry home."

Home. He wanted to be home. Other voices now. A man's. Something about Whitefield and taking the horses across. Was he speaking of George Whitefield, the evangelist? He'd like to meet him. Or had he already? He thought so, but he wasn't sure.

"I can conduct them safely across," the man was saying.

Does he mean us, or the horses?

"My friend is quite ill."

"There's a bridge you can use."

The moving about seemed endless. Motion, then more motion. When would it stop?

They had to get Henry back to Warminster before, before … She just couldn't think about *that*, although the subject filled her mind. They were so close, yet home had never seemed so far away, not even while they were in New England. "Is he going to make it?" she asked Whitefield, despising the way she sounded exactly like her mother not so long ago.

He frowned. "I hope so. We mustn't give up."

She rode next to Henry on the cart, oblivious to her wild, wet hair, mud-soaked clothes and shoes. *Oh, God, help me not to be faithless, but believing. I do believe—help my unbelief!*

Catherine entered what had been Henry's room before their marriage and where he now lay perspiring, his hands kneading the blanket. His mother was sitting next to him. Peter had done a good job of warming the chamber with a radiant fire, and little Sarah sat on a chair near the window, her face lined with what was likely the same brand of fear Catherine struggled with. Her father-in-law, Christian, William, and their grandfather stood just inside the door.

"There, now you look more comfortable," Dorothea said. "At least you're in dry clothes."

Catherine regretted every minute her clean-up had kept her from Henry's side. Dorothea rose from her chair and motioned for Catherine to sit down.

"Mother Sharp, I don't mean to replace you!"

She made a clucking sound. "You are his wife. Your place is next to him."

"Here, Mother." William brought a different chair to the foot of the bed.

Catherine leaned over Henry, stroking wet, blond hair away from his forehead. He looked up at her, eyes half-closed. Stubble covered his chin. "I'm home," he muttered. Then his eyes flickered like a spent candle, and he fell asleep.

"When did he take ill?" Dorothea asked, her voice low.

"As we left New York several days ago, he became especially tired. Of course, we were all depleted. He'd been losing weight, though, and his appetite was off."

His mother gave a half-smile. "That was always a sure sign he was sick."

Catherine felt strengthened by her hopeful attitude. Devoid of any trace of fear. "In Trenton, he developed a fever, but the next morning, he said he felt well enough to go home." She shuddered. "What a terrible journey." She suddenly remembered she didn't know what had happened to the evangelist. "Do any of you know where Mr. Whitefield is?" She looked from face to face.

"*Ja*," Papa Sharp said. "He is at the Tennent's."

"But he had other plans."

"He wants to be close to you and Heinrich for now."

Afterward, Whitefield came to the house along with William Tennent to pray with the family. An hour after that, Catherine walked them to the door of the farmhouse where she put her face into her hands. "You must forgive me." She fumbled for her handkerchief, trying to stop the flow. "I'm so afraid, and I know I need to have more faith, but I, he, might … like my father."

Whitefield took her hands. "My dear, our time on earth is appointed by the Almighty. For those left behind, we have his glorious presence to strengthen us, as well as ample grace."

"I have found this to be so in the past," she whispered.

Tennent pressed his lips together, thoughtful. "I don't believe this is Henry's time, but whatever happens, God will not forsake you. He never has."

"Would you like me to stay here tonight?" Whitefield asked.

"Oh, would you?" Her spirit brightened.

"Of course. I'll go speak to Mr. Sharp."

"Send someone if you need me," Tennent said, "although I leave you in especially good hands." She embraced him, and he left.

Throughout the day, Henry remained delirious, speaking about being on the road with Whitefield. Catherine prayed without ceasing at his bedside. *I want to glorify you, Lord, even in this, no matter what.* His family came and went, taking care of the farm and blacksmith shop as necessity demanded, then returning to Henry's side where Catherine and Whitefield kept a steady vigil.

"Do you want Papa and me to stay with you?" her mother-in-law asked at ten o'clock.

"If you want to," she said, but she hoped they wouldn't.

"We will be just next door, then. Call if you need anything." She turned to her guest. "Mr. Whitefield, do you require anything?"

"No, thank you very much, madam. I think I'll go downstairs and try to sleep in your parlor if you don't mind."

Catherine had given him the use of her and Henry's little house, but Whitefield preferred to be close at hand.

After everyone left, she laid down next to her husband, stretching out on the bed, feeling his warmth. Before drifting off to sleep, she prayed. "Lord, thank you for your faithfulness in providing all our needs according to your glorious riches in Christ Jesus, for this wonderful family and my good friends. For my dear husband, I am eternally grateful. If you should desire to take him home to yourself, I'm going to be thankful for the time I had with him on this earth." Her voice caught. Mercifully, peace filled her spirit, and she slept.

Climbing up from the edges of sleep, she thought she heard the singing of birds. *Where am I? New York? New Brunswick? Trenton, perhaps?* Darkness was lifting its thin veil outside the window. Henry was beside her breathing—snoring to be precise. Her eyes focusing on the outlines of the room, she remembered she was in Warminster, and this was her in-law's home. She reached over and touched Henry's face, then sat straight up when she realized his temperature was normal.

He stirred. "Catherine?"

"Yes, darling. I'm here." She kissed his cheek and felt him smile.

"I am so hungry."

The first streaks of dawn mingled with the crooning of birds. Somewhere on the farm a rooster crowed. Morning had come in its glory.

GLOSSARY OF GERMAN WORDS AND PHRASES

German	English
Chapter Two	
Komm Herein	Come here
Wie spat ist es?	What time is it?
Mir geht es gut.	I am well.
Verruckt	Crazy
Gott	God
Ja	Yes
Nein	No
Chapter Three	
Hier	Here
Was ist das?	What is that?
Vielen Dank.	Thank you.
Bitte sehr.	You're very welcome.
Opa	Grandpa
Sie est sehr hübsch.	She is very pretty.
Liebling.	Darling
Chapter Twenty	
Willkomen daheim!	Welcome home!
Lebuchken and brot	cake and bread
Chapter Twenty-Two	
Guten tag.	Good day.
Chapter Twenty-Five	
Ach! Danke! Danke!	Oh! Thank you! Thank you!
Chapter Twenty-Nine	
Deine Haare sind so hübsch.	Your hair is so pretty.

AFTERWORD

Henry Sharp and Catherine Harrison are fictional characters, who came alive in my imagination while I wrote *Morning Glory*. The Tennents, George Whitefield and his companions, along with Jonathan and Sarah Edwards, Benjamin Franklin, and Theodore Frelinghuysen are, of course, historic people who played key parts in the early 18th century's First Great Awakening. In addition, there was a Presbyterian school in Warminster, Pennsylvania, created by William Tennent around 1726 to educate American pastors, which his enemies derisively referred to as an inferior, "Log College." Nevertheless, in twenty years, many men graduated and went on to have distinguished careers in ministry and education—five of them became trustees of the College of New Jersey created in 1746, and later named Princeton University. One of them, Samuel Finley, became Princeton's fifth president.

Relying heavily on *George Whitefield's Journals*, I created many of the scenes based on his accounts, employing an ample measure of artistic license. Rather than cite references where they occur, I listed the works in the bibliography, because I didn't want to interrupt the flow of the story, and because this is a novel and not a text book. In addition, I tried to reflect the spirit of the times by using terms like *Thee*, *Thou* and *Thy* when my characters prayed, while employing a mixture of 18th- and 21st-century language when they spoke, in order to create a blend of authenticity and comfort for contemporary readers.

Revivals seem to happen during times when human wretchedness is greatest. Today, the harvest is plentiful. May the Lord once more send laborers, like Whitefield, Edwards, the Tennents, Frelinghuysen—Joseph Harrison and Henry Sharp.

BIBLIOGRAPHY

http://www.reformed.org/documents/index.html?mainframe=http://www.reformed.org/documents/Whitefield.html; Center for Reformed Theology and Apologetics (Various Whitefield sermons)

Sydney Ahlstrom. *A Religious History of the American People.* (New Haven: Yale University Press, 1972)

Jonathan Edwards, *A Faithful Narrative of the Surprising Work of God.* (Grand Rapids: Baker Book House, 1979)

Benjamin Franklin. *The Autobiography of Benjamin Franklin.* (New York: The Modern Library, 1981)

Christian Timothy George. *Jonathan Edwards: America's Genius.* (London: Christian Focus Publications, 2008)

John F. Hansen. *The Vision That Changed a Nation: The Legacy of William Tennent.* (Fort Mill, SC: MorningStar Publications, 2007)

Rebecca Price Janney, *Great Stories in American History.* (Camp Hill, PA: Horizon Books, 1998)

Rebecca Price Janney, *Who Goes There? A Cultural History of Heaven and Hell.* (Chicago: Moody Publishers, 2009)

J.I. Packer. *131 Christians Everyone Should Know.* (Nashville: Holman Reference, 2000)

J.C. Ryle. *Select Sermons of George Whitefield.* (London: The Banner of Truth Trust, 1958)

Seward, William. *Journal of a Voyage from Savannah to Philadelphia, and from Philadelphia to England.* (London: No publisher referenced, 1740) Found on the internet at http://bit.ly/2EVt61i.

George Whitefield. *George Whitefield's Journals.* (Carlisle, PA: The Banner of Truth Trust, 1992)

John R. Williams. *The Strange Case of Dr. Franklin and Mr. Whitefield. The Pennsylvania Magazine of History and Biography,* Vol. 102, No. 4 (Oct. 1978), pp. 399-421.

REBECCA PRICE JANNEY

At fifteen, Rebecca Price Janney faced-off with the editor of her local newspaper. He nearly laughed her out of the office. Then she displayed her ace—a portfolio of celebrity interviews she'd written for a bigger publication's teen supplement. By the next month she was covering the Philadelphia Phillies. She's now the author of twenty published books including two mystery series, as well as hundreds of magazine and newspaper articles. She, her husband, son, and their beloved and somewhat rascally dog, live in Media, Pennsylvania, just outside Philadelphia.

Other Books by Rebecca Price Janney

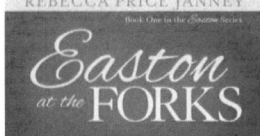

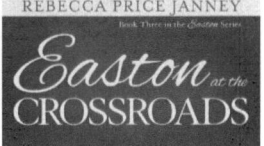

Great Events in American History (AMG)
Great Women in American History (Moody)
Great Stories in American History (Horizon)
Great Letters in American History (Heart of Dakota)

 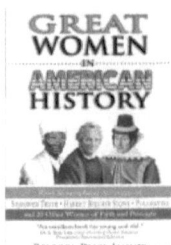  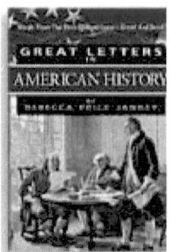

Harriet Tubman (Bethany House)
Who Goes There? (Moody)
Then Comes Marriage? (Moody)

 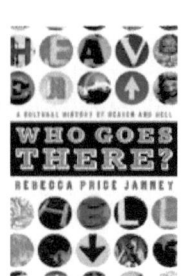 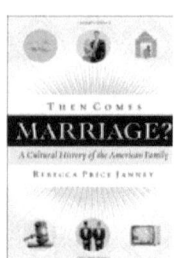

The Heather Reed Mystery Series (Word)
The Impossible Dreamers Series (Multnomah)

www.ingramcontent.com/pod-product-compliance
Ingram Content Group UK Ltd.
Pitfield, Milton Keynes, MK11 3LW, UK
UKHW041228200426
11947UKWH00034B/381